THE WIND BLOWETH

THE WIND BLOWETH

BY

DONN BYRNE

Author of *Messer Marco Polo.*

"The wind bloweth where it listeth, and thou hearest the sound thereof, but canst not tell whence it cometh, and whither it goeth: so is every one that is born of the Spirit."

The Gospel according to St. John

LONDON:

SAMPSON LOW, MARSTON & CO., LTD.

Printed in Great Britain by Fox, Jones & Co.,
Kemp Hall Press, High Street, Oxford, England.

TO

MADAME DOROTHEA DONN-BYRNE

CONTENTS

BOOK ONE

DANCING TOWN

THE WIND BLOWETH

DANCING TOWN

§ 1

BECAUSE it was his fourteenth birthday they had allowed him a day off from school, his mother doubtfully, his uncles Alan and Robin with their understanding grin. And because there was none else for him to play with at hurling or football, the other children now droning in class over Cæsar's Gallic War, he had gone up the big glen. It was a very adventurous thing to go up the glen while other boys were droning their Latin like a bagpipe being inflated, while the red-bearded schoolmaster drowsed like a dog. First you went down the gravelled path, past the greened sun-dial, then through the gate, then a half-mile or so along the road, green along the edges with the green of spring, and lined with the May hawthorn, white, clean as air, with a fragrance like sustained music, a long rill of rolling white cloud. There was nothing in the world like the hawthorn. First it put out little bluish-green buds firm as elastic, and then came a myriad of white stars. And then the white drift turned a delicate red, dropped, and the scarlet haws came out, a tasteless bread-like fruit you shared with the birds, and the stone of it you could whip through your lips like a bullet . . .

He left the main road and turned into a loaning that came down the mountain-side, a thing that once might have been a road, if there had been any need for it, or energy to make it. But now it was only a wedge of common land bounded on both sides by a low stone wall. Inside one wall was a path, and inside the other a little rill, and betwixt the two of them were firm moss and stones. And here the moss was yellowish green and there red as blood. And the rill was edged with ferns and queer blue flowers whose names he did not know in English, and now the water just gurgled over the rounded stones, and now it dropped into a well where it was colourless and cold and fresh as the air itself, and oftentimes at the bottom of a pool like that would be a great green frog with eyes that popped like the schoolmaster's. . . .

And to the left of the loaning as he walked toward the mountain was a plantation of fir-trees, twenty acres or more, the property of the third cousin of his mother's brother-in-law, a melancholy, thin-handed man who lived on the Mediterranean—a Campbell, too, though one would never take him for an Ulster Scot, with his la-di-da ways and his Spanish lady. But the queer thing about the plantation was this, that within half a mile through the trees were the ruins of a house, bare walls and bracken and a wee place where there were five graves, two of them children's. A strange thing the lonely graves. In summer the sun would shine through the clearing of the trees, and there was always a bird singing somewhere near. But it was a gey lonely place for five folk to lie there, at all times and seasons, and in the moonlight and in the sunlight, and when the rain dripped from the fir-trees. And all the company they had was the red fox slipping through the trees or the rabbit hopping like a child at play or the hare wide-eyed in the bracken. They must have been an unsociable folk in life to build a house in the woods, and they were an unsociable folk in death not to go to the common graveyard, where the dead folk were together, warm and kindly, lying gently as in their beds . . .

He turned now from the loaning to the mountain-side, passing through the heather on a little path the sheep made with their sharp cloven hoofs. In single file the sheep would go up the mountain-side, obedient as nuns, following the tinkle of the wether's bell, and then hunting a new pasture they would crop like rabbits. Now was a stunted ash, now a rowan-tree with its red berries—*crann caorthainn* they call it in Gaidhlig, — and now a holly bush would have red berries when all the bitter fruit of the rowan-tree was gone and the rolling sleets of winter came over Antrim like a shroud. Everywhere about him now was the heather, the brown, the purple heather with the perfect little flower that people called bells, all shades of red, and not often you would come across a sprig of white heather, and white heather brought you luck, just as much luck as a four-leaved shamrock brought, and fairer, more gallant luck.

A very silent place a mountain was, wee Shane Campbell thought, not a lonely but a silent place. A lonely place was a place where you might be afraid, as in a wood, but a mountain was only a place apart. Down in the fields were the big brooks, with the willow branches and great trout in the streams; and fat cattle would low with a foolish cry like a man wouldn't be all there, and come home in the evenings to be milked, satisfied and comfortable as a minister; wee calves shy as babies; donkeys with the cross of Christ on their back; goats would butt you and you not looking; hens a-cackle, and cocks strutting like a militiaman and him back from the camp; quiet horses had the strength of twenty men, and scampering colts had legs on them like withes. Up here was nothing, but you never missed them.

The only thing to break the silence up here was the cry of an occasional bird, the plaintive call of the plover, the barking of an eagle, the note of the curlew—a whinny as of a horse of Lilliput, the strange noise a pheasant makes on its rising from the heather: *whir-r-r*, like a piece of elastic snapping. Barring these you'd hear nothing at all. And barring a mountainy man or woman, and they cutting turf, you'd meet nothing unless it were the sheep.

You'd never hear the sheep, and you coming; you'd turn a wee bluff in the hill, and there they were looking, a long, solemn, grayish-white line, with aloof, cold eyes. You could never faze them. They'd look at you cool as anything, and "What license have you to be here?" you'd think they were saying. Very stupid, but unco dignified were the sheep.

But up to the top of the mountain, where wee Shane was going, you'd find no sheep; too bare and rocky there. There'd be nothing there but a passing bird. On the top of the mountain was a little dark lake into which you couldn't see more than a foot, though they said the depth of it went down to the sea. There were no fish in it, people said, and that was a queer thing, water without fish in it, wee Shane thought, like a country without inhabitants. In the sea were a power of fish, and in the rivers were salmon, long and thick as a man, and pike with snouts and ominous teeth, and furry otters, about which there was great discussion as to whether they were fish or animal . . . In the lake in the lowlands—Lochkewn, the Quiet Lake—were trout with red and gold and black speckles ; and perch with spiked fins ; and dark roach were easy to catch with a worm ; and big gray bream were tasty as to bait, needing paste held by sheep's wool ; and big eels would put a catch in your breath.

But in the lake on the mountain-top were no fish at all, and that was a strange thing . . .

There was another erie thing about the mountain, and a thing wee Shane was slightly afraid of. Oftentimes you'd be sitting by that lake, and sunlight all around you, and you'd turn to come down, and there'd be a cloud beneath you, a cloud that rolled in armfuls of wool that bound the mountain as by a ring ; and the lonely call of a bird . . . and you'd feel shut off from the kindly earth, as if you were on another planet maybe, or caught up into the air by some flying demon, and you knew the world was spinning like a ball through the treeless fields of space.

And what could a wee fellow do up there then but sit quiet and cry and be terribly afraid ? And your cry would be heard no more than the whinnying of the curlew . . . Or you might venture down through it, and that was more terrible still, for the strange host of the air had their domicile in the clouds, and there they held cruel congress, speaking in their speechless tongue, and out of the clouds they took shape and substance . . . their cold, malevolent eyes, their smoky antennae of hands . . . and nothing to turn to for company, not even the moody badger or the unfriendly sheep. There was no going down. You must stay there by the lake, and even then the cloud might creep upward until it capped mountain and lake, and enveloped a wee fellow scared out of his wits . . .

Nevertheless, he was going to the top of that mountain, clouds or no clouds. For he had heard it said that the mirage of Portcausey was being seen again—the Devil's Troopers, and the *Oilean-gan-talamh-ar-bith*, the Isle of No Land At All, and the Swinging City, and they were to be seen in the blue heat haze over the sea from the Mountain of Fionn . . .

And wee Shane was going to see it, clouds or no clouds, host or no host of the air.

§ 2

He had won half-ways up the mountain now, and from the brae of heather he could see the glen stretch like a furrow to the sea. The Irish Channel they called it on the maps in school, but *Struth na Maoile* it was to everyone in the country-side, the waters of Moyle. Very green, very near, very gentle they seemed to-day, but often they roared like giants in frenzy, fanned to fury by the winds of the nine glens, as a bellows livens a fire. But to-day it was like a lake, so gentle . . . And there was purple Scotland, hardly, you'd think, a stone's throw from the shore—the Mull of Cantyre, a resounding name, like a line in a poem. It was from Mull that Moyle came, *maol* in Gaidhlig, bald or bluff . . . a moyley was a cow without horns. The Lowlanders were coming into the Mull now, and the Highlanders being pushed north to Argyll, and westward to the islands, like Oran and Islay. He knew the Islay men, great rugged fishers with immense hands and their feet small as a girl's. They sang the saddest sea-chanty in the world:

'S tric sealltuinn o'n chnoc a's airde,
Dh' fheuch am faic mi fear a'bhata;
An tig thu'n aniugh, no'n tig thu amaireach,
'S mur tig thu idir, gur truagh a ta mi.

"From the highest hilltop I watched to see my boatman," went the sense of it. "Will you come to-day or will you come to-morrow? And if you never come—O God! help me!"

And there was a chorus to it that was like a keening for the dead:

Fhir a' bhata na horo eile! Fhir a' bhata na horo eile!
Fhir a' bhata na horo eile! Mo shoraidh slan leat, fhir a' bhata!

My heart's good-by to you, O man of the boat!

But nearer than Islay was their own Raghery—Rathlin Island the maps had it—he could see it now to the north. A strange little world of its own, with great caves where the wind howled like a starving wolf, and the black divers went into the water like a bullet. It was in the caves of Raghery that the Bruce took refuge, and it was there he saw the spider of Scots legend . . . Rathlin was queer and queer . . . There were many women with the second sight, it was told, and the men were very big, very shy, very gentle, except when the drink was in them, and then they would rage like the sea.

A strange, mystical water, the Moyle, to have two isles in it like Islay of the pipers and Raghery of the black caves. It was over Moyle that Columkill went in his little coracle to be a hermit in Iona, the gentlest saint that Ireland ever knew. And it was over the Moyle that Patrick came, landing whilst the Druids turned their cursing stones and could not prevail against him. And it was on the Moyle that the Children of Lir swam and they turned into three white swans, with their great white wings like sails and their black feet like sweeps . . . And in the night-time they sang a strange, sad music, and the echoes of it were still in the nine glens . . .

And northerly again were the pillars of the Giant's Causeway, blue-black against the sun. They were made so that the Finn MacCool, the champion of the giants, could take a running jump over to Scotland and he going deer-hunting in the forests of Argyll. So the country folk said, but wee Shane thought different, knew different. The Druids had made it for their own occult designs, the Druids, that terrible powerful clan with their magic batons, and their sinister cursing-stones, and their long, white, benevolent beards . . .

And there, green and well kept as a duke's garden, was the Royal Links of Portrush. And the Irish golfers said that it was harder than St. Andrew's in Scotland and better kept. There King James had played a game before he went down to the defeat of the Boyne Water.

"And if he golfed as well as he fought," Shane's Uncle Robin used to laugh, "they s'ould never have let him tee up a ball on the course!"

Eigh! how wonderful it all was! wee Shane felt: Raghery and the waters of Moyle; Portrush and the Giant's Causeway; the nine glens with the purple heather, and the streams that sang as they cantered to the sea; the crowing grouse and the whinnying curlew, and the eagles barking on the cliffs; the trout that rose in the summer's evening, and the red berries of the rowan; the cold, clear lakes, and the braes where the blueberries grow. He could well understand the stories they told of Napper Tandy, and the great rebel in the gardens of Versailles. Napoleon had found him weeping amid all that beauty.

"Don't be afraid, Napper Tandy. I shall keep my word and send General Hoche to Ireland."

"It's not that, sir; it's not that." And Tandy could not keep the tears back. "Och, County Antrim, it's far I'm from you now!"

§ 3

He had reached the cairn of round stones that marks the town land of Drimsleive, and was turning the brae when a voice called to him:

"Eh, wee fellow, is it mitching from school you are?"

An old woman in a plaid shawl was coming slowly down the hillside. He recognized her for Bridget Roe MacFarlane of Cushendhu, a cotter tenant of his Uncle Alan's.

"No, cummer," he told her; "I'm not mitching. I got the day off."

"For God's sake! if it isn't Shane Campbell! And what are you doing up the mountain, wee Shane?"

"Ah, just dandering."

"I was up mysel'," she went on, "to the top of it, because I heard tell there was a cure for sore eyes in the bit lake on the top. Not that I put much store in such cures, but there's no use letting anything by. I got a pair of specs from a peddling man of Ballymena," said she, "but they don't seem to do me much good. I'm queer and afeared about my eyes, hinny. It would be a hard thing for me to go blind and none about the wee bit house but mysel'."

"Ay! I should think it would be a terrible thing to be a dark person," wee Shane nodded.

"Och, it wouldn't be so bad if you were born that way, for you'd know no different. And if you went blind and you young, there's things you could take up to take the strain from your head, like a man takes up piping. When you're old it's gey hard. If you 're an old man itself, it's not so bad, for there'll always be a soft woman to take care of you. But if you're an old cummer, without chick or child, it's hard, *agra vig*. My little love, it's hard."

"Maybe it's in your head, Bridget Roe. My Uncle Robin says there's a lot of sickness that's just in your head."

"I trust to God so, and maybe your Uncle Robin's right, for there does be a lot in my head, and it going around like a spinning-wheel. I'm an experienced woman, wee Shane, too experienced, and that's the trouble. You've no' heard because you're too young and you would no' understand. I was away from here for twenty years," she said "for more nor twenty. And I knew a power of men in my time, big men, were needful of me. And a power of trouble I raised, too, and it does be coming back to me and me in my old days . . . But you'll be wanting to be getting on ?"

"Och, no, Bridgeen Roe; there's no hurry."

"It does me good to have a wee crack, the folk I see are so few . . . Aye ! There was a power of trouble. There were two men killed themselves and families broken up all by reason of me. I meant no harm, wee Shane, but it happened, and it does be troubling me in my old days. And I sit there afeared by the peat fire, and when I've thought too much on it, I get up and go to the half-door. And I look out on the Moyle, wee Shane, and I think : that's been roaring since the first tick of time, and I see the stars so many of them, and the moon that never changed its shape or size, and it comes to me that nothing matters in the long run, that the killed men were no more nor caught trout, and the rent families no more nor birds' nests fallen from a tree.

. . . None of us are big enough that anything we do matters . . . And than another feeling comes on me, that God is around, and that He'll be dreadful hard . . . And a wee bit of luck comes my way. The hens, maybe, are laying well, and there's a high price on the eggs, and I think, sure He's the Kindly Man, after all . . But if my eyes leave me, Shane Beg, what will I do? Sure, I won't have the moon or the stars or the waters of Moyle to put things in their place. And there'll be no luck about me, so as I'll know Himself is the Unforgiving Man."

"But someone will take care of you, Bridget Roe."

"And who, *agra*? 'T is not me to go to the poorhouse, and take charity like a cold potato. And my name is MacFarlane, wee Shane, and they're a clan that fights till it dies, that never gives in. And it is'nt to the big ones I knew I'd be writing for help . . . Sure I see them now, what's left alive of them, sitting by their firesides, figuring out their life, and tired with the puzzle of it; and then they'll remember me for an instant, and a wee joy will come to them in the dim twilight. They'll remember as you'd remember an old song you had'nt rightly got the air of. But you knew it was sweet and there was a grand swing to it . . . Aye, they'll remember me, and they looking into the heart of the fire . . . And you wouldn't have me write them now and tell them I'm only an old *cailleach* in a cabin on the mountain-side, and my eyes, that they'll remember, are dull like marbles . . . You wouldn't understand, wee Shane . . . But I'm blethering too much about myself. And where is it you were going, my little jo? Where is it?"

"I heard tell the Dancers were to be seen from the mountain-top over the sea, and I thought maybe I'd go up and gi'e them a look, cummer . . . just a look."

"So you would, wee Shane, so you would. You wouldn't be your father's son or your uncles' nephew if you were to let a marvel like that pass by. It's after adventure you are, and you only four and ten years old. 'T is early you begin, the Campbells of Cosnamara."

"But sure that isn't adventure, cummer, to be seeing the Dancers in the heat haze of the day. Adventures are robbers and fighting Indians and things like in Sir Walter Scott."

"Oh, sure everything's adventure, hinny, every time you go looking for something queer and strange, and something with a fine shape and color to it. Adventure isn't in the quick fist and the nimble foot; it's in the hungry heart and the itching mind. Isn't it myself that knows, that was a wild and wilful girl, and went out into the world for more nor twenty years, and came back the like of an old bitch fox, harried by hunting, and looking for and mindful of the burrow where she was thrown? . . . As we're made, we're made, wee fellow; you're either a salmon that hungers for the sea, or a cunning old trout that kens its own pool and is content . . . Adventures! Hech aye!"

"Well, I hope your eyes get better, cummer. I do so."

"I know you mean it, Shaneen Beg, and maybe your wish will help them, maybe it will."

"Well, I'll be going on my way, Bridget Roe."

"And I'll be finishing mines, wee Shane Campbell. And I hope to my God you're better off at the end nor me—me that once talked to earls and barons, and now clucks to a wheen o'hens; me that once had my coach and pair, and now have only an ass with a creel o' turf; and no care of money once on me, and now all I have is my spinning-wheel, and the flax not what it used to be, but getting coarser. And my eyes going out, that were the delight of many . . . I hope you're better off nor me at the end of the hard and dusty road, wee Shane. I hope to my God so . . ."

§ 4

He thought hard of what the cummer of Cushendhu had said about his family, and he on the last leg of the mountain. That he was his father's son puzzled him more than that he was his uncles' nephew, for there was little mention of his father in the house. At the dead man's name his prim Huguenot mother from Nantes pursed her mouth, and in her presence even his uncles were uncomfortable, those great, gallant men. All he knew was that his father, Colquitto Campbell, had been a great Gaelic poet, and that his father and mother had not quite been good friends. Once his Uncle Robin had stopped before a ballad-singer in Ballycastle when the man was striking up a tune:

"On the deck of this lonely ship to America bound,
A husk in my throat and a mist of tears in my eyes—"

His Uncle Robin had given the man a guinea.

"Why for did you give the singing man a golden piece, Uncle Robin?"

"For the sake of an old song, laddie, an old and sad song . . . A song your father made . . . It was like seeing his ghost . . ."

"But my father, Uncle Robin—"

"Your father was the heart of corn, wee Shane, for all they say against him . . . I never knew a higher, cleaner heart, but he was easy discourag't . . . Aye, easy thrown down and easy led away . . . I was fond of him . . . Am . . . always, and no matter . . . However . . . shall we go and see the racing boats, wee fellow?"

And that was all he ever got from Uncle Robin. But he knew some of his father's songs that were sung in the country-side . . .

Is truagh, a ghradh, gan me agas thu im Bla chliath!
No air an traigh bhain an ait nach robh duine riamh,
Seachd oidhche, seachd la, gan tamh, gan chodal, gan bhiadh,
Ach thusa bhi 'm ghraidh 's do lamh geal tharam gu fial!

"O God! my loved one, that you and I were in Dublin town! Or on a white strand, where no foot ever touched before. Day in, night in, without food or sleep, what mattered it? But you to be loving me and your white arm around me so generously!"

He couldn't understand the song, though the lilt of the words captured him. What should people accept being without food or sleep? And what good was a white arm generously around one? However, that was love, and it was a mystery . . . But that song could nor have been to his mother. He could not imagine her being generous with even a white arm. And none would want to be with her on a strand without food or sleep; that he instinctively felt. She was a high, proud cliff, stern and proud and beautiful, and that song was a song of May-time and the green rushes . . .

And other songs of his father's were sung: "Maidne Fhoghmhair—Autumn Mornings," and "In Uir-chill an Chreagain—In the Green Graveyard of Creggan. . ."

A queer thing that all that should be left of his father was a chill silence and a song a man might raise at the rising of the moon . . .

Silent he was in his grave, dumb as a stone, and all his uncles were silent, too, barring the little smile at the corners of their mouths, that was but the murmuring of the soul . . . There were paintings of them all and they young in the house, their high heads, their hawks' eyes, Alan and Robin and Mungo . . . And Mungo, too, was dead with Wellington in the Peninsula. He and three of his men were all left of the Antrim company. "Christ! have I lost this fight, too?" He laughed and a French ball took him in the gullet. "Damned to that!" He coughed. "He might have got me in a cleaner place!" And that was the end of Mungo . . .

And Alan had gone with Sir John Franklin to the polar seas, and come back with the twisted grin. "'T was a grand thing you did, Alan, to live through and come back from the wasted lands." "'T was a grand thing they did, to find the channel o' trade.

But me, I went to find the north pole, with the white bear by the side of it, like you see in the story-books. And I never got within the length of Ireland o' 't! Trade, aye; but what's trade to me? It's a unco place, the world!"

His father he could imagine: "Poor Colquitto Campbell! He wanted to bark like an eagle, and he made a wee sweet sound, like a canary-bird! Ah, well, give the bottle the sunwise turn, man o' the house, and come closer to me, a *bheilin tana nan bpog,* O slender mouth of the kisses!" His father, wee Shane thought, must have worn the twisted grin, too.

He knew what the twisted grin meant. It meant defeat. He had seen it on his Uncle Alan's face when he lost the championship of Ireland on the golf links of Portrush. And that morning he had been so confident! "'Tis the grand golf I'll play the day, and the life tingling in my finger-tips!" And great golf he did play, with his ripping passionate shots, but a thirty-foot putt on the home green beat him. All through the match his face had been dour, but now came the outstretched hand and the smile at the corner of the mouth:

"Congratulations, sir! 'T is yourself has the grand eye for the hard putt on the tricky green!"

The wee grin meant that Alan had been beaten.

And Uncle Robin, too, the wisest and oldest of them all, who had been to Arabia and had been all through Europe and was Goethe's friend, he had the twisted grin of the beaten man. Only occasionally you could get past the grin of Uncle Robin, as he had gotten past it the day Uncle Robin had spoken of his brother, Shane's father. And sometimes when a great hush was on the mountains and the Moyle was silent, Uncle Robin would murmer a verse of his great poet friend's :

"Ueber allen Gipfeln
  Ist Ruh,
In allen Wipfeln,
  Spürest du
Kaum einen Hauch.
Die Vögel schweigen im Walde
Warte nur, balde
  Rühest du auch !"

The sharp u's and heavy gutturals were so like Gaidhlig, it seemed queer wee Shane could not understand the poem ; but Uncle Robin translated it into Gaidhlig :

Os cionn na morbheanna
Ta sith—

And the melody of it was like the plucking of a harper's strings. So much in so little, and every note counted, and the last line like a dim quaint bar :

Beidh sith agad fein ! "You will rest, too !"

A queer thing, the men who were beaten and smiled. A queer thing the men who, beaten, were more gallant than the winners. A queer thing for the cummer of Cushendhu to say, she who was so wise after the hot foolishness of youth, that he was his uncles' nephew and his father's son. A queer thing that. A queer, dark, and secret thing.

§ 5

The memory of his Uncle Robin stuck in his mind and he going up the mountain. His Uncle Robin knew all there was to be known in the world, the immense learned man. When he was spoken to of anything strange, he had always an explanation of it. When the mirage off Portrush was mentioned, he could talk at length of strange African mirages that the travellers see in the desert at the close of day, oases and palm-trees and minarets, so you would think you were near to a town or a green pasture and you miles and miles away. And there was a sight to be seen off Sicily that the ignorant Italian people thought was the work of Morgan le Fay. And in the Alps was a horror men spoke of and called the Spectre of the Brocken.

All these strange occurrences were as simple as the alphabet to Uncle Robin. He would explain it as a sight reflected on the cloud and thrown on a sea of mist or a desert as on a screen, using difficult words, like "refraction," and words from Euclid, like "angles." But Uncle Alan would object, Uncle Alan mistrusting difficult words and words from Euclid. Alan would raise his head from splicing a fishing-rod or cleaning the lock of a gun or polishing a snaffle:

"You were ay the one for explanations, Robin. Maybe you've got an explanation for the gift?" By the gift Uncle Alan meant the second sight.

"Ah, sure: 't is only mind reading and sympathy."

"O my God! Now listen, Robin. You ken when you dragged me from the horse-show the last time we were in Dublin, to the library of the What-you-may-call-him—Archæological Society or so'thin'. You ken the book you showed me about Antrim, and what was seen off the cliffs one time. There was a great black arm in the air, and a hand to the wrist of it, and to the shoulder a crosspiece with a ring like one end of an anchor. And that disappeared. And then immediately there showed a ship, with the masts and sails and tackles and men, and it sailed stern foremost and it sank stern foremost, all in the red sky. And then there was a fort with a castle on the top of it and there were fire and smoke coming out of it, as if a grand fight was on. And the fort divided into two ships, that chased each other, and then sank. Then there was a chariot with two horses, and chasing that was a strange thing like a serpent, a snake's head at one end, and a bulk at the other like a snail's house. And it gained on the chariot and gave it a blow. And out of the chariot came a bull, and after it came a dog, and the bull and the dog fought as in a gaming-pit. And then suddenly all was clear, no cloud or mist or anything in the northern air. Am I right or am n't I ? Wasn't that in the book, Robin More ?"

"It was."

"And now, Robin, my man, wasn't that signed by respectable people : Mr. Allye, a minister, and a Lieutenant Dunsterville and a Lieutenant Dwine and Mr. Bates and twelve others, all of whom saw it near or around the time of the Boyne Water ? Wasn't it signed by the decent people ?"

"It was."

"And what explanation have you got for that, you and your master of arts of Trinity College !"

" They were daft—gone in the head. Daft or drunk."

" My song ! And maybe John was daft when he saw the vision of Patmos ! "

" I would no' be surprised."

" Na, Robin More ; you would not be surprised if you saw a trout that cantered or a horse that flew. You'd have an explanation. You're the queer hard man to live with, Robin, with your explanations."

Willie John Boyd, the servant boy, removed his cutty pipe and hazarded a suggestion.

" Queer things happened in the auld days."

" If there were queerer things nor you in the auld days," Alan laughed, " it must have been like a circus."

But mightn't they both be right ? wee Shane thought, and he trudging up the mountain-side. His Uncle Alan knew an awful lot. There was none could coax a trout from a glass-clear pool with a dry fly like Alan Campbell. He knew the weather, when it would storm and when it would clear, and from what point the wind would blow to-morrow. He could nurse along the difficult flax and knew the lair of the otter and had a great eye for hunting a fox, and a better eye for a horse than a Gipsy. Might there not be things in nature, as he said, that none knew of ? And mightn't there be explanations for them, as Uncle Robin, who had read every book, claimed there were ? Mightn't they both be right, who thought each other wrong, and they arguing by the red fire, fighting and snarling like dogs and loving each other with the strange soft love of lovers when the trees are a-rustle and the moon high ?

§ 6

He had thought to come up to the top of the mountain where the cairn was, and the dark and deepset lake, and to sit down in the heather and wait half-an-hour maybe while the curlew called, and then have Dancing Town take form and color before his eyes, hold it until every detail was visible, and then fade gently out as twilight fades into night. He had thought to be prepared and receptive.

But suddenly it was upon him, in the air, over the waters of Moyle. . .

A sweep of fear ran over him, and he grew cold, so strange it was, so against nature. Clear and high, as in some old print, and white and green, the town and shore came to him. The May afternoon was in it, hot and golden, but the town itself was in morning sunlight. A cluster of great houses and little houses, all white, a great church, and a squat dun fort, and about it and in it were green spaces and palm-trees that swayed to a ghostly breeze. And the green ran down to a white beach, and on the beach foamy waves curled like a man's beard. And in the air the town quivered and danced, as imaged trees seem to dance on running water . . .

On one side was Ireland, and on one side was Scotland, and high in the air between them was Dancing Town . . .

No one was in the streets that wee Shane could see, and yet the town was lifeful, some tropical city where the green jalousies were closed in the heat of the midday sun, and where no one was on the streets, barring some unseen old beggar or peddling woman drowsing in the shade. The town was sleeping not with the sleep of Scotland, that is the sleep of dead majestic, melancholy kings, nor with the sleep of Ireland, that is tired and harassed and old. It was not as lonely as sleeping lakes are where the bittern booms like a drum . . . It slept as a child sleeps, lips apart and chubby fingers uncurled, and happy . . . And all the time it quivered in the clear air . . .

In the morning, wee Shane thought, it woke to bright happiness, the green parrakeets chattered, the monkeys whistled, the lizards basked in the sun. And the generation of the town came out and gossiped and worked merrily, until the heat of the sun began to strike with the strokes of a mallet, and then they went into the cool, dark houses and slept as children sleep. And then came blue twilight, and lamps were lit in the green spaces, and into the odorous night would come the golden rounded women with smiles like honey, and the graceful feline men. . . . A woman's laughter, a man's song. . . . And the moon rising on tropic seas, while a guitar hummed with a deep vibrant note. . . . And the perfume of strange tropic trees. . . .

But meantime the town danced in the clear air . . . And—

" It's gone ! " said wee Shane.

One moment it was there, and the next there were only Ireland and Scotland and the waters of Moyle, and a ship going drowsily for the Clyde.

And for a long time he waited, thinking Dancing Town might come again. But it did not come. The schooner off the Mull lay over, and the Moyle awoke. A breeze rambled up the mountain, and the heather tinkled its strange dry tinkle. And afar off a curlew called, and a grouse crowed in defiance.

The moment of magic was by, and wee Shane went down the mountain.

§ 7

As he went down the mountain he tried to puzzle out the why and wherefore of Dancing Town.

Of course there were things you could not explain, like the banshee ; or the Naked Hangman, who strides through the valleys on midsummer's eve with his gallows under his arm ; or the Death Coach, with its headless horses and its headless driver. There was no use bringing these matters up to Uncle Robin. Uncle Robin would only laugh and shout : " Havers, bairn ! Wha's been filling your wee head with nonsense ? " But you could no more deny their existence than you could that of Apollyon, whom you read about in *Pilgrim's Progress,* and who wandered up and down the world and to and fro in it ; or of the fairies, whose sweet little piping many heard at night as they passed the forts of the little people ; or of the tiny cobbling leprechawns, who knew where the Danes had hid their store of gold in crocks such as hold butter. . . Of these there was no explanation but the act of God. And Uncle Robin was queer. He put no store in the act of God.

Now, if it had been an angel he had seen in the high air, it would have been the Act—or the banshee, and her crooning and keening by the riverside, with her white cloak, her red, burnished hair. . . . But it was an island he had seen, a dancing town, with his own hard wee Scots-Irish eyes. And that was not an act of God; it was a fact, and so outside his Uncle Alan's bailiwick and within his Uncle Robin's. His Uncle Robin would say it was the reflected image of some place in the world. Aye, he'd take his Uncle Robin's word for that. But where was it? Surely, as yet, it was undiscovered. It had the quiet of a June evening, that land had, and a grand shimmering beauty. . . . And if it was known where it was, wouldn't the mountainy folk be leaving their cabins, and the strong farmers their plowed lands, and the whining tinkers be hoofing the road for it? If it was known where that land was . . .

It occurred to him it must have been that land his father meant and he writing his poem of the Green Graveyard of Creggan. While he was sleeping under the weeping yew-trees the young queen had touched the sleeping poet on the shoulder.

"*A shiolaigh charthannaigh,*" she said, "O kindly kinsman, *na caithtear thusa ins na nealtaibh broin,* let you not be thrown under the clouds of sorrow! *Acht eirigh in do sheasamh,* but rise in your standing, *agas gluais liomsa siar' sa' rod,* and travel with me westward in the road. *Go Tir Dheas na Meala,* to the shimmering land of honey where the foreigner has not the sway. And you will find pleasantry in white halls persuading me to the strains of music."

Surely his father, too, had seen Dancing Town!

And it was an old story that Oisin had found it, when he rode with the princess over the waves on a white horse whose hoofs never touched water, and he abode with her in *Tir nan Og,* in the Land of Them Who are Young, for a thousand years or more, until the great homesickness for Ireland took him, that takes the strongest, and he came for a visit on the white horse; but the girths of the saddle broke, and he fell to the ground, and the horse flew away. And he who had been strong and young and beautiful became old and bald and blind, and Patrick of the Bells and Crosses took him, and put him with the groaning penitents, who beat their breast under the fear of hell. And he, who had known Tir nan Og and the Silver Woman, was a drooling ancient with a wee lad to lead him. . . . But that was just a winter's tale with no sense to it.

But there were other things in books that had the ring of truth to them. There was the voyage of Maeldun, who had set out in his coracle, and visited islands. The Island of Huge Ants was one, and wee Shane had seen in his geography book pictures of armadillos, and he shrewdly surmised that Maeldun had been to South America. And there was the Island of Red-Hot Animals, but that was a poser. Still and all, the rhinoceros had armor like an old knight's, and that would surely get red-hot under the suns of the equator. It would explain, too, why the rhinoceros favored the water, like a cow in July. . . . Sure that was it: Maeldun had been to Africa. And Maeldun, too, had found the Fortunate Isle. Brendan too, had known it. Wasn't it in old charts—St. Brendan's Isle? He said he found it, and surely a saint of God wouldn't lie. . . .

Och, it was there somewhere, but people were different from what they were in the ancient days. They didn't bother. If they had told his father about it, sure all Colquitto would have done was to call for pen and paper.

"*Mo bhron air an fhairrge*," he would have written ; "My grief on the sea—how it comes between me and the land where my mind might be easy—" And then he'd have lain back and chanted it. "*A vourneen*, did you ever in all your life hear a poem as good as my poem ? Sure old Homer's jealous in the black clouds. Was there ever a Greek poet the equal of a Gaelic one ? *Anois, teacht an Erraigh*—now the moment spring comes in, 'tis I will hoist sail, *inneosad mo sheol*. . . ."

And Alan Donn might have started to find it, but at the first golf links he'd stop, "to take the conceit out of the local people, and to give them something to talk of, and they old men," or to match his coursing greyhound against any dog in the world for a ten-pound note, or to deluther some red-cheeked likely woman. . . .

And Uncle Robin might hear of it, and he'd sit down and write a book, saying where it probably was, and how you might get there, and what the people were like, and whom they were probably descended from. . . . And the book would be in all the libraries of the world, and people would be writing him telling him what a great head was on him, and he'd mutter : "Nonsense ! nonsense ! All nonsense !" and stroke his great red beard. . . .

But wouldn't it be the funny thing, the queer and funny thing, if he himself, wee Shane Campbell, were to go out and discover that island, and to own it, and to have it marked in the maps and charts, "Wee Shane Campbell's Island," for all to read and see ? . . .

"Decent wee fellow, is it about here somewhere the house of the McFees?"

Shane had turned into the main road that ran along the sea-shore on the way homeward when the voice hailed him. It was a great black-bearded man, sitting on the ditch, holding his shoes in his hand. His face was tanned to mahogany, and in his ears were little gold rings. He wore clothes that were obviously new, obviously uncomfortable.

"If you keep on the road about half-a-mile and then turn to the left, and keep on there until you come to a loaning near a well with a hawthorn bush couching over it, and turn to the left down that loaning, you'll come to it. It's a wee thatched house, needing a coat of whitewash. It's got a byre with a slate roof, and a rowantree near it. You canna' miss it."

"Now isn't that the queer thing," the big man said, "me that thought I knew every art and part of this country, and that could find my way in the dark from Java Head to Poplar Parish, can't remember the place where I was born and reared? Forty years of travelling on the main ocean and thinking long for this place, and now when I come back I know no more about it than a fish does of dry land." He stood up painfully. "And me that thought I would come back leaping like a hare am now killed entirely with the soreness of my feet."

"You're not accustomed to walking, then, honest man?"

"'Deed, and you may say I'm not, decent wee fellow. I'm a sailorman, and aboard ship there's very little use for the feet. You've got to be quick as a fish with the hands, and have great strength in the arms of you. And you must have toes to grip, and thighs to brace you against the heeling timbers. But to be walking somewhere for long, hitting the road with your feet like you'd be hitting a wall with your head, it's unnatural to a sailing man. A half-a-mile, did you say ? "

" Honest man," said wee Shane, troubled, " are you looking for any one in the house of the McFees ? "

" For a woman that bore me and put me to her breast. An old woman now, decent wee fellow."

" You'll no' find her, honest man."

" She's dead ? "

" I saw her with the pennies on her eyes not two months ago."

" So my mother's dead," said the big man. " So my mother's dead. Ah, well, all her troubles are over. It's forty years since I saw her, and she the strapping woman. And in forty years she must have had a power of trouble."

" She looked unco peaceful, honest man."

" The dead are always peaceful, decent wee fellow. So my mother's dead. Well, that alters things."

" You'll be staying at home then, honest man ? "

" I'll be going back to sea, decent wee fellow. I had intended to stay at home and be with the old woman in her last days, the like of a pilot that brings a ship in, as you might say. But it would have been queer and hard. Herself, now, had no word of English ? "

" Old Annapla McFee spoke only the Gaidhlig."

" And the Gaidhlig is gone from me, as the flower goes from the fruit-tree. And there could have been little conversation betwixt us, she remembering fairs and dances and patterns in the Gaidhlig, and me thinking of strange foreign ports in the English tongue. Poor company I'd have been for an old woman and she making her last mooring. I'd have been little assistance. Forty years between us—strange ports and deep soundings. Oh, we'd have been making strange."

"Ah, maybe not, honest man."

"How could it have been any other way, decent wee lad? She'd have been the strange, pitiful old cummer to me, who minded her the strapping woman, and I'd have been a queer bearded man to her, who minded me only as a wee fellow, the terror of the glen. People change every day, and there's a lot of change in forty years.

"And, besides, it would have been gey hard on me, wee lad. The grape and spade would be clumsy to my hands, there being no life to them after the swinging spars. And my fingers, used to splicing rope, would not have the touch for milking a cow. And Id' feel lost, wee fellow, some day and me plowing a field, to see a fine ship on the waters, out of Glasgow port for the Plate maybe, and to think of it off the Brazils, and the pampero coming quick as a thrown knife, and me not aboard to help shorten sail or take a trick at the wheel. And it might have made me ugly toward the old woman. And I wouldn't have had that at all, at all. . . . But she's finished the voyage, poor cummer. . . . And it's a high ship and a capstan shanty for me again . . . ah, well. . . ."

"It's a wonder, honest man, you wouldn't stay on land at peace and you forty years at sea."

"Well, it's a queer thing, decent wee fellow, but once you get the salt water in your blood you're gone. A queer itching is in your veins. It's like a disease. It is so. It spoils you for the fire on winter nights and for the hay-fields in the month o' June. And it puts a great bar between you and the folk o' dry land, such as there is between a fighting man and a cowardly fellow. It's the salt in the blood, I think; but you'd have to ask a doctor about that.

"I'm not saying it's a good life. It's a dog's life. It is so. And when you're at sea you say: 'Wasn't I the fool to ever leave dry land; and if I get back and get a job,' says you, 'you'll never see me leave it again. It's a wee farm for me,' you'll say. And then somehow you'll find yourself back aboard ship. And you'll be off the Horn, up aloft, fighting a sail like you'd fight a man for your life, or you'll be in the horse latitudes, as they call them, and no breeze stirring, and not a damned thing to do but holystone decks, the like of an old pauper that does be scrubbing a poorhouse floor. And you say: 'Sure I'd rather be a tinker travelling the roads, with his ass and cart and dog and woman, nor a galley-slave to this bastard of a mate that has no more feeling for a poor sailorman nor a hound has for a rabbit. It's a dog's life,' you say, 'and when we make port I'm finished.'

"But you make port and you stay awhile, and you find that the woman you've been thinking of as Queen of Sheba is no more nor a common drab. And the publican you thought of as the grand generous fellow has no more use for you and your bit silver gone. It's a queer thing, but they on land think of nothing but money. And one day you think, and the woman beside you is pastier nor dough, and the man of the public house is no more nor a cheap trickster, and you're listening to the conversation of the timid urban people, and the house you're in is filthier nor a pig's sty. And you say : 'Is this me that minds the golden women of the islands, and they with red flowers in their hair ? Is this me that fought side by side with good shipmates in Callao ? Am I listening to the chatter of these mild people, me that's heard grand stories in the forecastle of how this man was marooned in the Bahamas, and that man was married to a Maori queen, by God? Me, the hero that dowsed skysails, and they crackling like guns. Is this lousy room a place for me that's used to a ship as clean as a cat from stem to stern ?' And you stand up bravely, and you look the man of the public house square in the shifty eyes, and you say : 'Listen, bastard ! Do you ken e'er a master wants a sailing man ? A sailor as knows his trade, crafty in trouble, and a wildcat in danger, and as peaceful as a hare in the long grass ?' And you're off again on the old trade and the old road, where the next port is the best port, and the morrow is a braver day. . . . So it's so long, decent wee fellow ! I'm off on it again. It's a dog's life, that's what it is, the life of a sailing man. But you couldn't change. I suppose it's the salt in the blood."

"You're off, honest man ?"

"Aye, I'm off, wee fellow. And thank you kindly for what you told me, and for telling me especially the old woman looked so peaceful and her with the pennies on her eyes."

"But aren't you going up to see the house?"

"I don't think I will, wee lad. I've had a picture in my mind for forty years of the big house was in it, and the coolth of the well. And maybe it isn't so at all. I'd rather not know the difference. I'll keep my picture."

"But the house is yours," wee Shane urged him. "You're not going to leave it as it is. Aren't you going to sell it and take the money?"

"Och, to hell with that! I've no time," said the sailing man, and he limped painfully back down the road.

§ 8

His Uncle Robin had gone off to discuss with some Belfast crony the strange things he used to discuss, like the origin of the Round Tower of Ireland or the cryptic dialect of the Gaelic masons or whether the Scots came to Scotland from Ireland or to Ireland from Scotland, all very important for a member of the Royal Irish Academy. And his mother had gone off shopping to buy linen for the house at Cushendhu, poplin for dresses, delft from Holland for the kitchen and glass from Waterford for the sideboard in the dining-room. And because he was to go to the boarding-school that night and thereafter would be harsh discipline, and because his Uncle Robin had known he was on the point of crying, he had been allowed to wander around Belfast by himself for a few hours with a silver shilling in his pocket. And wee Shane had made for the quays. . . .

The four of them had sat in a cold, precise room that morning, his Uncle Robin, his mother, wee Shane, and the principal, a fat, grey-eyed, insincere Southerner, with a belly like a Chinese god's, dewlaps like a hunting hound's, cold, stubby, and very clean hands, and a gown that gave him a grotesque dignity. And he had eyed wee Shane unctuously. And wee Shane did not like fat, unctuous men. He liked them lean and active, as glensmen are.

And the principal had spoken in stilted French to his mother, who had responded in French that crackled like a whip. And the principal had licked the ground before Uncle Robin. It was "Yes, Dr. Campbell!" And, "No, Dr. Campbell!" where the meanest glensman would have said "Aye, maybe you're right, Robin More," or, "Na, na, you're out there, Robin Campbell."

"The old hypocrite!" It was the only word wee Shane could describe the master by, a favorite word of his Uncle Alan's.

And in the corridors he had met some of the scholars, white-faced fellows; and the masters—they had mean eyes, like the eyes of badgers.

"I dinna want to go!" He blurted out on the quays of Belfast.

"Where dinna you want to go, wee laddie?" A black, curly-headed man with grey eyes and a laugh like a girl's stopped short. He had blue clothes and brass buttons and stepped lightly as a cat.

"I dinna want to go to school."

"Sure, all wee caddies go to school."

"I ken that. But I don't want to go to school with a bunch of whey-faced gets, and masters lean and mean as rats, and a principal puffed out like a setting hen."

" Oh, for God's sake ! is that the way you feel about it ? Laddie, you don't talk like a townsman. Where are you from ? "

" I'm from the Glens of Antrim. From Cushendhu."

" I'm a Rahgery man myself. *Tha an Gaidhlig agad ?*

" *Tha, go direach !* "

" So you've got the Gaidhlig too ? Who are your people, wee laddie ? "

" I'm a Campbell of Cushendhu."

" For God's sake ! you're no a relation of Alan Campbell's, wha sailed with Sir John Franklin for the pole ? "

" I'm his nephew."

" I've sailed under your Uncle Alan. He's the heart o' corn. And so they're going to make a scholar out of you, like your Uncle Robin. Oh, well, oh, well. Would you like to come around with me and see the ships ? "

" I'd like fine to see the ships."

" You'll see all manner of ships here. Square-riggers, fore-and-afters, hermaphrodites. You'll see Indiamen and packets from Boston. You'll see ships that do be going to Germany, and some for the Mediterranean ports. You'll see a whaler that's put in for repairs. You'll see fighting ships. You'll see fishers of the Dogger Banks, and boats that go to Newfoundland, where the cod do feed. All manner of sloops and schooners, barkantines and brigs, but the bonniest of them all lies off Carrickfergus."

" And who's she, Raghery man ? "

" The *Antrim Maid* is her nomination."

" And do you sail her ? "

" I sail in her, laddie Sail and sail in her. Mine from truck to keelson she is, and I'm master of her. Father and mother and brother to her, and husband, too. I'm proud of her." The Rathliner laughed. "You may notice."

" And why for shouldn't you be ? She must be the grand boat surely, man who sailed with my Uncle Alan."

§ 9

" Raghery man, you who've sailed the high seas and the low seas, did you ever put into an island that has great coolth to it and great sunshine, a town quiet as a mouse, a strip of sand like silver, the waves turning with a curl and chime ?"

" Where did you hear tell of that island, wee laddie? Was it in the books you do be reading at school ? "

"I saw it, and it dancing in the sun. From Slievenambanderg, I saw it, and it over the waters of Moyle."

The Rathliner sat on a mooring bitt on the quay and filled his pipe.

" I ken that island," he said. " I ken it well."

" And what name is on it, Raghery man ?"

" The name that's on it is Fiddlers' Green."

" Were you ever there, Raghery man ? " There was a sinking in wee Shane's heart.

" I was never there, laddie, never there. Oftentimes I thought I'd raised it, but it was never there, wee laddie, never there. There's men as says they've been there, but I could hardly believe them, though there's queer things past belief on the sea. There's a sea called Sargasso, and if I told you half the things about it, you'd think me daft. And there's the ghost of ships at sea, and that's past thinking. And there's the great serpent, that I've seen with my own eyes. . . .

" Aye, Fiddlers' Green ! Where is it, and how do you get there ? The sailormen would give all their years to know."

" Why for do they call it Fiddlers' Green ?."

" It's Fiddlers' Green, laddie, because it's the place you come to at the cool of the day, when the bats are out, and the cummers put by their spinning. And there's nou't there but sport and music. A lawn like a golf green, drink that is not ugly, women would wander with you on to the heather when the moon's rising, and never a thought in their mind of the money in your pocket, but their eyes melting at you, and they thinking you're the champion hero of the world. . . . And all the fiddlers fiddling the finest of dance music : hornpipes like ' The Birds among the Trees ' and ' The Green Fields of America ' ; reels like ' The Swallow-tail Coat ' and ' The Wind that Shakes the Barley ' ; slip-jigs would make a cripple agile as a hare. . . . And you go asleep with no mate to wake you in a blow, but the sound of an old piper crooning to you as a cummer croons. And the birds will wake you with their douce singing. . . . Aye, Fiddlers' Green. . . ."

And they were silent for a minute in the soft Ulster sunshine.

" Would you have any use for a lad like myself aboard your ship, Raghery man ? "

" Och, sure, what would you do with the sea, wee fellow ? "

"I ken it well already, Raghery man. And I'm no clumsy in a boat. I can sail a sloop with any man. On a reach or full and by, I'll keep her there. With the breeze biting her weather bow, I'll hold her snout into it. Or with the wind behind me, I'll ride her like you'd canter a horse."

"I might take you to learn you seamanship and navigation, but you'd be no use as a sailor, wee laddie, and it's not for a Campbell to be a cabin-boy."

"Take me to learn the trade, then. Take me now."

"I'd like fine, wee fellow, but I couldn't do it. You might be cut out for a scholar for all you think you're not. Or it might be a soldier you're meant for. I couldn't interfere with your life. It's an unco responsibility, interfering with a destiny, a terrible thing."

"Will you talk to my Uncle Robin? Will you?"

"Och, now, how could I talk to your Uncle Robin, him that's written books, and is counted one of the seven learned men of Ireland? Sure, I wouldn't understand what he'd be saying, and he'd have no ear for a common sailing man. If it was your Uncle Alan, now—"

"There's not a person in the world but has the ear of my Uncle Robin. And there's none easier to talk to, not even the apple woman at the corner of the quay. Will you come with me and talk to him?"

"I couldn't, laddie. Your Uncle Alan, now—"

"I'll do the talking, then; but will you come?"

"Och, wee fellow, it would be foolish."

"You wouldn't have me think hard of a man of Raghery?"

"No, I wouldn't have any one think hard of the

folk of Raghery, so I suppose I'll have to come. I don't know what your Uncle Robin will say to me for putting notions in your head. It's awful foolish. But I'll come."

§ 10

"So there'd never be the making of a scholar in me, Uncle Robin. A ship on the sea or a new strange person would be always more to me nor a book. I can read and write and figure! what more do I want? And, och, sir, the school would be a prison to me, the scholars droning and ink on their fingers, and the hard-faced masters at the desk. I'd be woe for the outside, for the sunshine and the water and the bellying winds—"

His Uncle Robin tapped the window-pane of the club and thought hard. The Rathlin sailor stood by, puzzled.

"But, childeen asthore, sure you don't know now what you want. Your career, laddie! Think a bit! The church, for instance—"

"Och, Uncle Robin, is it me in the church that must say my prayers by me lee lone, so loath am I to let the people see what's in me? I'd be the queer minister, dumb as a fish—"

"You once had a notion for the army, laddie."

"So I had, sir; and fine I'd like the uniforms and the swords and the horses, but I wouldn't have the heart to kill a man, and me never seeing him before. If a man did me a wrong, I'd kill him quick as I'd wash my hands, but never seeing him before, I could na, I just could na—"

"It's a clean thing, the sea," the Raghery man ventured.

"He's so very young," objected Uncle Robin.

"There's nothing but that or the books for me, Uncle Robin. A sailor or a scholar—and I don't think I'd make out well with the books."

"The books aren't all they're cracked up to be, wee Shane. I've written books myself, and who reads them but a wheen of graybeards, and they drowsing by the fire. Knowledge, laddie, I have that. . . . And it isn't even wisdom. Knowledge is like dry twigs you collect with care to make a big fire you can warm your shins at, and wisdom is the gift of God that's like the blossom on the gorse. I've searched books and taken out the marrow of dead men's brains, and after all, even all my knowledge may be wrong. . . . Your father's name will be remembered as long as the Gaidhlig lasts, for songs that came to him as easily as a woman's kiss. And your Uncle Alan's footprints are near the pole. And Mungo is remembered forever because he died with a laugh. Not that I'm saying anything against them, wee Shane; better men will never be seen. But Daniel Donelly's name is remembered because he beat Cooper in a fight, and songs were made about it. And I'll be remembered only when some old librarian dusts a forgotten book. And I was supposed to be the wise pup o' the litter, with my books and my study. And all I have now is a troubled mind in my latter days. Aye, the books! . . ."

"Shall I go to sea, sir?"

"Is it up to me? And how about your mother, laddie?"

"Oh, there's little warmth within her for me, sir. She's a bitter woman. She does na like my father's breed."

"Are you your father's breed through, wee caddie? Are you Campbell all? Here, gi' us a look at your face. Aye, the eyes, the nose, the proud throw to the head of you. I'm afeared there's little of your mother in you, laddie; afeared there's none at all."

"I'm no' ashamed o' my kind, sir."

"And you're set on going to sea?"

"I'd like it fine, sir."

"And if it does na turn out the way you thought it would, you're not going to cry or turn sour?"

"I thought you knew me better nor that, Uncle Robin."

"I do." The big man laid his hand on the boy's shoulder and smiled at the shipmaster. "Take him, Raghery man!"

§ II

Though all was wonder to wee Shane, there was so much of it that it flicked through his head like a dream: the hazy September afternoon; the long, lean vessel like a greyhound; the sails white as a swan's wing; the cordage that rattled like wood; the bare-footed, bearded sailors; the town of Carrickfergus in the offing; the *lap-lap-lap* of water; the silent man at the wheel; the sudden transition of the friendly Raghery man into a firm, authoritative figure, quick as a cat, rapping out commands like a sergeant-major.

The town of Carrickfergus began to slip by as if

drawn by horses. The mate ran up the ladder of the poop.

"Topsails, McCafferty!" the Raghery man ordered.

"Topsails, sir."

A minute later there came the mate's voice from amidships:

"Sheet home the topsails—and put your backs into it!"

Patter of feet. An accordion began to whine like a tinker. Creak and strain. Faster lapping of water. A song raised in chorus:—

As I came a-tacking down Paradise Street—
  Yo-ho! Blow the man down!
As I came a-tacking down Paradise Street—
  Give us some time till we blow the man down!

A trim little bumboat I chanced for to meet!
  Blow, bullies, blow the man down!
A trim little bumboat I chanced for to meet!
  Give us some time till we blow the man down!

She was round in the counter and bluff in the bows!
  Yo-ho! Blow the man down!
She was round in the counter and bluff in the bows!
  Give us some time till we blow the man down.
    Blow the man down!
  Blow, bullies! Blow the man down!

BOOK TWO

THE WAKE AT ARDEE

§ I

THE WAKE AT ARDEE

THE feeling that was uppermost in him as he sat outside the thatched cottage in the moonlight, while the wake was within, was not grief at his wife's death; not a shattered mind that his life, so carefully laid out not twelve months before, was disoriented; not any self-pity; not any grievance against God, such as little men might have: but a strange dumb wonder. There she lay within, in her habit of a Dominican lay sister, her hands waxy, her face waxy, her eyelids closed. And six guttering candles were about her, and women droned their prayers with a droning as of bees. There she lay with her hands clasped on a wooden crucifix. And no more would the robins wake her, and they fussing in the great hawthorn-tree over the coming of dawn. No longer would she rake the ash from the peat and blow the red of it to a little blaze. No longer would she beat his dog out of the house with the handle of the broom. No longer would she foregather with the neighbours over a pot of tea for a pleasant vindictive chat. No longer would she look out to sea for him with her half-loving, half-inimical eyes. No longer in her sharpish voice would she recite her rosary and go to bed.

And to-morrow they would bury her—there would be rain to-morrow: the wind was sou'east,—they would lower her, gently as though she were alive, into a rectangular slot in the ground, mutter alien prayers in an alien tongue with business of white magic, pat the mound over as a child pats his castle of sand on the sea-shore, and leave her there in the rain.

A month from now they would say a mass for her, a year from now another, but to-morrow, to-day, yesterday even, she was finished with all of life: with the fussy, excited robins of dawn; with the old dog that wanted to drowse by the fire; with the young husband who was either too much or too little of a man for her; with the clicking beads she would tell in her sharpish voice; with each thing; with everything.

And here was the wonder of it, the strange dumb wonder, that the snapping of her life meant less in reality to him than the snapping of a stay aboard ship. The day after to-morrow he would mount the deck of Patrick Russell's boat, and after a few crisp orders would set out on the eternal sea, as though she were still alive in her cottage, as though indeed she had never even lived, and northward he would go past the purple Mull of Cantyre; past the Clyde, where the Ayrshire sloops danced like bobbins on the water; past the isles, where overhead drove the wedges of the wild swans, trumpeting as on a battle-field; past the Hebrides, where strange arctic birds whined like hurt dogs; northward still to where the northern lights sprang like dancers in the black winter nights; eastward and southward to where the swell of the Dogger Bank rose, where the fish grazed like kine. Over the great sea he would go as though nothing had happened, not even the snapping of a stay, down to the sea, where the crisp winds of dawn were, and the playful, stupid, short-sighted porpoises; the treacherous sliding icebergs; and the gulls that cried with the sea's immense melancholy; and the great plum-coloured whales . . .

§ 2

To his nostrils, sterilized as they were by the salt air of the sea, the rich scents of Louth came in a rushing profusion. The wild roses of June were like the high notes of a violin, and there was clover, and mown hay. In the southeast the clouds were banking, but still the moon rose high, and the cottage was clear as in daylight, clearer even in the mind's eye—the whitewashed walls, the thatch like silver, the swallows' nests beneath the eaves. The hard sea-cobbles beneath his feet were clear and individual, and to where he sat in the haggard came a girl's song from down the road:

"Oh, Holland is a wondrous place and in it grows much green.
It's a wild inhabitation for my young love to be in.
There the sugar-cane grows plentiful, and leaves on every tree,
But the low, lowlands of Holland are between my love and me."

He listened with a cocked ear, and smiled as he thought how easy it would be to stroll down the road to where the singing girl was, and accost her pleasantly: "So he's in Holland, is he? That's the queer and foolish place for him to be, and I here!" There would be banter, quick and smart as a whip, a scuffle, a clumsily placed kiss, laughter, another scuffle, and a kiss that found its mark somehow, then a saunter together down the scented loaning while the June moon rode high and the crickets sang.

O my God ! here he was thinking about love, and his wife lay inside and she dead !

And a new light wonder sprang up and whirled within the big dumb wonder that was on him : that here was he, a lad not yet twenty-two, with a dead wife on his hands, while his shipmates were off with the laughter of young women in their ears after the silent and tense watches of the sea. His captain had gone home to Newry to where his wife awaited him, the tall, graceful woman with the hair like black silk and the black eyes and the black ear-rings and the slim, white, enigmatic hands. And the first mate had gone to Rostrevor with a blond, giggling girl, and the crew were at Sally Bishop's in Dundalk, draining the pints of frothy porter and making crude material love to Sally Bishop's blowsy brown girls, some chucking their silver out with a laugh—the laugh of men who had fought hurricanes, and some bargaining shrewdly . . But here he was, home, with his wife, and her dead. And if she hadn't been dead, she would have been half loving, half inimical toward him, her arms and bosom open, but a great stranger . . . He couldn't understand. Well, she was dead, and . . . he didn't know . . .

A bent, fattish figure in a shawl came toward him through the haggard, his wife's mother. There was the sweetish, acrid odor of whisky.

"Shane *avick*, are you there all alone, mourning for the pleasant, beautiful one who's gone?"

"I was just sitting down."

"You wouldn't like a wee drop of consolation?"

"Whisky? No, thanks."

"Just the least taste?"

"No, thanks."

"And I after bringing it out to you in a naggin bottle. Just the wetting of your lips, *agra*, would cheer you up, and you down to the ground."

"No!"

The old woman sat on the stone ditch beside him and began swaying backward and forward, and the keening note came into her voice:

"Is it gone? Is it gone you are, Moyra *a sthore?* Sure, 't was the kindly daughter you were to me, and me old and not worth my salt, a broken *cailleach* hobbling on a stick. Never did you refuse me the cup o' tea so strong a mouse could walk on it. And the butcher's meat o' Christmas, sure your old ma must have a taste, too. And many's the brown egg you let me have, and they bringing a high price on the Wednedsay market. And the ha'porth o' snuff—sure you never came home without it, and you at Dundalk fair. Kindly you were as the little rains of April, and my heart is ashes now you're gone . . ."

Shane paced off through the haggard. There was the *glug-glug* of a bottle, and again the sweetish, acrid odor of whisky. He turned back.

"Only to one were you kinder nor to myself and that was to the lad here, whose heart is broken for you. Dumb with grief he is, now you're gone. And all you did for him! You might have married a strong farmer, would have a dozen cows, horses would pull a cart or plow, hens by the dozen, and flitches of bacon hanging in the kitchen. Or you might have married a man who had a shop and sat at your ease in the back room, like a lady born. Or you might have married a gager and gone to Dublin and mixed with the grand quality. And your mother would have a black silk dress, and shoes with buttons on them. But you married this young fellow who goes to sea, so much was the great love on you for him. Love came to you like a thunder-storm, and left you trembling like a leaf, and now you're dead—ochanee! ochanee! ochanee! o!"

Her voice changed from the shrill keen to a shrewd whine:

"You'll be leaving me something to remember her by, Shane Oge, and her a fathom deep beneath me in the cold ground. And a trinket or two, or a dress, maybe, or a bangle would keep my heart warm?"

"You can have them all."

"All is it? Ah, sure, it's the grand big heart is in you, lad o' the North. And are they all to be mine, the silver brooch you bought her from the Dutch city, and the ring with the pearl in it, and the dresses of silk from France, and the shoes that have buckles? Are they for me, hinny?"

"Yes, yes. Take them."

"And the wee furnishings of the house, the feather-bed is soft to lie on, and the dresser with the delft, and the creepy stool beside the fire, the noble chairs? You wouldn't be selling them to the stranger, Shane Oge?"

"No, you can have those, too."

"And the house, too? Young noble fellow, where is your wife's mother to lay her gray hairs? Couldn't you fix the house, too?"

"The house is not mine, and I can't afford to buy it."

"But 't is you you are rich the Protestant family. Your uncles and your mother, hinny. Rotten with gold they are, and me just a poor old *cailleach* that gave you the white lamb o' the flock."

"We'll look after you. My uncle Alan Campbell will be here in a day or so and fix everything. But I'm afraid the house is out of the question."

"Oh, sure it would be a noble thing to have the house, and they around me dying with envy of my state and grandeur. At fair or at wake great respect they would pay me, and the priests of God would be always calling. The house, fine lad, give me the house!"

"You'll have to speak to my Uncle Alan."

"Alan Campbell is a hard Northern man."

"Nevertheless, you'll have to speak to him."

"*A mhic mheirdrighe!*" Her mouth hissed. "O son of a harlot!"

Shane wheeled like a sloop coming about.

"You forget I've got the Gaelic myself, old woman."

"Oh, sure, what did I say, fine lad, but *avick machree*, son of my heart? *Avick machree*, I said. O son of my heart, that's what you are. You wouldn't take wrong meaning from what an old woman said, and her with her teeth gone, and under the black clouds of sorrow!"

A glint in the moonlight caught Shane's eyes. He gripped her right hand.

"Is that Moyra's wedding-ring you have on? Did you—did you—take it—from her hand?"

"Oh, sure, what use would she have for it, and she in the sods of Ballymaroo? And the grand Australian gold is in it, worth a mint of money. And what use would you have for it, and you in strange parts, where a passionate foreign woman would be giving you love, maybe? The fine lad you are, will draw the heart of many. But it's drawing back coldly they'd be, and they seeing that on your finger, or on a ribbon around your neck. Drawing back they'd be, and giving the love that was yours to another fellow. A sin to waste the fine Australian gold it is. And you wouldn't begrudge me the price of a couple o' heifers that would grow into grand cows? You wouldn't, fine lad—."

He flung her hand from him so savagely that she fell, and he went swiftly toward the house where the dead woman was. Back of him in the haggard came the *glug-glug* of the naggin bottle, and from down the loaning came the rich, untrained contralto of the singing girl:

"Nor shoe nor stocking will I put on nor comb go in my
hair.
And neither coal nor candlelight shine in my chamber
fair.
Nor will I wed with any young man until the day I die,
Since the low lowlands of Holland are between my love
and me."

§ 3

As he paused at the half-door, the laughter and the chatter in the kitchen ceased, and he was aware of the blur of faces around the room, white faces of men and women and alien eyes. Over the peat fire—there was a fire even in June—the great black kettle sang on the crane, to make tea for the mourners. Here and there were bunches of new clay pipes scattered, and long rolls of twisted tobacco, for the men to smoke, and saucers full of snuff for both men and women. A great paraffin lamp threw broad, opaque shadows, making the whole a strange blur in the kitchen, while in the bedroom opening off it, where the tense, dead woman lay, was a glare of candles as from footlights, and there gathered the old women of the neighbourhood, discussing everything in hushed, vindictive whispers—the price of cows, morbid diseases, the new wife some man had, and whether such a girl was with child . . . And the dead woman, who had loved talk such as this, as a drunkard loves the glass, gave no heed . . . Strange ! . . . And every hour or so they would flash to their knees, like some quick instinctive movement of birds, and now carelessly, now over-solemnly they would say a rosary for the dead woman's soul :

" *Ar n-Athair, ta ar neamh* . . . " Our Father, Who art in Heaven—" and then a long suspiration ; " *'Se do bheatha, 'Mhuire !* " " Hail, Mary ! Full of grace ! "

But in the kitchen they would be laughing, chatting, playing crude forfeits, telling grotesque stories, giving riddles, and now, to the muted sound of a melodeon, a man would dance a hornpipe . . . And men would sneak out to the byre in twos and threes for a surreptitious glass of whisky . . . And suddenly they would rush in and join in the rosary:

"*Ar n-Athair, ta ar neamh*—" they would gabble, "'*Se do bheatha, Mhuire!* . . ."

It was all so grotesque, so empty, so play-actor-like—so inharmonious with Death! Death was very terrible or very peaceful, thought Shane Campbell of the sea and the Antrim Glens. "Down from your horse when Death or the King goes by," went the Antrim old word. But here the house of death was a booth of Punchinello.

More aware even than of the indignity of it all was he of the hatred about him. They hated him for his alien race, his alien faith. Not one of the men but would have killed him had they had courage, because his head was high, his step firm. The women hated him because he had chosen one from among them and given her honor and gifts. And his wife's mother hated him with the venomous, nauseous hatred that old women bear. And yet they'd have loved him if he'd given way to hysterical, unprofound grief, or become . . . drunk! They'd have understood him. But all they had for him was hatred now. Even the dead woman on the bed hated him . . . Ah, well, only a day or so more, and he'd shake them off as a great ship leaves behind it the troublesome traders' bumboats.

There came to him the shrill keening of the old woman as some one brought her toward the house:

"Ochanee! Ochanee! Ochanee o! the Shepherd's lamb! She's gone from us! The high branch on the pleasant little tree! And what's to become of me in my latter days! Me that thought I'd have the beautiful house to live in, and a horse and cart, and a wake would be the envy of many, and not the curate, but the parish priest himself, to be at the head of the funeral. And now I'm to be thrown against the great cruelty of the harsh Northern men! Nine black curses against them and theirs, and on my bare knees I say it. Och, white gull o' the harbor, why did you die? Ochanee! Ochanee!"

The gabbled rosary, the low laughter in the kitchen, the clink of glasses, the howling of the *cailleach*—all these noises repulsed him like a forefront of battle. So he did not go into the house, but took his hand from the half-door and returned to the haggard, to the grave, understanding silence of the moon.

§ 4

Because he was so young, and thought he knew so much when in reality he knew so little, young Shane had thought, when he met Moyra Dolan, that he had discovered the morning star. Five and a half years at sea, as apprentice and navigator, had shown his eyes much and his heart little. He knew Bermuda and the harbor of Kingston. He had beaten up the China Seas. He had seen the clouds over Table Mountain. He knew Baltimore. He had seen the bowsprits of the great Indiamen thrust over the quays of Poplar parish like muskets levelled over a barricade. And to him it was just a wonder, a strange spectacle. The streets were strange as in a dream, and the folk were strange as in a play. One wandered down an avenue, seeing the queer commodities in the shops and booths. One wandered to the right. One wan- to the left. And there was great delight to finding a street one had seen before, maybe only five minutes ago, and one felt one was getting somewhere, was understanding the new country.

But one never did understand the new country. All the people were strange. One could not imagine them about the daily business of life, waking, eating, buying, and selling. Black men and ochre-coloured folk. There seemed to be a mystery somewhere. One imagined them gathering at night in secret to begin their real understood life. At times it seemed impossible that it was the same world. Surely the sun that struck like a hammer in Jamaica could not be the gracious warm planet that gilded the gorse of the Antrim glens. And up the Baltic in mid-winter it was bleak as a candle, and even then in Antrim it had a great kindliness. Nor were the winds the same. The hot puffs of the Indian Ocean, the drunken lurching flaws of Biscay Bay, the trades that worked steadily as ants, had not the human quality of the winds of the Nine Glens, that were now angry as an angry man, now gentle as a gentle woman.

Only one thing was constant, and that was the women whom sailors know in ports. And they wore masks. The same easily forced laughter, the same crude flattery, the complacent arms, the eternal eager hand. . . .

And then one day the new port palled, like a book one has read too often, or a picture one has looked at over long. And it was sheet home the royals and off to a new port, where there were new strange people, and streets laid another way, and other things in the merchant's booths, and a new language to pick up a phrase or two of.

But in the end all palled for a time, the aphrodisiac tropic smell; the coral waters, clear as well water at home; the white houses with the green jalousies; the lush, coarse green. And the melancholic drums of the East palled and palled the grimness of the North. And the unceasing processional of strange secret faces wearied the eye and the mind. And the angular spiritual edges of shipmates wore toward one through the uniform of flesh, became annoying, sometimes unbearable.

And then an immense yearning would come over young Shane for the beloved faces in the lamplight, for the white road over the purple heather, for the garden where the greened sundial was, with its long motto in the Irish letter:

Is mairg a baidhtear in am an anaithe
Na tig an ghrian in dhiaidh na fearthainne—

as if anybody didn't know that, that it was a pity to be drowned in time of storm, for the sun shines brightly when the rain goes!

But the sun-dial was mirrored in his heart, and the purple mountain and the great dun house. The winds he sniffed as a hunting dog does, and each tack to port or starboard either thrilled or cast him down. . . . When would be get there, would it be cool of the evening, when the bats were out? or would it be in the sunshine of the morning, when a great smell was from the heather? And who would hear the wicket-gate click as the latch was lifted, and put a welcome before him with a great shout, uncles Alan or Robin, or a servant girl or boy, or the bent old gardener who kept the lawn true as a bowling-green ? . . . Or would it be his mother ?

§ 5

Aboard ship the young apprentices had their problems, problems of conduct, or of girls at home, or of money in port, but for young Shane there was always the problem of his mother.

At home he had regarded as a matter of fact that she should come and go in her hard, efficient French way. It had not seemed strange to him that her mouth was tight, her eyes hard as diamonds. It was to him one with his Uncle Robin's solemnity and Alan Donn's gruff sportsmanship. But away from home he thought of it, brooded over it. Her letters to him were so curt, so cut and dried ! She wrote of the birth of another child to young Queen Victoria—as if that mattered a tinker's curse !—or how her Holland bulbs, which she had bought at Belfast, had withered and died. She directed him " to pray God to keep him pure in mind and body, your affectionate mother, Louise de Damèry Campbell." Alan Donn's letters had the grand smell of harness about them. " You'll mind the brown gelding we bought at Ballymena. He disgraced us at Dublin in the jumping competitions. You know he can jump his own height, but he got the gate after three tries. I could have graet like a bairn. Well, this will be all from your loving Uncle Alan. P.S. I caught the white trout in Johnson's Brae burn. I was after him, and he was dodging me for six years. Your loving Uncle Alan. P.P.S. The championship is at Prestwick this year, and I think I've a grand chance. If you're home, you can caddy for me. Your loving Uncle Alan."

Uncle Robin's letters had vast wisdom. "Ay be reading the books, laddie. An ill-educated man feels always at a disadvantage among folk of talent. Aboard ship you can read and think more than at a university I've got a parcel for you to take when you go again. Hakluyt's Voyages and a good Marco Polo. And the new book of Mr. Dickens, *The Haunted Man*. And there's a great new writer you'll not want to miss, by name of Thackeray." And there'd be the Bank of England note, "for fear you might be needing it on a special occasion, and not having it, and feeling bad." Dear Uncle Robin! And then the flash of tenderness, like a rainbow: "God bless you and keep you, my brother's son!"

His Uncle Robin's letters he would greet with a smile, and perhaps a bit moistness in the eye; Alan Donn's with a grin, as an elder brother's. But his mother's letters he would approach with a coldness akin to fear. He hated to open them. It was like an unpleasant duty.

The realization of her was always a chilling disappointment, but the dream of her was a great hope. And in the black waters of the China Seas, or in the night watches off the Azores, where the porpoises played in the phosphorescence, there would come a sea-change over the knowledge he had of her. All the spiritual, all the mental angles of her faded into gracious line, and on the tight lips of her a smile would play as a flower opens, and her eyes, hard as diamonds, would open and become kindly as a lighted house. And the strange things of the heart would come out, like little shy rabbits, or like the young tortoises, and bask in that kindly picture. And the things that were between them, that could not be said, but just sensed, as the primroses of spring are sensed, not seen, not felt, hardly smelt even, but sensed. . . . The hesitant deep things he would say and the dignified, smiling answer, or the pressure of the hand even, and the inclination of the shoulder. . . .

And the people he would meet who would ask him about his mother, and he could answer nothing, so that they thought him stupid and unthoughtful. But really what was there to say ? . . . And once when he sprang into Biscay Bay after a cabin-boy who had fallen over the taffrail, and the lad's mother had thanked him in Plymouth for saving the child's life : " Your mother will be very proud of you," the old woman said. But the reality of the harsh Frenchwoman came to him like a slap in the face. " Christ, if she only were ! " his heart cried. But the clipped little Scots-Irish voice replied, " Aye, I suppose she will."

And again the soft mood would come, and then he would have a letter from her, ending with that harsh command, that was a gust of some bleak tempest of her own life, where his father had perished : " Pray God to keep you pure in mind and body ! "

And homeward bound again, in the soft murmur of the wind among the shrouds, and the little laughter of the water at the bows, there would abide with him again the dream-mother of the night watches, until he said to himself that surely the reality was false, and at the garden-gate she would be waiting for him with a great depth of kindness in her eyes, and arms warm as sunshine, and a bosom where a boy might rest his head for a moment after the great harshness of the strange places.

But the kindliness came not from her. It came from Robin More, who ran down the garden faster than his dignity should have allowed him. " Are you all right, wee Shane ? Is everything all right with you ? You're looking fine, but you haven't been sick, wee fellow ? Tell me, you haven't been sick ? " Or from Alan Donn, with his great snort of laughter : " Christ ! are you home again ? And all the good men that's been lost at sea ! Well, the devil's childer have the devil's luck. Eigh, laddie, gie's a feel o' ye. *A Righ*—O King of Graces, but you're the lean pup ! Morag, Nellie, Cassie, some tea ! and be damned quick about it ! "

And then his mother would come into the room, like a cold wind or a thin ghost, and there would be a kiss on the cheek, a cold, precise peck, like a bird's. And, " Did you have a good voyage ? " just as if she said, " Do you think we'll have rain ? "

Oh, well, to hell with it ! as Alan Donn said when he flubbed his approach to the last green for some championship or other, " What you never had, you never lost ! "

Aye, true indeed. What you never had you couldn't very well lose. Aye, there was a lot in that. Just so ; but—

Boys do be thinking long. . . .

§ 6

Because his Uncle Alan was in Scotland somewhere shooting deer and would not be home for several days, and because Uncle Robin was in Paris, and because the *Goban Saor* put into Dundalk to take a cargo of unbleached linen, young Shane decided to stay there for a few days before proceeding northward to the Antrim Glens. He felt he couldn't face the house at Cushendu with his cold, precise mother alone there, so he accepted the hospitality of an apprentice friend.

It was at a country barn dance during these few days that he met Moyra Dolan.

A tallish, tawny-haired woman with the dead-white skin that goes with reddish hair, with steel for eyes, there was a grace and carriage to her that put her aside from the other peasant girls as a queen may masquerade as a slave and yet betray herself as a queen. Other girls there were as pretty, with their hair like flax and their eyes like blue water; with hair like a dim blue cloud and eyes like a smudge of charcoal. But none had her teeth, her small ankles, her long, sensitive hands. Some strain of the Stuart cavaliers had crept into that hardy peasant stock on the way to defeat of the Boyne Water. . . . She might have seemed nothing but a pretty lady's maid in London or Dublin, but in North Louth she was like a queen. . . .

Her looks were her tragedy, for she held herself too good for a labouring man to marry, and, having no dower, no farmer would have her. Among the peasantry romance does not count, but land. And if the Queen of Sheba, and she having nothing but her shift, were to offer herself in marriage to a strong farmer, he would refuse her for the cross-eyed woman in the next townland who had twenty acres and five good milch cows. . . . Only for the very rich or the very poor is romance!

Her only chance for marriage was a matter of luck. She would have to meet some government official, or some medical student home on his holidays, or some small merchant whom her beauty would unbalance, as drink would unbalance him. And she must dazzle, and her old mother play and catch him, as a jack pike is dazzled by a spoon bait, hooked, and brought ashore. She might marry or might miss, or grow into an acidulous red-headed woman. It was a matter of luck. And her luck was in. She met young Shane Campbell.

They danced together. They wandered in the moonlight. They met in the country lanes. And they were very silent, she because she played a game, and a counter is better than a lead, and he because he was in love with her. Had it been only a matter of sweethearting, he would have been merry as a singing bird, full of chatter, roughing it with her for a kiss. But it was love with him, and a thing for life, and life was long and more serious than death. . . . So he was silent.

He was silent when he went home for a week, silent with uncles Robin and Alan, who sensed he was going through one of the crises of adolescence, and knew the best thing to do was to leave him alone. He was silent with his mother, who saw nothing, cared nothing, so intent was she on revolving within herself as inexorably as the planets revolve in space. He decided to spend the last days of his leave in Dundalk. And at the railroad station in Ballymena he hazarded a look at Alan Donn.

" Uncle Alan—" and he stopped.

" What is it, laddie ? Is it a girl troubling you ? Take my advice and look her in the eyes and, 'You can love me or leave me, and to hell with you !' tell her. 'Do you see this right foot of mine ?' says you. 'Well, it's pointed to the next town-land, where there's just as pretty a one as you.' And you'll find her come around ; maybe there'll be a bit of an argument, but she'll come around. And if she doesn't there'd have been no hope for you, anyway. A touch o' the spur for the lazy mare and a bit of sugar for the jumper ! And when you've done loving her, gie her a chuck under the chin: 'Good-bye ! Good luck ! What you keep to yoursel' 'll worry nobody,' says you. And to hell with her !"

" Alan Donn !"

" Oh, it's that way, is it, Shaneen ? If you're in deep water, there's none but yourself can help you, laddie. I thought it was just maybe a case o' laugh and kiss me. But it's different, is it ? There's no use giving advice. What's in you will out. But remember this: when it's over, for good or bad, your Uncle Alan's here, to laugh with you or greet with you or help you out of a hole. So—

" Good-bye, laddie. *Beannacht leat !* My blessing with you !"

§ 7

"Young lad, what is this you have done to my fine young daughter ?"

"I have done nothing, Bhean 'i Dolain," young Shane flared up, "save in honour, and the man or woman who says other lies."

"Agra, I know that. I know there's no harm in you from head to foot. And the trouble you've put on her is in her heart. All day long she sighs, and is listless as a shaded plant that does be needing the sun. All night she keeps awake, and the wee silent tears come down her face. And before my eyes she's failing, and her step that was once light now drags the like of a cripple's. Young lad of the North, you've put love in the heart of her and sorrow in the mind."

"I'm not so sprightly in the mind myself, woman Dolan."

"I know, avick. I know. Isn't it myself that's suffered the seven pangs of love and I a young girl ? But it's easy on a man, avick. He can go into the foreign countries, and put it out of his mind, or take to the drink and numb the great pain. But for a woman it's different. It's the like of a disfiguration that all can see. And when you're gone away, sure all will remember, for men do be minding long. The marrying time will come, and they'll look at my grand young daughter : strong farmer, and merchant of the shop, and drover does be going to England for the cattle-fairs, and they'll say : 'Isn't that the red girl gave love to the sailing fellow, and burnt her heart out so that there's no sap in it for me ?' And they'll pass her by, my grand young daughter, that's the equal of any."

"And what would you have me do, woman of the house?"

"What would any decent man do but marry her?"

"Aye! . . . Aye! I thought of marrying her, if she'd have me. . . . But we hardly know each other yet. . . . and maybe I'm too young . . ."

"If you're able to handle a ship, you're able to handle a woman, young lad. And what time is better for marriage nor the first flush of youth? Sure you grow together like the leaves upon the tree. Let you not be putting it off now, but spring like a hero."

"But isn't the matter of her faith between us, woman of the house?"

"And sure that can be fixed later. Will the priest mind, do you think, so long as she does her duty? And a sixpence in the plate on Sunday is better nor a brown ha'penny, and a half-sovereign at Easter will soothe black anger like healing grass. Very open in thought I am, and I knowing the seven pangs of love. Let you go to your own clergyman, and she'll go with you, I'll warrant, so eaten is she by love."

"My people, woman o' the house—"

"Your people is it? Sure it isn't your people is marrying my grand young daughter, but you yourself. The old are crabbit, and they do be thinking more of draining a field, or of the price of flax, nor of the pain and delights of love. And it's always objections. But there can be no objecting when the job 's finished."

She looked at him shrewdly.

"A grand influence, a grand steadying influence is marriage on a sailing man. It keeps you from spending your money in foreign ports, where you only buy trickery for your silver. And when you have a wife at home, you'll have little truck with fancy women, who have husbands behind the screen, sometimes, and them with knives. . . . So I've heard tell. . . . Or maybe get an evil sickness. Listen to an old woman has wisdom, bold lad."

"When I come from my voyage. . . ."

"Dark lad, if anything happens to you, and you drowning in the black water, the great regret that will be on you and the water gurgling into your lungs, and, 'Wasn't I the fool of the world,' you'll say, 'that might have heard the crickets singing in the night-time and my white love by my side? And might have had power of kissing and lovemaking, but was young and foolish, and lay be my lee lone. . .'"

But this was the wrong track, the old woman noticed, and came about.

"And all the time you're away, my daughter will be pining for you, drooping and pining, my grand young daughter, and the spring will go out of her step and the light from her eyes and the lustre from the hair that's a wonder to all. . . . Oh, isn't it the cruel thing?"

"My ship sails the day after to-morrow."

She saw surrender in his face, rose quickly, and went to the door.

"Come inside, Moyra, Moyreen! And be putting your cloak on, with the ribbons that tie beneath your chin. And your dress of muslin that the lady in Newry gave you. And stockings. And your shoes of leather. And I'll be putting on my Paisley shawl. And this young boy will be getting Michael Doyle's horse and trap. Come in, Moyreen, come in and put haste on you, for it's going to Dundalk we are, this day, this hour, this minute even!"

§ 8

It occurred to him as he sat in the haggard under the riding moon, not a pitch shot from the house where his wife was being waked, that nothing was disturbed because she was dead. It was not strange that the stars kept on their courses, for the death of neither king nor cardinal nor the wreck of the greatest ship that ever sailed the seas would not move them from their accustomed orbit. But not a robin in the hedge was disturbed, not a rabbit in the field, not a weasel in the lane. Nature never put off her impenetrable mask. Or did she really not care? And was a human soul less to her than a worm in the soil?

There was a stir in the house. They would be making tea now for the men and women who said they were mourners. . . . The querulous voice of his wife's mother came to him as someone led her from the heated house into the cool of the June night.

"Great sacrifices we made for him, myself and the white love that's stretched beyond in the room. All we had we gave him, and all she found was barren death, and I the barren charity of Northern men . . ."

"Oh, sure, 'tis the pity of the world you are, Pegeen," a neighbour comforted her.

"On his bended knees he came to her, asking for love," the *cailleach* went on. "On his bare and bended knees. And her heart melted toward him as the snow melts on the hills. 'And hadn't you better wait,' said I, 'Moyreen Roe? With the great looks and the grand carriage of you, 'tis a great match you can make surely. A gentleman from England, maybe, would have a castle and fine lands, or the pick of the dealing men, and they going from Belfast to Drogheda and stopping overnight at Ardee. Or wouldn't it be better for you to marry one of your own kind, would go to church with you in a kindly way?"

"'But if I don't marry this lad, he'll kill himself,' she says to me.

"'But your faith,' says I, ''avourneen, your holy faith, surely, you will not be forsaking that for this boy!'"

"And what did she say to that, Pegeen?" the neighbour asked.

"'Sure it's promised to turn he has,' she answered. 'And do everything is right by me, so much I love him!'"

"The treacherous Ulster hound!" The neighbour inveighed.

"Treacherous by race and treacherous by nature. Sure, can't you see it, the way he treats me? Sorrow word he has for me, that bore the wife of his bosom, barring, 'Alan Donn Campbell will see you and fix up everything.' And haven't I met Alan Campbell once before, and it's the cold eye he has and the hard heart. And this is all the return I get for bearing the white darling would be fit mate for a king. There was a publican of Dundalk had an eye on her, a big red-faced, hearty man. And she might have married him but this lad came and spoiled everything. And if she'd married him, I'd have been sitting in the parlour of the public house, in a seemly black dress and a brooch in the bosom of it, taking my pinch of snuff and my strong cup of tea with a drop of Hollands in it would warm the cockles of your heart, and listening to the conversation of the fine customers and them loosening up with the drink. And the ould grannies would have courtesied to me and hate in their hearts. But now a leaf on the wind am I, a broken twig on the stream. And the black men of Ulster have me for a plaything, the men that have a hatred for me and my kind, so that it's a knife they'd put in you, or poison in your tea—"

" Let you be coming in now, Pegeen. Let you be coming in now. And take a cup of tea would put heart in you, or something strong, maybe. And then we'll be saying a prayer for her who's gone—"

" Dead she is, the poor heart, dead she is, and better off nor I am—"

Her high querulousness died away as she went into the house, and again was the silence of the riding moon. All her grief, all her lies, all her bitterness had not stirred a leaf upon the bough. Not a robin in the hedge was disturbed by her calamity, not a rabbit in the field, not a weasel in the lane. . . .

§ 9

He thought to himself: had they rushed him into this marriage? And he answered himself truthfully, they had not. He could have said no, and stood by his no, young as he was, against every old woman and every young woman in the world. No, fast as they had worked, they hadn't worked faster than his thought had.

And did he marry because he was in love with Moyra Dolan He was in love with her, he conceded that. For what the term was accepted at, he was in love with her. Women he had met in his twenty years, great ladies of the Ulster clans; shy, starched misses from the Friends' School; moody peasant girls; merry women of the foreign ports, and to none of them had he felt that strange yearning he had felt toward Moyra Dolan, the strange pull that sends the twig in the diviner's hands down toward the hidden water. Yes, he was in love with her, but was it because of that he had married her? And he truthfully answered, no.

He remembered, the mood coming back to him as concretely as an action, what he had thought while the old woman had wheedled him with her voice like butter. All he had thought in his prentice days at sea, all he had thought of in the night watches, all he had thought of in the loneliness of his mother's house, had gathered like great cloud-banks at night, and had suddenly taken form and colour and purpose in that one moment, as a cloud-bank at the coming of the sun. . . . Life had appeared to him in one brief moment, and he had tried to grasp it.

It had seemed to him right that he would go down to the sea in ships all his days, and trade in foreign ports, and work, transmuting effort into gain, and should come home to rest.

And for whom was the gain? And where was home? Surely not for himself was the gain, and home was not his cold mother's house? And now that he had come to manhood as boys come at sea, braving danger and thinking mightily, it was for him to decide.

A mirage, a seeming, a thing to look at, to go get bravely had come into his mind in little pictures, like prints in a book. A thing of simplicity, simple as the sea, and as colourful and as wholesome and as beautiful. He thought of a little thatched and whitewashed house with a cobbled yard clean as a ship's decks, and a garden where the bluish green stalks and absurdly pretty flowers of potatoes would come in spring, and one side would be the red and white of the clover, and on the other would be the minute blue flower of the flax; and an old dog drowsing on the threshold . . . And this would be in his mind as he wandered the far foreign streets . . . And there would be the droning of the bees in the clover, and the swish of the swallows darting to and from the eaves, and in the evening would be the singing of the crickets . . . And these he would hear over the capstan's clank . . . When he tumbled into his cabin after his watch, into the heeling room where the lamp swung overhead like a crazy thing, and all was a litter of oilskins and sea-boots, and a great dampness everywhere, he would know there was a swept cottage in Louth where the delft shone on the dresser in the kindly light of the turf, and there would be a spinning-wheel in the corner, and a big rush-bottomed chair, and the kettle singing on the hob . . . And when his comrades would leave the ship in port of nights to go to the houses where music and dancing were, and crazy drinking, and where the adroit foreign women held out their arms of mystery and mercenary romance, he would lean over the taffrail and laugh and shake his head:

"No, I think I'll stay on board." "Come on, young Shane. There's a woman down at Mother Parkinson's and they say she's an Austrian arch-duchess who has run away with a man, and got left. Come on." Or, "There's a big dance over on the beach to-night, and a keg of rum, and the native women. Jump in." "No, I think I'll stay on board and read." "Come on. Don't be a fool." "No, go ahead and enjoy yourselves. I'll stay on board." And there would be the plash of oars as they rowed shoreward, and maybe a song raised. . . . And he would make himself comfortable under the awning of the after deck, and read the bundles of newspapers from home, of how Thomas Chalmers, the great Scottish preacher, was dead, or how a new great singer had been heard in London, a Swedish girl, her name was Jenny Lind, or how Shakspere's house had been bought and a great price paid for it, three thousand pounds . . . Or he would read one of the new books that were coming out in a flood, a new one by Mr. Dickens, the bite of the new writer, Mr. Thackeray with his "Vanity Fair," or that strange book written by a woman, "Wuthering Heights." . . . But in a little minute the volume would fall to his knees, and the people of the book would leave the platform of his mind, and a real, warmer presence come to it . . . He could see the gracious, kindly womanhood now move through the house, now come to the door to watch the far horizon . . . Of evenings she would stand dreaming at the lintel while he was leaning dreaming over the taffrail, and though there were ten thousand miles between them their hearts would be intimate as pigeons . . . And he would think of coming home to the peaceful cottage and the wife with the grave eyes and kindly smile, and if he were a day ahead of time, she would forget her reserve in great joy, and low, pleased laughter would jet from her throat . . . And if he were on time, there would be the quiet, grave confidence : " I knew your step ! " . . . And if he were late, there would be the passing of the cloud from the brows : " Thank God ! I—I was—just a trifle worried ! " . . . And the greetings over, she would look at him with a smile and a little lift of the eyebrows, and he would give her what he had brought from the voyage : a ring from Amsterdam, maybe, where the great jewellers are, or heavy silken stockings of France ; or he had gone to the West Indies, a great necklet of red coral ; or some fancy in humming-birds' feathers from the Brazils ; lace from Porto Rico, that the coloured women make with their slim brown fingers ; things of hammered brass from India ; and were he to China in the tea-trade, a coat such as a mandarin's lady would wear. . . . And with each gift there would be gasp of incredulous surprise, and "O Shaneen, you shouldn't have ! " . . . And then the evening would come, and they would stand on the threshold, and he would listen to the sounds the sea-men never hear : the swish and ripple of the wind among the trees, the birds settling themselves to sleep amid the boughs, the bittern that boomed like a horn, and the barking of a distant dog, and the crickets that do be singing when the evening falls. . . . And he would turn from that to find her arms out and her lips apart, who could wait no longer, and together they would go into their house, where the red turf had turned yellow—together, over their own threshold, into their own house . . . And when the time came for him to go to sea again, she would be grave with unshed tears and a brave smile . . . And one day after a long voyage, when she had greeted him, she would say, " Someone has come to our house ! " and he wouldn't understand, and be annoyed, until she showed him the little warm head in the cradle, and he would drop on his knees reverentially, and there would be great silent tears from him, and all her heart would show in her quiet smile . . .

And never an old woman on Naples quay would ask him for an alms but would get it, he thinking all the time of the old woman with the tow-like hair who abode in his house, his wife's mother. And she would be comfortable there in her old days, with always a fire to warm her, and always a cup of tea to cheer her up, and a kindly ear for her stories of ancient days, and a thanks for the alien rosaries she would say, praying for his safe return from the almighty waters. . . . And never a dog on his travels but would get a pat and a whistle, and he thinking of the grizzled terrier in Louth that guarded the threshold of quiet beauty . . .

And so he would have been content to live all his days, so he thought he would live, going down to the dangers of the sea, trading in strange ports, and transmuting hard, untiring effort into gain for her at home and her children, and he would grow old and grizzled, until he could no longer brace to a heeling plank or stand the responsibility of a ship's mastery, and then they would buy a little house on some harbour, while their sons went rolling down to Rio or fought the typhoon in the China Seas, and he could sit there with his telescope, watching the ships go by, or come in and out hauling up mainsail or making their mooring, and grumbling pleasantly at how good seamanship fades and dies. . .

All this he had thought out in the loneliness of foreign ports, in the night watches aboard ship, in the inhospitality of his mother's house, and on the jaunting-car to Dundalk. All this he had thought out, and on its basis gone into marriage. And it would just have been as well for him, better perhaps, had he thrown a coin into the air to find out whether he should marry or no.

And that was what human thought was worth —a brown penny thrown into the empty air !

"*Gloir do'n Athair, agas do'n Mhac, agas do'n Spiorad Naomh,*" went the drone of the rosary within. "Glory be to the Father, and to the Son, and to the Holy Ghost, Amen ! "

§ 10

And the house that he had known in a dream was no more in reality than a cold strange dwelling ; all was there, the whitewash, the thatch, the delft on the dresser, but as a home it was still-born. The turf did not burn well and the swallows shunned the eaves, feeling in nature's occult way, that the essential rhythm was wanting. Nor would bees be happy in the skips, but must swarm otherward. One would have said the house was built on some tragic rock . . .

Only the old dog was faithful, and stayed where his master put him.

And the face he had dreamed would not look toward him over the illimitable ocean. Seek as he would, it was never there, with warm gravity. His eyes might strive, but all they would see was the oily swell of the Dogger Bank, and the great plowed field of Biscay Bay, and the smash of foam against the Hebrides. Never would a space in the watery horizon open and show him a threshold of beauty with quiet, brooding face . . . And when he came home, either late or early, or on time to the moment, it was, "Och, is it yourself ?" And the only interruption to the house was the little more trouble he caused. And his gifts were treated tepidly, though with cupidinous eyes. In the evening, if he stood on the threshold, it was : "Wisha, is it going out you are ? And isn't it enough of the fresh air you have, and you on the salt water ?" And her embraces were half chastity, half sin, tepidly passionate, unintimate . . . so that shame was on him, and no pride or joyousness . . . Cold ! cold ! cold ! . . . A cold house, a cold woman . . . No light or warmth or graciousness . . .

And the old woman whom he had thought of as warm and peaceful by the fire was a hag with a peasant's cupidity : "And isn't it a little more you can be leaving us, darling lad, what with the high price that does be on things in this place and you are not spending a brown ha'penny aboard ship? . . . And herself might be taken sick now, and wouldn't it be a grand thing, a wee store of money in the house? Or the wars might come, find you far on the sea! An extra sovereign now, brave fellow, a half-sovereign itself!"

And when he left it was of less import than the cow going dry. Only one mourned him, the old dog. Only one remembered him, the half-blind badger hound, that dreamed of ancient hunting days . . .

And he would go down to his ship, heart-broken, when none was looking a mist of tears in his eyes, —he was not yet twenty-one,—but in a day or so that would pass, and the sea that was so strong would give him of its strength and heal him, so that after a few days he could stand up and say: "Well . . . Huuh . . . Well . . ."

A trick had been played him, like some tricks the sea and sun play. Afar off he had seen an island like an appointed dancing place, like the Green of Fiddlers, and he had asked to be put ashore there, to live and be a permanent citizen. And when he was landed, he found that his dancing place was only a barren rock where the seagulls mourned. Past the glamour of the sun and sea mists, there were only cold, searching winds and dank stone . . .

But he came of a race that are born men, breed men, and kill men. Crying never patched a hole in a brogue, and a man who's been fooled is no admirable figure, at least to Antrim men. So shut your mouth! When a master loses a ship he gets no other. That is the inexorable rule of the sea. So when a man wrecks his life . . .

What he had decided was this: go ahead. He had been fooled; pay the forfeit. Retreat into his own heart, and go ahead. Thirty, forty years. . . . He had himself to blame. And it wasn't as if he had to live in the house all the time; he had only to come back there. All that was killed was his heart. His frame was still stolid, his eye clear . , . There would be little oases here and there, some great record of a voyage broken, friends bravely made, a kiss now and then, freely, gallantly given . . . But . . . go ahead!

And then suddenly death had come, and the scheme of life was broken, like a piece from the end of a stick. Death he had seen before, but never so close to him. A good man had died and he had said: "God! there's a pity!" though why, he didn't know. And a young girl might die, and it would seem like a tragedy in a play. And a child would die, and he would feel hurt and say, "Yon's cruelty, yon!" And death had seemed to be an ultimate word.

But never before now had he seen the ramifications of death. Life had seemed to him to be a straight line, and suddenly he was inspired to the knowledge that it was a design, a pattern, a scheme . . . And now he felt it was only a tool, like a knife, or scissors, in the hands of what? . . . What? Destiny? . . . or what? . . .

§ II

"*A chraoibhin oaibhinn!* O pleasant little branch, is there regard in you for the last words of the dead woman ?" The old *cailleach* had come again to ruffle the grave silence about young Shane in the haggard.

"Was it—was it anything for me?"

"And whom would it be for, *acushla veg?* Sure the love of her heart you were, the white love of her heart. You and me she was thinking of, her old mother that saw a power of trouble. Ill-treated I was by Sergeant Dolan, who fought old Bonaparte in the foreign wars, and took to drinking in the dreadful days of peace. Harsh my life was, and peaceful should my end be, the like of a day that does be rainy, and turns at evening-time. And that was what she wanted, *a charaid bhig*, little friend o' me."

"What now?"

"She said to me, and she dying in my arms, and the blue spirit coming out of the red lips of her,—och! ochanee!— 'Sure it's not in that grand Northern lad to see you despised in your old age, and the grannies of the neighbourhood laughing at you who boasted often. The wee house he'll give you—the wee house is comfortable for an old woman—'"

"But the house isn't mine. It's Alan Donn Campbell's. It isn't mine to give, and I haven't the money to buy it. All the money I have is my pay and what my uncles give me—and they won't see you want."

"But isn't it the grand rich Northern family you are? And won't there be money coming to you when your uncles and mother die?"

"I suppose so."

"Well now, agra, a few of us have been thinking. And Manus McGinty, the priest's brother, is willing to advance you the money at interest, to be paid him when your people die. And you can buy the house, and a slip of a pig I can be fattening against the Christmas market."

"No!"

"Och, agra," she whined, "you wouldn't go back on the words of the poor girl, and her dying in my arms? And she was thinking of you when she should have been thinking of her God! And the grand subtle things she said of you, that only a woman can understand! Sure it was of love for you she died, you being away so long from her on the salt and bitter sea—"

"Listen, woman Dolan. I heard how Moyra died as I came through the village. She died as she was beating my poor old hound. She dropped dead from the passion in her, like a shot man. So where's all your love and your long dying wishes as she lay in your arms?"

He arose and walked away from her, through the haggard, under the sky, where the southeast cloud-banks rolled steadily toward the placid moon. And there was silence for an instant, so speechless he left her. And then suddenly her ancient shrill voice cut the air like a drover's whip:

"You Orange bastard!"

§ 12

The feeling that was uppermost in him as he sat outside the thatched cottage in the moonlight while the wake was within was not grief at his wife's death;

not a shattered mind that his life so carefully laid out not twelve months before was disoriented; not any self-pity; not any grievance against God such as little men might have. But a strange dumb wonder . . . There she lay within, in her habit of a Dominican lay sister, her hands waxy, her face waxy, her eyelids closed. And six guttering candles were about her, and women droned their prayers with a droning as of bees. There she lay with her hands clasped on a wooden crucifix. And no more would the robins wake her, and they fussing in the great hawthorn-tree over the coming of dawn. No longer would she rake the ash from the peat and blow the red of it to a little blaze. No longer would she beat his dog out of the house with the handle of the broom. No longer would she foregather with the neighbours over a pot of tea for a pleasant vindictive chat. No longer would she look out to sea for him with her half-loving, half-inimical eyes. No longer in her sharpish voice would she recite her rosary and go to bed.

And to-morrow they would bury her—there would be rain to-morrow: the wind was sou'east,—they would lower her, gently as though she were alive, into a rectangular slot in the ground, mutter alien prayers in an alien tongue with business of white magic, pat the mound over as a child pats his castle of sand on the sea-shore—and leave her there in the rain.

A month from now they would say a mass for her, a year from now another, but to-morrow, to-day, yesterday even, she was finished with all of life—with the fussy excited robins of dawn; with the old dog that wanted to drowse by the fire; with the young husband who was either too much or too little of a man for her ; with the clicking beads she would tell in her sharpish voice ; with each thing ; with everything. . . .

And here was the wonder of it, the strange dumb wonder, that the snapping of her life meant less in reality to him than the snapping of a stay aboard ship. The day after to-morrow he would mount the deck of Patrick Russell's boat, and after a few crisp orders would set out on the eternal sea, as though she were still alive in her cottage, as though, indeed, she had never even lived, and northward he would go past the purple Mull of Cantyre ; past the Clyde, where the Ayrshire sloops danced like bobbins on the water ; past the isles, where overhead drove the wedges of the wild swans, trumpeting as on a battlefield ; past the Hebrides, where strange arctic birds whined like hurt dogs ; northward still to where the northern lights sprang like dancers in the black winter nights ; eastward and southward to where the swell of the Dogger Bank rose, where the fish grazed like kine. . . . Over the great sea he would go, as though nothing had happened, not even the snapping of a stay—down to the sea, where the crisp winds of dawn were, and the playful, stupid, short-sighted porpoises ; the treacherous, sliding icebergs ; and the gulls that cried with the sea's immense melancholy ; and the great plum-coloured whales. . . .

BOOK THREE

THE MOUTH OF HONEY

THE MOUTH OF HONEY

§ I

IT was all like a picture some painter of an old and obvious school might have done. First, there was the port, with the white ships riding at their moorings in the blue sea. Then greyish white Marseilles, with its two immense ribbons, the Cannebière running northward, and the Rue de Rome and the Prado intersecting it. The great wooded amphitheatre rising like a wave and little Notre Dame de la Garde peeking like a sentry out to sea. And eastward from the quays were the little jagged islands the Phœnicians knew, If, and Rion, Jaros, strange un-French names . . . the sunshine yellow as a lamp, and the sea blue as flax, and the green woods, and the ancient greyish white city—all a picture some unimaginative painter would have loved. Next to Belfast, Marseilles was to Shane Campbell a second home. There it was, like your own house !

Obvious and drowsy it might seem, but once he went ashore, the swarming, teeming life of it struck Shane like a current of air. Along the quays, along the Cannebière, was a riot of colour and nationality unbelievable from on board ship. Here were Turks, dignified and shy. Here were Greeks, wary, furtive. Here were Italians, Genoese, Neapolitans, Livornians, droll, vivacious, vindictive. Here were Moors, here were Algerians, black African folk, sneering, inimical. Here were Spaniards, with their walk like a horse's lope. Here were French business men, very important. Here were Provençals, cheery, short, tubby, excitable, olive-coloured, black-bearded, calling to one another in the *langue d'oc* of the troubadours, "*Té, mon bon! Commoun as? Quézaco?*"

And the bustle of the shops and the bustle of cafés, until Shane was forced to go out to the olive-lined roads to the rocky summit of La Garde, and once there, as if drawn by a magnet, Shane would enter the chapel in the fort, where the most renowned Notre Dame of the Mediterranean smiles mawkishly in white olive-wood. After the blinding sun of the Midi, the cool dark chapel was like a dungeon to him, so little could he see anything; but in a while the strange furniture of the place would take form before his eyes: the white statue of the Virgin, the silver tunny-fish, the daubs of sea hazards whence the Virgin had rescued grateful mariners, the rope-ends, the crutches . . . And though none might be in the chapel, yet it was full of life, so much did the pathetic ex-votos tell . . . And he would come out of the chapel, and again the Midi sun would flash in a shower of gold, and he could see the blue Mediterranean, pricked with minute lateen-sails, and the greyish town beneath him, so old and yet so vital, and the calm harbour, with the forest of spars, and Monte Cristo, white as an egg . . .

A queer town that, as familiar as a channel marking, teeming as an ant-hill, and when darkness came over it, and he viewed it from the after deck, mystery came, too . . . For a while there was a hush, and around the hills gigantic ghosts walked . . . One thought of the Phocæans who had founded it, and to whom the Cannebière was a rope-walk, where they made the sheets for their ships . . . And one thought of Lazarus, who had been raised from among the silent dead and who had come there, so legend read, a grey figure in ceramic garments, standing in the prow of a boat . . .

One thing Robin More had told him remained in his mind and captured his fancy, and that was that Pontius Pilate had been governor of Marseilles after his office in Judea. And of him Shane would think when the mysterious dusk came on the Midi hills . . . Pilate, who had smiled, " What is truth ? " and who had turned Christ over to the mob . . . A big man, he imagined the Roman to have been, with clever eyes, and a great black beard covering a weak chin . . . A man who knew all the subtleties of mind, and had no backbone . . . And he could see the Roman, sitting on his villa porch in the dusk with tortured eyes, and fingering his beard with fingers that shook . . . Paul was going through Greece and Rome like a flame, and the Pilate wondered . . . Could it have been possible ? . . . Ridiculous ! a Jewish carpenter ! A crazy man ! . . . And yet . . . Could it have been possible . . . No ! no ! no ! And yet . . . People had seen Him walk on the waves . . . But people never knew what they saw, exactly . . . No ! How foolish ! . . . He raised a man from the dead, they said . . . And that centurion—what was his name ?—his daughter ! . . . No, a stupid Jewish legend . . . And yet . . . Could it be possible ? Could it ? Could it ?

" Lights ! Lights ! Do you hear me ! Bring lights ! Lights ! " Pilate would all put scream, panic-striken in the Midi dusk. . . .

To Shane Campbell Marseilles had been all this for

two years while he journeyed from Liverpool for silk and scented soaps—a landmark familiar as the Giants' Causeway, a strange, motley human circus, a veil behind which hid gigantic ghosts . . . Until he met *La Mielleuse* on the road to Aix.

§ 2

For six years, now, since the day they had buried his wife in the green divots of Louth, women had been alien to him. It was not that he hated them, not that he was uncomfortable among them; but the thought of close mental or spiritual or physical contact with them put him in a panic, as one might be in a panic at the thought of contact with some Chinaman, or Eskimo. The women of the better class in ports importuned him, but he passed with a grave humorous smile and an unexpected courtesy. His friends' wives or acquaintances could get nothing out of him but a grave answer to any question they might put, so that they characterized him as a stick. And at home in Ulster, whither he went after occasional voyages, where Robin More still drowsed over his books; where Alan Donn still hunted and fished and golfed, haler at five and fifty than a boy in his early twenties; and where his mother sat and did beautiful broidery, dumbly, inimically, cold as a fish, secretive as a badger, there he would meet the women of the Antrim families, women who knew of the disaster of his marriage, and they would look approvingly at his firm face and smiling, steady eyes, and they would say: "A man, thon! He could be a good friend. You could trust him, a woman could." They were unco good folk, Antrim folk.

For the peasant girls around he had always a laugh and a joke. And for the young girls from school he had always a soft spot in his heart somehow, appreciating them as one appreciates the first primrose or a puppy dog playing on the lawn or the lark in the clear air. There came such a current of beauty and freshness from them . . . New from the hand of the Maker . . . They were pausing now, as the wind pauses on the tide. . . . And in a little while the world, the damned world ! . . . And so he treated them with a great gravity, answering their questions on geography, telling them what an estuary was, and what the trade-winds, and how a typhoon came and paused and passed : and how jute and grain and indigo were taken from Calcutta, and of the Hooghly, the most difficult river in the world to navigate, and of the shoal called "James and Mary" . . . And they listened to him with wide-open, violet eyes . . .

And there were two women, Leah Fraser, a slight woman with hair smooth and reddish like a gold coin, and eyes that thought and saw back of things, and slender, beautiful hands, and she moved with the dignity of a swan . . . And there was Anne MacNeill, who handled a horse as a man would, and was a great archer—she could shoot as far as Alan could drive a golf-ball with a spoon . . . Shane could always see her, a Diana on the greensward, leaning forward, listening to hear the smack of the arrow on the target . . . And both these women were his good friends, the thought of them filling his mind like sweet lavender . . . But when they were each alone with him, and a little silence would come, then panic would fall on him, and he would make an undignified escape from their company proffering any old excuse . . . And they would watch him go, with little twisted smiles . . . Poor Leah ! Poor Anne !

All the love in him, that some sweet, gracious woman should have had, was anesthetized, or it was deflected, perhaps, to the great three-masted schooner he was now owner and master of, a beautiful boat that had been christened the *Ulster Lady*, and came from the yards at Belfast, taking the water as nobly as a swan. From truck to keelson there was no part of her imperfect ; from stem to stern. Barring a little tendency to be cranky before the wind in a seaway, nothing better sailed. Jammed, or on the wind, she was like a hare before the hounds, so quickly did she go. Her slim black body, her white, beautifully set sails—not a strake or an inch of canvas on her that he did not know and love. And more thought was given by him to the proper peaking of a spar and the exact setting of a leech than to the profits of the cargo. It was like having one's own country, and his cabin aboard was like his own castle—the little stateroom with the swinging-lamps, and the compass above the fastened bed, the row of books, the Aberdeen terrier, *Duine Uasal*, who slept peacefully on the rug, and who would go on deck and sniff the wind like a connoisseur . . . And there was a manuscript poem of his father's in the Irish letter, *Leaba Luachra*, "The Bed of Rushes," which he had discovered and had framed. And there was a prized thing of his boyhood there, a dagger the

Young Pretender wore in his stocking, and he in Highland dress, as he swung toward London with pipe and drum. Alan Donn had given it to him, and he after getting it on a visit to Argyll. "Not only is it Charlie's, but it's a nice handy thing, thon!" . . . A beautiful piece of work it was, perfectly balanced, keen as a razor, with a handle of the stag's horn . . . It was the only weapon Shane had, and about it curled romance and the smoke of dead, royal hopes . . . A bonny, homy place that cabin, peaceful as a garden of bees, when the water slipped past the beam. It was like a warm hearth-fire to come down there after a strenuous time on deck while the sou'wester crashed on the Welsh coast. Or in the roll of the Bay of Biscay, after a space watching the swinging fields of stars, to come down there was to drop into a welcoming circle of friends, to throw one's self down and pick up a book, the Laureate's "In Memoriam" or Mr. Thackeray's latest—and to glance from the pages of "Henry Esmond" to Prince Charlie's dagger lying peacefully on the desk . . . How near! how near! . . . And up forward the look-out paced, or leaned over the bows, humming in Gaidhlig:

'S tric me sealtuinn do'n chnoc is airde
D'fheac a faic mi fear a bhata
An dtig tu andiu no'n dtig tu 'maireach?
Is mur dtig tu eader gur truagh mar ta mi!

Will you come to-day or will you come to-morrow?
If you never come how piteous for me!
Fhir a' bhata, na horo eile!
Hi horo, fhir a bhata—

All the nostalgia of the Scottish isles was in the minors of that song . . . And it was like a lullaby . . . And the wind hummed through the rigging . . . And underneath was the flow and throb of the immense circulation of the sea . . . And overhead the helmsman rang the ship's bell. *Tung-tung, tung-tung, tung-tung, tung*. And all was well on board the *Ulster Lady*. And she was his only sweetheart and delight . . . until he met *La Mielleuse* on the road to Aix . . .

§ 3

The babble of the Greek merchants in the Café Turc at last began to bore him, and hiring a horse and sort of gig he decided to drive toward Aix. He had always wished to see the Provençal countryside, but somehow the opportunity had always passed by, or something . . . But on this bright September afternoon it seemed such a pity to go back on board ship . . . He examined the old white horse with interest.

"Are you sure he'll take me there? You see his—" Shane wanted to say suspensory ligaments, but his French didn't quite go that far—" his legs—"

"But, Monsieur, he has won several races—"

"Well, in that event"—Shane grinned, "K-k-k-k!"

The white horse trotted steadily out the Prado, the Rue de Rome, trotted out in the country, passed Bains de la Méditerranée. A northerly breeze was out rippling the gulf and giving promise of autumn, and the heavy heat of the Midi had disappeared for the instant. Soon they would be plucking the grapes of Provence. The olive-trees were black on the white road. The white horse trotted on . . .

There were peasants on the road going into town, and townspeople going out to the country . . . And children who insulted one another shrilly . . . But the white horse plodded on. On a stretch of level road he passed a pair talking, noting casually that the woman was a lady from her carriage, and from his threatening cringe that the man was a cad. Italian riffraff of some kind . . .

"But you are mistaken," the woman was saying. "You are making an error."

The man's reply was low, inaudible.

"But I assure you, you are mistaken."

The white horse plodded on.

"Please, please"—the woman's voice followed Shane, and there was embarrassed fear in it,—"please let me pass! You are mistaken."

And then again: "I swear to you . . . please . . . please!"

The white horse was surprised at a firm pull on his mouth, a crack of the whip, and a turn . . . He broke in a lolloping canter . . . Shane jumped down . . .

"Madame, is this man annoying you?"

"*Sirvase, signor—*"

But one look at the woman's face was sufficient. Shane turned on the fawning Sicilian with a snarl.

"Get to hell out of here, quick!" The man shuffled off, walked quickly, ran, disappeared . . .

The great dark eyes had agony in them. Her mouth quivered. Shane knew her knees were shaking as she stood.

"Better get in here. I'll drive you home.' He helped her into the trap. "I ought to have held that fellow," he grumbled. "Marseilles? No! Oh, Les Bains! We'll be there in a minute. You're all right now, Madame."

"He mistook me—for—somebody else—" She had a voice deep and sweet as a bell, but there was a tremor in it now—a marked accent of fear, past, but not recovered from.

He was aware of a great vibrant womanhood beside him, as some people are aware of spirits in a room, or a mother is aware of a child. He was aware, though he hardly saw them, though he didn't know he saw them, of the proud Greek beauty of her face, so decisively, so finely chiselled, so that it seemed to soar forward, as a bird soars into the wind; of the firm, dark ellipsis of the eyebrows; of the mouth that quivered, and yet in repose would be something for a master of line and colour to draw; the little hands that plucked nervously at the dark silk gown, unquiet as butterflies. Her eyes, he knew, were wide with fear, great black pupils, deep, immensely deep. And he was aware, too, of something within her that vibrated, as a stay aboard ship vibrates in a gusty, angry wind, or as an ill-plucked harpstring will vibrate to and fro, unable to stop.

"I live here, Monsieur."

It was a little white villa, with green jalousies such as the Midi has in thousands. He pulled up, and she was down before he could help her. Her face was quiet now but for the tremor of her eyes.

"Thank you ever so much," she said.

"But this man, Madame. Are you safe? Ought not one to—the police?"

"It was nothing, Monsieur." She laughed, but her voice still quivered. "Some good-for-nothing who took me for someone else, whom he had seen somewhere else, and knew—something—about. Nothing at all, a bagatelle, that might happen to anyone. But I thank you so much! You were going somewhere?"

"Toward Aix, Madame."

"But your horse is lame!"

"So he is, poor old boy! I hadn't noticed."

"Then—*àdieu, Monsieur.* And thanks again."

He drove back to town. "I didn't get very far," he thought. "Just another wasted afternoon!" .... At the livery post he got down and examined the horse's fetlock.

"So you won several races, eh?" But the white horse seemed to shake its head. "No! Oh, well, no matter, old codger!" And he stroked the long lugubrious muzzle....

And thus, casually as he would light a match for his cigarette, casually as he would stumble over something, casually as he would pick up a book, he met *La Mielleuse* on the road to Aix....

§ 4

For days now he had been aware of her presence in Marseilles without thinking of her—aware of her as he was aware of the Hôtel de Ville, or of the Consigne, or of the obelisk in the Place Castellane. These things were facts, had their place, and she was a fact.

She had become imprinted on his memory as on a sensitive plate. So one dusk night on the Prado, as he met her, he was no more surprised than if, in their appointed places he had come across the obelisk or the Consigne or the Hôtel de Ville.

She was standing looking out to sea, and the little wind from Africa blew against her, and made her seem poised for flight, like a bird.

And because he saw no reason why he shouldn't and because he was direct and simple as the sea itself, he went to her.

"Are you a sea-captain's wife?"

"No, Monsieur." She seemed to know him without turning. Perhaps she recognized his voice.

"I saw you looking out toward the Pharo. I thought perhaps you were waiting for someone to come home on a ship."

"No," she said slowly. "No. I—I come here some dusks, and look out to sea. There is something. It seems to pull me. The great waters and the blinking lighthouse—I seem to stand out of myself. And miles and miles and miles away there is a new land with a new life where one might go . . . and begin . . . What is in me seems to struggle to go out there, but it never gets more than an inch or so outside. But even that . . And the wind . . . so clean. Are you a sailor?"

"Yes, I am a sailor."

"It is very beautiful and very pure, the sea?"

"Yes, sometimes it is very beautiful. I think it is always beautiful. And it must be pure—I never thought . . . It is strong, and sometimes cruel.

It heals, and sometimes it is very lonely. One never quite understands. It is so big."

"Yes, so big and strong . . . and it heals. One seems, one's self, one's little cares, to be so little."

And they were silent for a while.

"But perhaps I intrude, Madame. Your husband ——"

"My husband is dead in Algiers these six years."

"I am sorry."

Everything was hushed, the tideless sea, the silent wind. Behind them, and still about them, hung the strange dusk of Pontius Pilate. Before them blazed Marseilles.

"You are married?"

"I was married."

"Then your wife is—dead?"

"Yes, Madame, she is dead."

"You grieve?"

"No, I do not grieve."

"Did you not love her?"

"I loved someone I thought was she. It wasn't she."

There was another instant's silence as they walked.

"Ah, I think I understand," she said. And they walked into the blaze of the city. She paused for a moment.

"Will you pardon me for asking things like that? I don't usually . . . But in the dusk I seem to be another person."

"No. In the light we are other persons."

"Ah," she smiled understandingly. "You are going to your ship now?"

There was a finality in her voice. It was more an affirmation than a question.

"Madame," Shane said, "will you please let me see you to your door?"

She looked at him for an intense second, and a little cloud of—was it fear?—flitted across her face.

"Madame, there are thieves and villains of all kinds abroad. You have had one experience. Please let me protect you from a possible second."

"If you wish." She smiled. He called a carriage.

In the light she was a different person. Along the sea-shore walking in the dusk, she was a troubled phantom, a thing of beauty, but without flesh, without the trappings of clothes—as if a spirit had been imprisoned in cold white statuary. But now she was a beautiful woman, gravely gay, a woman of the world, not of the great world, perhaps, and not of the half-world—just a woman aware of and experienced in life. And poised.

"You are English?"

"Not English. Irish."

Poised she was, but she was like a player playing a game, and the breaks against her. He knew the smile. He had seen it often on Alan Donn's face, playing in some of the great title matches. Four holes to go, and he must better par. It's all right, the smile said; there's nothing wrong. But in Alan Donn's was the glint of a naked knife, and in this woman's eyes, down deep, veiled, but ill-concealed, was appeal.

They stopped at her house. He helped her out.

"*Adieu, Monsieur.* And again a thousand thanks."

"*C'était un vrai plaisir!*"

" Monsieur ! "

" Madame ! "

The cabman looked surprised when ordered to return. He turned and regarded his fare with amazement.

" *Quai de la Fraternité*," I said.

" *Hup, alors !* " The cabby shrugged his shoulders. And they trotted ploddingly through the dusk of Pontius Pilate to the burning cloud which was Marseilles. . . .

§ 5

He knew he should meet her again, and where he should meet her ; and he did, on the Prado. He knew when. In the Midi dusk. A touch of mistral was out, and the wind blew seaward. She was sitting down, looking towards Africa.

" You oughtn't to come out here alone," he said. " Marseilles is a bad port."

" I know," she said. " I know. But it draws me, this spot. You leave soon ? " she asked.

" In a few days."

" But you will be back."

" Yes, I will be back," he told her. " I don't know why, but I think I'd rather die than not see Marseilles again. It is a second home, and yet I know so few people here."

" If one has the temperament, and conditions are —as they should be—Marseilles is wonderful."

" One could be happy here."

" Yes," and she sighed.

The spell of the archaic dusk came on him again ;

a dusk old as the world. About them brooded the welter of passion and romance that Marseilles is. Once it was a Phocæan village, and hook-nosed Afric folk had stepped through on long, thin feet. And then had come the Greeks, with their broad, clear brows, their grey eyes. And further back the hairy Gauls had crept, snarling like dogs. And Greece died. And came the clash of the Roman legions, ruthless fighting hundreds, who saw, did massive things. And Rome died. And over the sea came the Saracens, their high heads, their hard, bronzed bodies, their scarlet mouths. And they conquered and builded and lived. . . . And were hurled back. . . . Years hummed by, and passion died not, or romance, and it was from Marseilles that a battalion had come to Paris gates singing the song that Rouget de Lisle had written in Strasburg :

Allons, enfants de la Patrie,
Le jour de gloire est arrivé.

And passed that day, and came another, when a handful of grizzled veterans left the gates to join their brothers and meet the exiled emperor. . . . Passion and romance ! Their colours were in Marseilles still. . . . Over in *Anse des Catalans* weren't there the remains of the village of the sea-Gipsies, who had come none knew whence ? . . . And along the gulf there were settlements of Saracen blood . . . *les Maures,* the Provençals called them . . . and the shadow of Pontius Pilate wild-eyed in the dusk. . . .

" It's strange "—her voice came gently to him,—" but I can hear you think."

"And I can feel your silence," he said. "Just feel—you—being silent—"

The wind whipped up, grew shrill, grew cold. She shivered in her thin frock.

"You are becoming cold."

"I am cold."

"Then hadn't you better go home—to your house."

She rose silently. It seemed to him somehow that she had put herself under his care. She was like some gentle craft that had anchored humbly under the lee of a great ship. He felt somehow that she was a thing to be protected. He hailed a carriage, and she made no protest—all the time under his lee, so needful of protection. It was a shock when they came into the lights of Marseilles to find a proud, grave woman there and not a shrinking, wide-eyed child. . . . Her face, poised for flight, like a bird's wing; the beautiful, half-opened mouth, the hands, the little feet in their shoes. She was like some beautiful shy deer. And somewhere hovered disaster, like a familiar spirit. . . . And yet she was smiling. . . .

At the door he made to bid her good-bye.

"Would you—would you care to come in?"

"Why—why, yes." He sent the carriage away.

He followed her up the path to the little villa and with her entered the house. There were no servants to answer the door; she let herself in with a latch-key, but so scrupulously clean was the place, so furnished in its way, that there must have been servants somewhere. The living-room into which she conducted him was spacious and a little bare, though not bare for the Midi—a plain white room, high in the ceiling, with chairs of good line. Here was a big piano, here a fireplace, here a few paintings, colourful landscapes, on the wall. Together they lit candles.

" Back of here is a garden," she said, " where I spend most of the day. And I have a cook "—she smiled—" and a maid who waits on me. And yet I go out to walk on the Prado. . . ."

Shane wasn't surprised. It wasn't home, somehow. The room was like a setting in a play, here light, here shadow. . . . The paintings, the instrument of music, the chairs, they were not things owned and loved. They were properties. . . . In the golden candle-light, as she moved, she was like an actress of great restraint. Every step, posture, gesture seemed to have an occult significance. Even her bedroom, away off somewhere, he felt, was not a place where one slept easily and dreamed. It would be like the dressing-room of some woman mummer. . . . It was all like a play, of which he was seeing a fragment from the wings. . . . What was it all about? Who was she? And why was his heart a-flutter?

She had taken off her hat, and her hair was coiled close about her exquisite head. White and black, regular, significant, antique—like a cameo of some Greek woman, long dead. She stood by a little table, one hand on it, the other like some butterfly against her gown. . . . It was like a pose—but unconscious, he knew, utterly unconscious. . . .

" Tell me," she said, " why did you speak to me?"

" I don't know," he said, " I just spoke."

" You weren't "—her words were weighty, picked —" looking for a flirtation with a pretty woman?"

"Why, no. Of course not," he answered. "I never thought——"

"No. No, you didn't." She decided for herself.

She came toward him suddenly in the candlelight. Stood before him.

"Tell me, who are you? What are you?" There was a tragic appeal in her face. "Where do you come from? Where are you going?"

"I don't know." His throat was dry, his heart pounding. "A few days ago I was a contented man, unhappy but contented. And now I don't know."

"And I don't know who I am." Her mouth quivered. "I am two people—three people."

They looked at each other with a sort of agony, as though they had lost something dear to each, and to both of them. They were immensely intimate. He put out his hand. . . . .

"Poor . . . poor . . ."

Their hands touched, and there seemed to rush between them, through them, some powerful current; and how it happened he did not know, but they were kissing each other. . . . He thought with a queer shock, was a woman's mouth so soft, so sweet, so vibrant? He hadn't known. And was he kissing her? And how had it happened? It was impossible! . . . Or was he dreaming? . . . Or was he—was he dead? . . .

She released herself from him for an instant, putting her hands on his shoulders, her eyes looking into his eyes. . . .

"What is your name?"

"Campbell. Shane Campbell."

"Campbell. Shane Campbell. Shane—Shane Campbell. Mine is Claire-Anne—Claire-Anne Godey."

§ 6

It seemed to him as he went to Les Bains next evening that the world had somehow changed into another dimension, so much clearer the air was, so much brighter the stars. . . . He had discovered a higher, more rarefied stratum of life, in the dim, keen atmosphere of which things took on incomparable beauty and mystery, so that the water on his left hand, unseen, yet so blue, was not the Gulf of Lyons, but the whole Mediterranean, which washed Genoa and Naples and Sicily, and the little islands of the Greeks, and the barbaric shores of Africa, Morocco, and Algiers ; and Gibraltar, where the English were, like an armed sentry in a turret. The ships in the harbour were not ships of commerce, but stately entities each whispering to each in the *shush-shush* of water and wind, telling of the voyages they had made, adventurous as sturgeons. Even from the mud-and-rush huts along the seashore came the note of brave romance. And the softly singing trees ! And in the great amphitheatre of the woods no longer the shade of Pontius Pilate gnawed his bitten nails, but more gallant presences were, grey-eyed Greek women, with proud composed faces and eloquent hands, and Saracens calmly awaiting the morrow's battle, and troubadours puzzling keenly for a rhyme. . . . They were not coloured thoughts, but sentient presences. Spirit and thought had united in him into a being like a bird, leaving the earth, and flying into a realm of ancient forgotten beauty, spirit being the will, and thought the vibrating wing. . . . How harmonious everything was, the stars, the earth, the sea, the people! How clear it had all become! How one! . . .

He came to her in her garden where she sat beneath a tree. Around, the cicadas whirred in the speaking trees. *Zig-zig-zig-zig.* But they were no longer strident. They seemed but a vibration of the high atmosphere in which he was. . . .

"Claire-Anne! Claire-Anne. . . ."

"Yes . . . yes, lover . . ."

"Claire-Anne!"

She stood up as he took her lovely, pale hands. There was no shame to her glance, nothing but a wonderful frankness, her eyes going to his like brave winged things.

"Claire-Anne, I want to ask you something."

"Yes . . . lover . . ."

"Claire-Anne, when will you marry me?"

Her hands never quivered, but he was aware that her mouth did, in the high diluted starlight.

"Why do you want to marry me? Is it because . . . ? Do you feel bound? . . . or . . . just why?"

"I want to be with you, Claire-Anne."

"Then—dearest, does it matter to go before the mayor and arrange about property? And to go before a priest and make promises—to God! . . . Sit down, lover; sit down with me here, in the dusk, under the tree."

She still clasped both his hands. He might have been talking to some beautiful disembodied spirit, as Pontius Pilate was a poor panic-stricken spirit, or to something he had conjured out of his head, but for her firm, warm hands. To-night it was she had strength. . . .

"Dearest, promises are so easy to make. I have made promises, oh, so many promises! . . . And life or destiny . . . And when you can't keep them, your heart breaks. You know nothing of me—Shane." . . .

"I don't want to know; I just want you, Claire-Anne!"

"You must know something. I was just a girl, well brought up, well educated . . . I dreamed of being a great actress. I was an actress, but I was . . . *manquée* . . . didn't succeed, get success . . . And then I married, and my husband died . . . And here I am. . . . And there are other things you mustn't know. . . . Not that they are dear to me; oh no! . . . . but you must never hear them . . . O Shane, if seven years ago. . . . But destiny or life wouldn't let us. And now we can only cheat him, and that only for a while. . . . Because destiny is all-seeing and jealous and cruel. . . . Only for a while, a sweet while. . . ."

"But, Claire-Anne, I don't understand—"

"Don't understand, don't, my lover. Don't anything . . . Only let me give all I have, can give to you, and let me take what you care to give in return, only that . . . O Shane, we are two people in a dark wood, and it is lonely and terrifying . . . And we have met, and our hands . . . *se sont serrées* . . . gripped and held. . . . And we aren't lonely any more, or afraid. And you have a picture in your mind of me, a beautiful, warm picture. . . . But if the night passed, and we came to the meadow-lands . . . Oh Shane, don't let's go into the light—not into the open, not into the light. . . . Oh, no! no!"

"But, Claire-Anne . . . "

"Come closer, Shane. The night is empty. There are only we two in the world . . . Come close. Closer. Closer still . . ."

§ 7

He was sitting in her garden one sunset, under the mulberry-tree, and she had gone into the house for a minute, moving with the firm, gracious walk of hers that was like the firm swimming of swans. In the little hush of sunset, and she gone, there came a sudden knowledge to him. . . . For a space of time, how long he knew not, he was in an Antrim study. . . . Without, the sun had gone down, and there was the purple, twilight water and the gentle calling of the cricket. . . . And within was a grey head that had fallen on a book . . . fallen . . . fallen as the sun went down.

"Why, Uncle Robin!" he called.

Then came a great gush of tears to his heart and eyes. . . .

She came from the house, as again he became cognizant of the Midi garden instead of the Antrim glen, of the Mediterranean instead of the waters of Moyle. She came down the dusky pathway. At a little distance she saw his face. She stopped short, her face white. . . .

"Shane! Shane! what is wrong? Are you hurt? Ill?"

"My Uncle Robin is dead, Claire-Anne."

She looked at him for a little instant, not quite understanding. She came to him swiftly as a swallow. She sat close beside him. Her arm went through his. Her hands clasped his hands.

"Why didn't you tell me, heart?" she whispered.

"I just knew this instant. I felt, saw . . . We were that close . . . my Uncle Robin! *Beannacht De ar a anam!* God's blessing on his soul!"

She never spoke. She never stirred. She hardly breathed. She was just there, her hands, firm and strong, on his, did he want her.

"Was it . . . a hard death, Shane?"

"No; I seemed to see him, asleep, among his books."

"His books were his friends . . . you told me. . . ."

"Yes, dear. His life was with them."

"And he wasn't a young man, your Uncle Robin?"

"Eight and sixty years of age."

"Is it so ill, heart, to go quickly, quietly, with your friends about you, on an autumn afternoon?"

"No, dear, not ill. Very rightly . . . I think. But there is something . . . something is gone from the world, like a fine tree from a garden . . . And he was awful dear to me, my Uncle Robin. . . . It will be a hard thing to go home and he not there to come and ask: 'Are you all right, laddie? You're no sick?' Claire-Anne, I'll be thinking long. . . ."

She sat with him in silence in the garden, and after a little while got up and went without a word. . . . And he sat in the garden thinking to himself, had he been lax to Uncle Robin in any way? He might have written oftener. It wasn't fair to have kept the old man worried and he an apprentice at sea. Yes, he could have written, could have written oftener. And thought more. And there were books he might have brought the old man—books from 'Frisco and

New York and Naples. The book stores were so far from the quays, and he had put it off. And he could have so easily. . . When one is young, one is so thoughtless. . . . A message from somewhere ran into his consciousness like a ripple of code-flags : " It doesn't matter, dear laddie. Don't be taking on. Don't be blaming yourself. You were the dear lad . . . and I'm happy. . . ."

Ah, yes, but a great tree was gone from the garden. An actuality had been converted into thought and emotion, and thought and emotion may be all that endure, and an actuality be unreal . . . but an actuality is so warm . . . so reassuring . . .

He rose and went toward the house, and as he walked he met her. . .

" Claire-Anne, do you mind if I go back to the ship ? . . . . Somehow, I'm a little lost. . . . "

" There is a carriage waiting for you outside."

For the first time it occurred to him that in this occult experience she had not uttered one jarring note. She had not asked questions, nor had she tried to argue with him, as other women would have, telling him he fancied all this. Nor had she bothered him with vain, unwelcome sentiment. She had just —stood by, as at sea. And how swiftly she had divined his need of privacy, of his own ship ?

" There are none like you in this world, Claire-Anne," he told her.

" I am what you make me, Shane—what you need of me." Her hand sought his in the stilly dusk. " Come back only when you are ready, dearest . . . dearest . . . I am here ! Always here ! "

§ 8

Though she never said so, yet he knew she wanted to go on board the ship that was so much of his life, and one day he had her rowed across to the *Ulster Lady*. He smiled as he saw how firmly she got on board, though ships were unknown to her. Queer, how she never lost dignity, grace. And it was so easy for a woman to look silly, undignified, getting on board ship. She never disappointed him. . . .

She mused over the sweet line of the schooner, the tapering masts, the snug canvas, the twinkling brass. The wake of a passing paddle-steamer made the boat pitch gently. It was like breathing.

" She is so much a pretty lady," Claire-Anne said. " So much like you, Shane, in a way. She might be a young sister—a young, loved sister. And where is your place on board when she sails ? "

He pointed out the space behind wheel and binnacle. " Whenever there's any need, I'm there, just there."

" And, Shane, great waves like you see in pictures —great enormous waves, does she stand those ? "

" Yes, great waves, like you see in pictures, she stands those. Drives through them, and over them, and under them."

" And Solomon said "—she was just thinking aloud—" that he couldn't understand the way of a ship on the sea. And he was immensely wise. Dearest . . . it can't be just wood and canvas, a ship . . . power and grace and beauty. . . . It's like great people. . . ."

" They're as different as people are, Claire-Anne."

"Are they, Shane? I knew they weren't . . . just things."

He took her below in the dusk of his cabin. She filled the space like some gracious green tree.

"And here is where I live on board ship."

The Aberdeen terrier came forward to greet her, his tail waving gently, his ears up, his brown eyes grave and warm.

"*Duine uasal! Duine uasal!*" she knelt to him.

"You remember?" He minded he had told her casually of the dog's name.

"Of course I remember! Shane, what does *Duine uasal* mean?"

"*Gentilhomme,*" he translated.

"He has the eyes," she said.

The framed manuscript of his father's verses caught her eyes, and she looked at him in inquiry.

"What is it?"

"A poem of my father's, in Gaidhlig, Claire-Anne. 'The Bed of Rushes.'"

"How queer the letters are! Slim and graceful, and powerful, too. Would you read it, Shane?"

"*Leaba luachra,*" he read, "a bed of rushes, *bhi fúm aréir*, was beneath me last night, *agas do chaitheas amach é le banaghadh an lae*, and I threw it out with the whitening of day. *Thainic mo chéad grádh le mo thaobh*, my hundred loves came to my side; *guala le gualainn*, shoulder to shoulder, *agas béal re béal*, and mouth to mouth."

"Now I know you better, Shane."

"How, dearest?"

"I know how you come by your—your sense of beauty, Shane. It's from your father. You have it just as he had. But he could say and you can't, Shane. You have it, but it doesn't come out that way. It comes out in the sailing of the ship Shane. You must sail beautifully. Shane, I should love to see you sail."

With a quick movement she dropped on her knees, and her beautiful dark head on the pillow of his bed.

"Couldn't you take me with you once, Shane, when you sail? Away on just one voyage?"

"Of course I could, dearest, and will."

"Would you, my heart? Would you?" She stood up again, and swift tears came to her eyes.

"I couldn't come," she said.

"But, Claire-Anne—"

"No," she said. She turned her back to him, so that he shouldn't see her face, and her voice vibrated. "No, Shane dear. No. You go to sea and sail your ships, and take care of them in the tempest and coax them in light weather. And go from port to port, watching the strange cities and the peoples, and seeing into them, with . . . *tes yeux d'enfant* . . . your eyes of a child . . . And have your life, free, big, clean . . . And just in a corner . . . *le plus petit coin* . . . keep me . . . so when you come to Marseilles, you will come up the garden path in the dusk, and call, 'Claire-Anne!'" There was something like a sob from her. "Just say, 'Claire-Anne' . . . ."

She turned around and caught his hands for a minute, looked at him, smiled, laughed . . . From his desk she picked up the Young Pretender's dagger.

"What is this for, Shane? Is this yours?"

"Mine now, Claire-Anne; but it was—someone else's once. My Uncle Alan, Alan Donn, gave it to me."

" Yes ? . . . "

" It belonged once to Charles Edward Stuart, the Young Pretender. He wore it at his knee in '45. Do you remember, Claire-Anne ? He landed in Scotland and advanced on England, and got as far as Derby at the head of the Scottish clans and Jacobite gentlemen. ' Black Friday ' they called it in London."

" But he never got to London."

" No, he never got to London. Crash and whir of battle, and when the smoke cleared, there were the gallant Highland clansmen scattered, and the sturdy English nobles, and the bonny Irish gentlemen. And a king on the run ! "

" And Shane, what happened to him after that ? "

" I think—my history may not be right, but I think he spent the rest of his life a pensioner of the king of France, playing petty politics, drinking, and accepting love from romantic women, and loyalty from the beaten clans."

" What a pity, Shane ! What a pity."

" That he failed, dearest ? I don't know."

" Not that he failed, Shane ! No ! The most gallant fail, nearly always fail, for they take the greatest odds. But that he lived too long, Shane . . . the high moment gone . . . "

She looked at the dagger again that had once snuggled to Prince Tearloch's knee, hefted it, caressed it.

" Shane dearest, why didn't he use his own knife to—set himself free ? "

" I don't know."

" I think I know."

She faced him suddenly.

" Shane, why didn't somebody do it for him ? "

" I suppose they couldn't see the end, Claire-Anne. They couldn't foresee the king of France's charity, the tricked women, the wine-stained cards. There's many the Scots gentlemen who would have —set him free."

" But they didn't, Shane dearest. It seems destiny must always win. Shane, what is that poem in Gaidhlig about the world, the verses you once said ? "

" *Treasgair' an saoghal, agus tigeann an gaoth mar smal.*
Alaistir, Cæsar, 's an méad do bhi d'a bpairt
Ta an Theamhair na fear agas feach an Traoi mar ta—
Life goes conquering on. The winds forever blow
Alexander, Cæsar, and the crash of their fighting men
Tara is grass, and see how Troy is low— "

He stopped with a little shock, for her face was a mask of tears.

" Dearest, dearest, it's only an old, sad story. It has nothing to do with us. Claire-Anne—"

" Is any story old, Shane ? Is any story ever new ? Isn't it always the same story ? "

She looked at the dagger for an instant more, and put it down with a little sob.

" Poor gentleman ! "

§ 9

From his cabin below he could hear the Belfast mate roaring at the helmsman :

" What kind of steering do you call that ? Look at your damned wake. Like an eel's wriggle. Keep her full, and less of your damned luffin'."

" Keep her full, sir ! " the steersman repeated.

" Look at your foretopsail ! Bouse it, blast ye ! Bouse it ! You Skye cut-throats ! "

If the nor'easter held, Shane calculated, he could run through Biscay full, come into the Mediterranean on a broad reach, and jam her straight at Marseilles. About him was the tremor as she took the head seas. Plunge! Tremble! Dash on! Overhead the squeaking of the sheets, the squeal of blocks, the *thrap-thrap-thrap* of the lee halyards, the melancholy whining of the gulls. With luck he would be in Marseilles within the week. And if the wind swung westward after he left Gibraltar to port, he would nip off hours, a day even. And every hour counted until the moment he went up the dusky path and called " Claire-Anne ! "

He had never before driven the *Ulster Lady* as he was driving her now. Before, he had been content to get what he could out of her, coaxing her, nursing her, as a trainer does a horse he is fond of ; but now he was riding her like a jockey intent on winning a race. On deck the crew wondered what had got into the old man, as they called him, for all his twenty-eight years.

" Before he was a sailor," the isles crew complained. " Is he now a merchant at last. *A Righ is truagh!* O King, the pity ! "

But it was not interest in cargoes that compelled him ; it was the thought of a face like the wing of a bird, ready to soar. The dark, gracious face, with the eyes where emotion swirled like a mill-race, the parted, ruddy lips—*la Mielleuse*—mouth of honey. And the word he must not say aloud, like some occult word of magic until a certain moment should come :

"Claire-Anne!" Just "Claire-Anne!"

Before he had left Marseilles he had not been able to think of her, to weigh what happened, to understand. Things were too close. But at sea, and in the dusk of the Antrim glen, and in Belfast and Liverpool, he had had time to view the incident in perspective; to stand aside, as one stands back from a picture, and appreciate the colour, the line, the truth; to see that that rich purple, that splash of orange, that rippling, rich silver-gray are not spots like flowers, but a definite design. . . .

In Antrim he had remembered Dancing Town, the vision of Fiddlers' Green. Fourteen years before!

And now that he remembered, it seemed to him foolish not to have known he was sailing somewhere. He was always sailing. . . . And unexpectedly, after he had given up all hope, under his lee bow had risen suddenly Fiddlers' Green. . . . Once before he thought he had made port there, but that only made this island the true one. . . . For there were always two things, and the second was right. . . . False dawn and dawn; the False Cape and Cape Horn; the Southern Crosses, the false and true. . . .

And he would tell her this, when he met her again, of how he had been thinking, and discovered her to be the true life. . . . .

The wife he had married and buried seven years before he thought of now; she was the second woman he had known, his mother the first. And from the cold precipice of his mother he had fled into the flinty fields of Moyra Dolan. . . . He felt a little sorry for the boy he was seven years before—so young, so gallant, so wrong. . . . He had thought that all there was in life was a home to return to, a wife, children. . . . He had wanted an acre of land in the sun, where all the world was his. When one was young, one knew so little. . . . Wisdom came with the lapping of the waves, and years of quiet thinking under the gigantic stars. . . . A plot of land he had wanted then, and now he had the stars, they belonging more to him than to the astrologers who conned them, the fields, more than to the tillers who cultivated them, the sea than to the fishermen who trawled. . . . He was one with everything, understanding everything, its immense harmony. . . . From hard earth and wet sea he had arisen on swift, dark pinions until he had been one with the spirit that infused all earth and sea and sky holding the multitudinous atoms in One with immense will and scheme. . . . And it was she who had given them to him—Claire-Anne . . . the wings of the morning. . . . The flutter of her white hands . . . the eyes that looked and drooped looked, drooped . . . the little catch in her breath . . .

His life opened before him now, like a fair seaway. About his appointed tasks he would go in his appointed life . . . sailing ships with needed cargoes . . . a despatch messenger for the peoples of the world over the vast solitudes of sea . . . doing his work well and willingly . . . and asking no reward but that the bird of dusk, the mouth of honey, be his to love and be loved by . . . to melt with and be one in occult alchemy of soul and mind and body . . . to get strength and knowledge, and the understanding which is more than strength and knowledge.

He was twenty-eight, she was twenty-five. There

were twenty years before them still, twenty years of love and understanding, and then a strange happy twilight, like the dusk of Antrim, that gives way hardly to the short night . . . Some day she would marry him and come to his house . . . some day when something that was wrong in her heart was righted and forgotten, something he had no wish to intrude upon, so closely did she conceal it . . . There was a locked, haunted room in her heart . . . poor heart! . . . but one day the presence would be exorcised, and the room swept and garnished . . . Some day she would marry him, and he would bring her home to Ulster . . . And who better than she could understand the springy heather and the blue smoke-reek, the crickets of the evening and the curlew's call? And in the house where his mother was cold and arrogant, would be a warm and gracious lady . . . Claire-Anne! . . .

God! he was thinking long to be in Marseilles again, to go up the dusky path, to call, "Claire-Anne!"

The big Belfast mate larruped down the short companionway.

"How's she doing, Mr. McKinstry?"

"She's doing fine, sir. If I may say so, there's not a better boat sail the water, not the *Sovereign of the Seas* itself. Nor a better crew to handle things, not on board the king's yacht."

"Not a better mate, Mr. McKinstry."

"Ah, well, sir; we do wir best."

He tumbled on deck again, and Shane could hear him roar from amidships:

"Lay forward a couple of you damned farmers,

and see if you can't get more out of those jibs. Faster ! faster ! You're as slow as the grace of God at a miser's funeral. . . . If I only had a crew . . ."

§ 10

She stopped in her swift flight to him through the dusk of the Midi garden.

" Dearest, why is your face so white ? Your hands bruised ? "

" The consul said something to me—about you—and I knocked him down."

" Oh ! " she said, a shocked little cry, and : " Oh !" a drawn-out wail of pain. " Why did you strike him ? "

" Because he lied about you."

Her face was turned from him, in the dusk of the crickets, towards the wooded amphitheatre, where dead Pontius roved wild-eyed in the dusk, where Lazarus tossed uneasily in his second sleep, where the Greeks lay in alien soil, and the shadows of Roman legionaries looked puzzled at the flat sea, nor recognizing busy Tiber—her back was to him, her head up in pain, her nerve-wrenched hands uneasy, white . . .

" He didn't lie," she said at last. " Oh, you'd have known it sooner or later. No ! no ! He didn't lie."

" Claire-Anne ! "

" He didn't lie. I was just a fool to think—oh, well, he didn't lie. No, no ! " she repeated. " He didn't lie." She threw out a hand hopelessly. " He didn't lie."

He went up to her in the dusk, put his hands

gently on her shoulders. The quivering frame became still suddenly, with a greater nervousness. She was like a deer ready to bound away . . .

" I don't see what I could have done, Claire-Anne. But—can I do anything now ? "

She turned toward him suddenly. Her face was a mask of pain—and surprise.

" Then you haven't grown cold to me, unmerciful, . . . or gross ? "

" Why, no, Claire-Anne ! "

" And you know."

" I—know, but I don't understand . . . "

She gave a queer, little shuddering cry, half laugh, half sob. She moved over to the seat by the whispering mulberry-tree, and dropped in it, her hands covering her face.

" All the wrong," she said, " that people call wrong I've done I didn't mind. But the one decent thing—of loving you—that's kept me awake all the time you were away. It's been like a sin, letting you love me. The rest was destiny, but this one thing was—I."

She suddenly raised her face, her eyes shining through the humid mask of it.

" Would you—could you—understand ? "

" Tell me, Claire-Anne, what you want to."

She drew a short gasping breath, turned her head away, looked up, turned it away again, paused for breath, gripped his hand by the wrist. . . .

" I . . . I . . . I was the child of actors, and they died, and there was enough money to bring me up and educate me, and give me my chance on the stage . . . And I wasn't good enough . . . I was too much myself. Couldn't quite be other characters. I don't know if you understand . . . But . . . then a man got infatuated with me and married me . . . And later he wished he'd married a comfortable woman with a fortune . . . And then he died and left me . . . not very much . . . But that was not the reason . . . I was left, how do you say ? . . . stranded. I had no career, no husband, no child, no business. France, it is not easy . . . not easy anywhere . . . Friends ? People are too busy . . . And I was . . . just there . . . And all around me life bubbled and flowed, and I was . . . not dead, not alive . . . and alone . . . I might have been a leper, but even lepers have colonies, and some one to be kind to them . . . not dead, not alive . . . and alone. I was so young . . . It was unfair. Life was everywhere like a sparkling wine . . . but where I was, was flat . . .

"And then—then I met a man . . . it was pleasant for a while—to have some one to talk to, to go around with. It's so pleasant to laugh. You don't know how pleasant until you haven't laughed for a long time. . . . He didn't want to marry . . . and in the end it was a choice of—oh, well . . . or going back to being not dead, not alive . . . and I couldn't go, just couldn't. And he gave me presents and money. . . . And then he got married. I don't blame him . . . a comfortable woman with a fortune . . . but I wasn't left for long . . . where one goes, others always follow. . . . There's a sort of . . . *sentier intuitif*, a psychic path. . .

"And I wasn't so ashamed . . . I was a little glad I had a place in the world . . . a work even. . . . And everyone might despise me, but I had a place

. . . I was no longer not dead, not alive . . . I was even thankful for that . . . until I met you with your—terrible courtesy, with your understanding. . . . My head and my heart melted, and my body, too, and all had been so firm, so decided. . . . And I dreamed that I could snatch a while from destiny. . . . But—you see. . . . What the consul said was true, so . . . dearest—but I mustn't ever call you dearest again."

"Claire-Anne!"

"Well, then—dearest, you see why I couldn't marry you when you asked." She laughed bitterly. "If you had only known. . . ."

He took a terrible grip on himself, faced her, looked at her.

"Claire-Anne, will you marry me now?"

"I don't know why you say it, but I know one thing: you are true. And I thank you . . . but please don't make me cry any more. I have cried so much when you were away. . . . If only five years ago before I was . . . *estropiée* . . . crippled. . .

"Destiny . . ."

§ II

Dusk had gone; darkness had come, and now darkness itself would leave soon, for the third quarter of a great saffron moon showed its edge in the eastward. Marseilles was like the pale light of a candle. And a great palpable darkness had settled like water in the hollow of the woods.

"Dearest"—her voice took sudden strength—"will you forgive me? I don't say that just as if

I'd done a small wrong. But will a big power come out of your heart and say: 'It's all right, Claire-Anne. I understood.' It will be so much for me to know that—in the days when you are gone——"

"But, Claire-Anne, I'm not gone——"

"You must go, dearest. You must go now. Don't you see?" Her voice grew gentle. "You couldn't stay any more. It wouldn't be like you, somehow. And I wouldn't have you spoiled in my eyes . . . darling, you could never be . . . but you must go . . ."

"And you, Claire-Anne——"

"Destiny . . . a long, lean finger . . . a path . . ."

"But you never know——"

"We know, we poor women, Shane. We know . . . Shane, don't you understand . . . what makes the . . . girl in the archway, the emperor's mistress, drink, take ether . . . do strange horrors? . . . They know . . . and they want to escape from seeing it . . . for an instant even . . . the terrible story of the *Belle Heaulmière* . . . the 'Armorer's Daughter':

"*Ainsi le bon temps regretons*
Entre nous, pauvres vielles sotes,
Assises bas, à crouppetons,
Tout en ung tas commes pelotes,

A petit feu de chenevotes.
Tost allumées, tost estaintes;
Et jadis fusmes si mignotes! . . .
Ainsi emprent à maintes et maintes.

"Do you understand, Shane, do you understand? So we regret the good old times, poor old light women, gathered together like faggots, and hunkering over a straw fire, soon lit, soon out—*tost allumées, tost estaintes* . . . and once we were so dainty. To many and many's the one it happens. *Pauvres vielles sotes!* Poor old light women, Shane . . . *Et jadis fusmes si mignotes!* . . . Dainty as I am, they were once . . . and do you blame them now when they see it coming . . . the drink, the ether . . . the abominable things. . . ."

"O my God! Claire-Anne!"

"Hearts of hearts, Shane. I once escaped to light, where they escape to oblivion. . . . Once I had you, and all my life I'll remember it. . . . All my life I'll remember: I once knew a man . . . and it will be a help, so much a help. . . ."

"Oh, Claire-Anne, it can't be!"

"It must be, dearest heart. It is—decreed. Darling, sometimes I thought—— Do you remember your showing me the poor prince's dagger, and our talking about him—setting himself free—and I said I thought I could understand why he did not. . . . I've wanted to, myself. . . . But . . . there's a way you're brought up, when you're young. . . . They put such fear of God in you . . . such fear of hell . . . you never could—throw things down and go straight to Him, and say: 'I couldn't. I just simply couldn't. I hadn't the strength. I couldn't . . . just . . .' And they never think of Him saying: 'Of course you couldn't . . . and it was all My fault. I wasn't looking. . . . I've so much to think of. . . . You did right to come to Me. . . .' But, no! no! One fears. They teach you so much fear, Shane, when you are young . . . so that even this is better—this —game, where none win. . . . And so—one goes on. . . ."

She rose suddenly and clutched his shoulders in panic. Her mouth twisted in piteous agony. . . .

"Oh, but dearest, dearest, *pauvres vielles sotes,* poor old light women. . . . Shane, *assises bas, à crouppetons,* in an archway, hoping for a drunken farmer with a couple of sous . . . and so cold, so cold, with a little fire of straw stalks . . . *tost allumées, tost estaintes!*" . . .

"No, Claire-Anne! no!"

"A drunken farmer, or travelling pedlar. . . . *Et jadis fusmes si mignotes* . . and so dainty once!"

"No!" His voice took the ring of decision. She didn't hear him. Her voice broke into a torrent of sobs.

"Take me in your arms, Shane, once more. And let my heart come into your heart, where it's so warm . . . and I'll have something to remember in the days when it will be . . . so cold, so cold . . . and I'll be there warming old bones. . . . *A petit feu de chenevotes.* . . Shane, dearest, please. . . ."

He took her in his arms, and her body seemed to be some light envelope in which a great turmoil of spirit beat, as a wild bird beats against a cage. . . . He could hardly hold her body so great was her tortured sobbing. . . So much did what was within wheel and beat, beat and wheel, in unendurable panic. Her voice murmured in his wet shoulder:

"*Pauvre vielle sote!* O Shane, Shane . . *pauvre vielle sote!* . "

§ 12

Above him, to starboard, he could hear the churning of the tug that was to take them from the docks to the open sea. Overhead the pilot was stamping impatiently. Forward the mate was roaring like a bull:

"Where is that damned apprentice? Tell him to lay aft and bear a hand with the warps."

In a minute or so he would have to go on the poop and give orders to let go and haul in. The tug was blowing, "Hurry up . . ." He ought to be on deck now. . . . He hated to go up . . . he hated to see the last of Marseilles . . . he would never see Marseilles again. . .

Was all ready? Yes, all was ready. Cargo, supplies, sea-chest, everything for the long voyage he had decided—had to decide—on at the last minute. Forward across the Atlantic to where the sou'-east trades blew, and then south'ard reaching under all sail—the fleecy clouds, the bright constellations of the alien pole, the strange fish-like birds, the flying-fish, the bonita, the albacore; the chill gust from the River Plate; the roar of the gales of the forties; the tremendous fight around the Horn, with a glimpse of land now and then as they fought for easting—the bleak rocks of Diego Ramirez and the Ildefonsos, and perhaps the blue ridge of Cape Horn, or of the False Cape; then, northward to Callao . . . anywhere, everywhere . . . new seas, new lands, new cities . . but never again Marseilles. . . .

And he would never see her again, *La Mielleuse*—couldn't if he wanted to . . never again . . irrevocable . . . Her head, her dark, darling head! . . . And last night he had seen it for the last time, dark, smiling in sleep, on a snowy pillow. . . . He remembered as he might remember a strange pantomime. . . . His going to his coat for—what he had there . . . the silent tiptoe . . . the gentle raising of her left arm, as she smiled in her sleep . . . the sudden weakness at her soft, warm beauty . . . the decision. . . . Of course he had done right ! . . . Of course !

Of course ! . . .

Overhead the pilot stamped on the deck in a flurry of impatience. The tug wailed in irritation. He must get on deck. . . .

He threw one last glance around. . . . He had everything he needed for himself. . . . Nothing lacking. . . His eyes paused for a moment on his desk. Wait ! Where was the dagger ? Prince Charles' dagger ?

He gripped himself in fright. Was he going—had he gone—mad ? He knew where that was . . he knew . . . he knew . . It was—

" Ogh ! " A flash of horror went over him. . . But he had done right . . . of course he had done right. . . .

" All's ready, sir," the mate called in to his cabin

" Yes ? . . . "

" Man, you're no' ill ? " the mate looked at him queerly.

" Of course I'm not ill." He swung on deck. " All right ? Let go aft, then, and haul in. Tug a little westward : a little more westward. Hard a port, Mr. McKinstry. All right ! Let go all, for'a'd. . . . She's off. . . . "

BOOK FOUR

THE WRESTLER FROM ALEPPO

BOOK FOUR

THE WRESTLER FROM ALEPPO

§ I

"YA ZAN," came his wife's slow, grave voice, "O Shane, when your ship is in trouble, or does not go fast, do the passengers beat you ?"

"Of course not," Campbell laughed. "What put that in your little head ?"

"When I went with my uncle, Arif Bey, on the pilgrimage to Mecca—Arif was a Moslem that year," she bit the thread of the embroidery she was doing with her little sharp teeth, *tkk !*—"our ship anchored for the night in *Birkat Faraun*—Pharaoh's Bay. In the morning it would not move, so the Maghrabi pilgrims beat the captain terribly. And once at Al-Akabah, when the captain lost sight of shore for one whole day, the Maghrabis beat him again. They said he should have known better. Don't—don't they ever beat you, *ya Zan ?*"

"Not yet, Fenzile. They only beat bad skippers."

"But our *Rais* was a good sailor. He must have been a good sailor, Zan. He was very old. He was very pious, too. He said the prayers. Do you ever say the prayers, Zan, when the sea looks as if it were about to be angry ?"

"What sort of prayers, Fenzile ?"

"Oh, prayers. Let me see." Her dark eyes had the look he loved, as if she had turned around and were rummaging within herself, as a woman seeks diligently and yet slowly in a chest. "Oh, like the Moslem's *Hizb al-Bahr.* You ought to know that prayer, *ya Zan.* It will make you safe at sea. I wonder you, a great *Rais*, do not know that prayer."

"What is the prayer, Fenzile?"

"'We pray Thee for safety in our goings forth and our standings still . . . Subject unto us this sea, even as Thou didst subject the deep to Moses, and as Thou didst subject the fire to Abraham, and as Thou didst subject the iron to David, and as Thou didst subject the wind and the devils and djinns and mankind to Solomon, and as Thou didst subject the moon and *Al-Burah* to Mohammed, on whom be Allah's mercy and His blessing! And subject unto us all the seas in earth and heaven, in Thy visible and Thine invisible worlds, the sea of this life and the sea of futurity. O Thou Who reignest over everything and unto Whom all things return, . . . You must know that prayer, and say that prayer, *ya Zan*. What do you do when it is very stormy?"

"Oh, take in as little sail as possible and keep shoving ahead."

"I don't understand," she let the embroidery fall in her lap. "I see your ship from the quays and I can't understand how you guide such a big ship. And how you go at night, Zan, that I cannot understand. It is so dark at night. There is a terrible lot I do not understand. I am very stupid."

"You are very dear and darling, Fenzile. You understand how to take care of a house and how to be very beautiful, and be very loving—"

"Do I, Zanim? That is not hard. That is not very much. That is not like sailing a ship on the sea."

Without, Beirut seethed with life. Thin, gaun

dogs barked and snarled in the narrow staired streets. Came the cry of the donkey-boys. Came the cry of the water-sellers. Came the shouts of the young Syrians over the gammon game. Loped the laden camels. Tramped the French soldiers. Came a new hum. . . .

Fenzile rose and went through the courtyard, past the little fountain with the orange-trees, past the staircase to the upper gallery, came to the barred iron gates, looked a moment, moved modestly, back into the shadows. . . .

" O look, *ya Zan*," her grave voice became excited. " Come quickly. See. It is Ahmet Ali, with his attendants and a lot of people following him."

" And who is Ahmet Ali ? "

" Ahmet Ali ! don't you know, Zanim ? The great wrestler, Ahmet Ali. The wrestler from Aleppo. . . "

§ 2

Through the grilled door, in the opal shade of the walls, Shane saw the wrestler stroll down the street ; a big bulk of a man in white robe and turban, olive-skinned, heavy on his feet, seeming more like a prosperous young merchant than a wrestling champion of a vilayet. Yet underneath the white robes Shane could sense the immense arms and shoulders, the powerful legs. Very heavily he moved, muscle-bound a good deal, Shane thought ; a man for pushing and crushing and resisting, but not for fast, nervous work, sinew and brain co-ordinating like the crack of a whip. A Cornish wrestler would turn him inside out within a minute ; a Japanese would pitch him like a ball before he had ever even taken his stance. But once he had a grip he would be irresistible.

" So that's Ahmet Ali."

" Yes, Zan," Fenzile clapped her hands with delight, like a child seeing a circus procession. " Oh, he is a great wrestler. He beat Yussuf Hussein, the Cairene, and he beat a great Russian wrestler who came on a pilgrimage to Jerusalem. And he beat a French sailor. And he beat a Tartar. Oh, he is a great wrestler, Ahmet Ali."

The wrestler had come nearer. Behind him came four or five supporters, in cloth white as his. Behind them came a ruck of Syrian youths, effeminate, vicious. Came a crowd of donkey-boys, impish, black. The wrestler walked more slowly as he approached to pass the iron doors. And Shane was startled into a sudden smile at the sight of his face—a girl's face, with a girl's eyes. And in his hand was a rose. A wrestler with a rose !

" Why, a man could kill him."

" Oh, no ! Oh, no, Zan !" Fenzile said. " He is very strong. He conquered Yussuf Hussein, the Cairene, and Yussuf Hussein could bend horseshoes with his bare hands. He is very strong, very powerful Ahmet Ali."

The wrestler was walking slowly past the house throwing glances through the grill with his full girl's eyes. A quick suspicion came into Campbell's mind. He turned to his wife.

" Does he come past here often ? "

" Yes, yes, Zan. Every day."

" Does he stop and look into the court like that, every time ? "

"Yes, Zan. Every time," she smiled.

"Do you know whom he's looking for?"

"Yes, Zan. For me."

Campbell's hand shot out suddenly and caught her wrist.

"Fenzile," his voice was cold. "You aren't carrying on with, encouraging this—Ahmet Ali?"

"Zan Cam'el," her child's eyes flashed unexpectedly "I am no cheap Cairene woman. I am a Druse girl. The daughter of a Druse Bey."

"I am sorry, Fenzile."

She looked at him steadily with her great green eyes, green of the sea, and as he looked at her sweet roundish face, her little mouth half open in sincerity, her calm brow, her brown arch of eyebrow, she seemed to him no more than a beautiful proud child. There was no guile in her.

"You mustn't be foolish, you know, Fenzile."

"*Severim seni*. I love only you, Zan. But it is so funny to see him go by, I must always smile. Don't you think it funny, Zan?"

"No, I don't think it at all funny."

"Oh, but is is funny, Zan. A big strong wrestler like that to be foolish over a very little woman. And for a cheap showman of the market-place to be lifting his eyes to a daughter of the Druse emirs. It is funny."

"It isn't funny. And he isn't much of a wrestler anyway"

"Oh, but he is Zan. He is a very great wrestler. They say he threw and killed a bear."

"O kooltooluk. Hell! I could throw him myself."

She said nothing, turning her head, and reaching for her embroidery.

"Don't you believe me, Fenzile? I tell you I could make mince-meat of him."

"Of course, Zan. Of course you could." And she smiled. But this time it wasn't the delighted smile of a child. It was the grave patient smile of a wise woman. And Shane knew it. Past that barrier he could not break. And on her belief he could make no impress. There was no use arguing, talking. She would just smile and agree. And her ideal of strength and power would be the muscle-bound hulk of the Aleppo man, with the girl's face and the girl's eyes, and the rose in his hand. And Shane, all his life, inured to sport, hard as iron, supple as a whip, with his science picked up from Swedish quartermasters and Japanese gendarmes, from mates and crimps in all parts of the world, would always be in her eyes an infant compared to the monstrous Syrian! Not that it mattered a tinker's curse, but—

Oh, damn the wrestler from Aleppo!

§ 3

He had thought, when he left Liverpool on a gusty February day, of all the peace and quiet, of the colour and life there would be on the Asian shore. . . . Europe had somehow particularly sickened him on this last voyage. . . . All its repose was sordid, all its passion was calculated. England and its queen mourned the sudden death of the prince consort, but it mourned him with a sort of middle-class domesticity, and no majesty. So a grocer's family might have mourned, remembering how well papa cut the mutton. . . . He was so damned good at everything, Albert was, and he approved of art and science—within reason. . . . There was a contest for a human ideal in America, and in the ports of England privateers were being fitted out, to help the South, as the Greeks might, for a price. . . . And Napoleon, that solemn comedian, was making ready his expedition to Mexico, with fine words and a tradesman's cunning. . . . And the drums of Ulster roared for Garibaldi, rejoicing in the downfall of the harlot on seven hills, as Ulster pleasantly considered the papal states, while Victor Emmanuel, sly Latin that he was, thought little of liberty and much about Rome . . . Aye, kings!

And so a great nostalgia had come over Shane Campbell on this voyage for the Syrian port and the wife he had married there. He wanted sunshine. He wanted colour. He wanted simplicity of life Killing there was in Syria, great killing too. But it was the sort of killing one understood and could forgive. A Druse disliked a Maronite Christian, so he went quietly and knifed him. Another Maronite resented that, and killed a Druse; and they were all at it, hell-for-leather. But it was passion and fanaticism, not high-flown words and docile armies and the tradesmen sneaking up behind. . . . Aye, war!

And he was sick of the damned Mersey fog, and he was sick of the drunkenness of Scotland Road, and he was sick of the sleet lashing Hoylake links. He was sick of Pharisaical importers who did the heathen in the eye on Saturday and on Sunday in their blasted conventicles thumped their black-covered craws in respectable humility. . . . In Little Asia religion was a passion, not a smug hypocrisy; and though the heathen was dishonest, yet it was not the mathematical reasoned dishonesty of the Christian. It was a childish game, like horse-coping. . . . And in the East they did not blow gin in your face, smelling like turpentine. . . .

And he was sick of the abominable homes, the horsehair furniture with the anti-macassars—Lord! and they called themselves clean. . . . He wanted the spotlessness of the Syrian courtyard. . . . The daubs on the British walls, sentimental St. Bernard dogs and dray-horses with calves' eyes, brought him to a laughing point when he thought of the subtlety of colour and line in strange Persian rugs. . . .

And he was sick of British women, with their knuckled hands, their splayed feet. Their abominable dressing, too, a bust and a brooch and a hooped skirt—their grocer's conventions, prudish, almost obscene, avoiding of the natural in word, deed, or thought. . . . He wanted Fenzile, with her eyes, *vert de mer*, her full childish face, her slim hands with the orange-tinted finger nails, her silken trousers, her little slippers of silver and blue. . . . Her soft arms, her back-thrown head, her closed lids. . . . And the fountain twinkling in the soft Syrian night, while afar off some Arab singer chanted a poem of Lyla Khanim's:

"*Beni ser-mest u hayran eyleyen ol yar; janim dir* . . . The world is a prison and my heart is scarred . . . My tears are like a vineyard's fountain, O absent one. . . ."

And here was Beirut again: here the snowy crest of Lebanon, here the roadstead crowded with craft; here the mulberry groves. Here the sparkling sapphire sea; here the turf blazing with poppies; here the quiet pine road to Damascus; here the forests, excellent with cedars. Here the twisting unexpected streets. Here his own quiet house, with the courtyard and its fountain. Here the hum of the bazaars, here the *haha* of the donkey boys, here the growling camels. Here the rugs on the wall; here the little orange-trees. Here the two negress servants, clean, efficient. Here colour, and peace, and passion. Here Fenzile. . . .

And this damned wrestler from Aleppo must go and spoil it all.

§ 4

He might have shipped with one of the great American clippers racing around Cape Hope under rolling topsails, and become in his way as well known as Donald Mackay was, who built and mastered the *Sovereign of the Seas*, with her crew of one hundred and five, four mates and two boatswains. He might have had a ship like Phil Dumaresq's *Surprise*, that had a big eagle for her figurehead. He might have clipped the record of the *Flying Cloud*, three hundred and seventy-four miles in one day, steering northward and westward around Cape Horn. He might have had a ship as big as the *Great Republic*, the biggest ship that ever took the seas. He might have had one of the East Indiamen, and the state of an admiral. He might have had one of the new adventurers in steel and steam.

But fame and glory never allured him, and destiny did not call him to be any man's servant. He was content to be his own master with his own ship, and do whatsoever seemed to him good and just to do. If they needed him and his boat anywhere, he would be there. When they needed boats to America, he was there. But if they didn't need him, he was not the one to thrust himself. Let destiny call.

Success, as it was called, was a thing of destiny. When destiny needed a man, destiny tapped him on the shoulder. Failure, however, was a man's own fault. There was always work to do. And it was up to every man to find his work. If there were room for him in a higher work it was no excuse for his not working in a lower plane. There would be no failures he thought, if folk were only wise. If a man came a cropper in a big way, it was because he had rushed into a work before destiny, the invisible infallible nuncio of God, had chosen her man. Or because he was dissatisfied, ambition and ability not being equal Or because he was lazy.

Always there was work to do, as there was work for him now. Clouds of sail and tubby steamboats went the crowded tracks of the world's waters, not to succour and help but for gain of money. And Lesser Asia was neglected now that the channel of commerce to the States was opened wide. Syria needed more than sentimental travellers to the Holy Land. It needed machinery for its corn-fields and its mines. It needed prints and muslins from the Lancashire looms. It needed rice and sugar. And it had more to give than a religious education. Fine soap and fruit and wine and oil and sesame it gave, golden tobacco, and beautiful craftsmanship in silver and gold, fine rugs from Persia. Brass and copper and ornamental woodcarving from Damascus, mother of cities; walnuts, wheat, barley, and apricots from its gardens and fields. Wool and cotton, gums and saffron from Aleppo, and fine silk embroidery.

Others might race past Java Head to China for tea and opium. Others might make easting around the Horn to the gold-fields of California. Others might sail up the Hooghly to Calicut, trafficking with mysterious Indian men. Others might cross to the hustle and welter of New York, young giant of cities, but Campbell was content to sail to Asia Minor. He brought them what they needed, and they sent colour and rime to prosaic Britain, hashish to the apothecaries, and pistachios from Aleppo, cambric from Nablus and linen from Baghdad, and occasionally for an antiquary a Damascene sword that rang like a silver bell.

For others the glory and fame to which destiny had called them. For others the money that they grubbed with blunted fingers from the dross-heaps of commerce. But for Campbell what work he could do, well done—and Lesser Asia. . . .

§ 5

Of all the seas he had sailed it seemed to Shane that Mediterranean had more colour, more life, more romance than any. Not the battles round the Horn, not the swinging runs to China, not the starry southern seas had for him the sense of adventure that Mediterranean had. Mediterranean was not a sea.

It was a home haven, with traditions of the human house. Here Sennacherib sailed in the great galleys the brown Sidonian shipwrights had made for him. Here had been the Phoenicians with their brailed squaresail. Here had been the men of Rhodes, sailors and fighters both. Here the Greek penteconters with their sails and rigging of purple and black. Here the Cypriotes had sailed under the lee of the islands Byron loved and where Sappho sang her songs like wine and honey, sharp wine and golden honey. Here had the Roman galleys splashed and here the great Venetian boats set proud sail against the Genoese. Here had the Lion-heart sailed gallantly to Palestine. Here had Icarus fallen in the blue sea. Here had Paul been shipwrecked, sailing on a ship of Andramyttium bound to the coast of Asia, crossing the sea which is off Cilicia and Pamphylia, and transhipping at Myra. How modern it all sounded but for the strange antique names.

" And when we had sailed slowly many days "—only a seaman could feel the pathos of that—" and scarce were come over against Cnidus, the wind not suffering us, we sailed under Crete, over against Salmone;

" And, hardly passing it, came unto a place which is called The Fair Havens——"

Was Paul a sailor, too, Campbell often wondered? The bearded Hebrew, like a firebrand, possibly epileptic, not quite sane, had he at one time been brought up to the sea? " Sirs," he had said, " I perceive that this voyage will be with hurt and much damage, not only of the lading and ship, but also of our lives." There spoke a man who knew the sea—

not a timid passenger. But the master of the ship thought otherwise, and yet Paul was right. And then came "a tempestuous wind, called Euroclydon." And that was the Levanter of to-day, Euraquilo, they call it—hell let loose. Then came furious seas, and the terrors of a lee shore; the frapping of the ship and the casting overboard of tackle, the jettisoning of freight—

"And when neither sun nor stars in many days appeared, and no small tempest lay on us, all hope that we should be saved was then taken away." Somehow the absolute fidelity of the sea-life of the story went to Campbell's heart, and the figure of Paul the mariner was clearer than the figure of Paul the Apostle.

"Howbeit, we must be cast upon a certain island.

"But when the fourteenth night was come, as we were driven up and down in Adria, about midnight the shipmen deemed that they drew near to some country——"

The intuition of seamanship. The flash. How modern! Oh, Paul lived in that sea. His ghost and memory were forever there, as were the ghosts of the Lion-heart; and of Sappho, singer of songs; and of the stout Phoenician sailing men; and of the doges of Venice, lovers and husbands of the sea. On the tideless Mediterranean beauty still abided, as nowhere else; would abide, when nowhere else——

Would it, though? Would it abide anywhere? A pang came into Campbell's heart. Off Finisterre he had been passed by Robert Steel of Greenock's *Falcon*, every sail drawing, skysails and moonrakers set, a pillar of white cloud she seemed, like some majestic womanhood. And while boats like the *Fiery Cross* and the *Falcon* tore along like greyhounds, there were building tubby iron boats to go by steam. The train was beating the post-chaise with its satiny horses, the train that went by coal one dug from the ground. And even now de Lesseps and his men were digging night and day that the steamboat might push the proud clipper from the seas. Queer! Would there come a day when no topgallants drew? And the square-rigged ships would be like old crones gathering fagots on an October day. And what would become of the men who built and mastered great racing ships? And would the sea itself permit vile iron and smudgy coal to speck its immaculate bosom? Must the sea, too, be tamed like a dancing bear for the men who are buying and selling? It seemed impossible

But the shrewd men who trafficked said it must be so. They were spending their money on de Lesseps' fabulous scheme. And the shrewd men never spent money without a return. They would conquer.

Poor sea of the Vikings! Poor sea of the Lion-heart and of the Sappho of the songs! Poor sea of Admiral Columbus! Poor sea to whom Paul made obeisance! Sea of Drake and sea of Nelson, and sea of Philip of Spain. Poor sea whom the great doges of Venice wed with a ring of gold! Christ! If they could only bottle you, they would sell you like Holland gin!

§ 6

He had figured his work. He had figured his field. It seemed to him that this being done life should flow on evenly as a stream. But there were gaps of unhappiness that all the subtle sailing of a ship, all the commerce of the East, all the fighting of the gales could not fill. Within him somewhere was a space, in his heart, in his head, somewhere, a ring, a pit of emotion—how, where, why he could not express. It just existed. And this was filled at times with concentration on his work, at times with plans of the future and material memories of the past or thoughts of ancient shipmates, of his Uncle Robin. It was like a house, that space was, with a strange division of time, that corresponded not with time of day, but with recurrent actions, memories, moods. There would be the bustle of his work, and that seemed to be morning. There would be the planning of future days, and that seemed like an afternoon of sunshine; and there would be memories, as of old shipmates, as of Uncle Robin—God rest his dear soul; as of Alan Donn with his hearty cursing, his hearty laugh. And that was like an evening with golden candlelight and red fire burning. And then came the quietness of night, all the bustle, all the plans, all the memories gone. The fire out, the rooms empty. And in the strange place somewhere within would come a strange lucidity, blue and cold and absolute as the stars, and into that place would walk, as players stalk upon the stage, each of three ghosts.

The first was his mother, who was dead, an apparition of chilling terror. From afar she beheld him with eyes that were queerly inimical. She had done nothing to him, nor he anything to her. She had done nothing for him, nor he for her. Between them was nothing. When she had died he had felt nothing, and that was the tragedy. No tears, no relief, nothing. She had carried him in her womb, borne him, suckled him ; and he had always felt he had been unwelcome. There had been no hostility in her body ; just constraint. She had had no welcome for the little guest of God ; her heart had been hard to him and he at her breasts. Nothing common to them in life and now joined through the horrible significant gulf of death. She could be with him always now, being dead. But where a man's mother should come to him smilingly, with soft hands, with wisdom and comfort passing that of life, she came with terrible empty eyes. He could see her gaunt profile, her black brows. She was like an engraving he had once seen of the witch Saul had used at En-dor, to call up Samuel, who was dead. She had the same awful majesty, the same utter loneliness.

"You gave me nothing in life. In death give me peace," he would cry. But she stayed until it suited her to go, as she would have done in life. Her haunted, haunting eyes . . . !

And there would come another ghost, the ghost of the girl he had married and he a boy—fourteen years ago. It was strange how he could remember her—her red hair, her sullen mouth, her suspicious eyes. Her shoulders drooped a little, there was no grace to her stance. She complained against something, but she did not accuse him. He had married her, and she had married him, and she had died. That was all there was to it. And though she had sorrowed his younger days, yet he felt very kindly to her. There she was, with her sullen mouth, her drooping shoulders complaining. "Life is so short, and there was so little to it, and others have so much," she seemed to say. "I had a right to have my man and a place in the country, the like of other girls, but all I got was you. And death at the end of a short year. Wasn't it hard, och, wasn't it so!" And he had to comfort her. "It was nobody's fault, Moyra. It just happened. We were awfully young." But her lips were still sullen, her eyes suspicious as she went away. "A short life and a bitter one. A hard thing surely!" When she left him there was a sigh of relief. Poor girl!

And the third ghost was hardly a presence, but an absence, or a presence so intangible that it was worse than an absence—Claire-Anne, who was dead, whom he had—made dead, whom he had taken it upon himself to set free. For a year after he had left Marseilles she had seemed to be always with him, closer in spirit, now she was dead, than she had ever been in flesh and spirit when alive. A part of him she seemed always to be. Always there, in the quiet cabin, on the heeling decks, on the solid shore. And the long thoughts of him seemed to be conversation with her, on strange beautiful things, on strange terrible things, on the common commodity of life. . . . And then one day she left him. . . .

He was coming into Southampton Water and waiting for the pilot's cutter from the Solent, one bright July morning. And all the Solent was dotted with sails, the snowy sails of great yachts and the cinnamon sail of small ones. Little fishing-craft prowled near the shore. And afar off, in fancy, he could see the troops of swans, and the stalking herons. The pilot's cutter ploughed toward him, her deep forefoot dividing the water like a knife. Immense, vibrant beauty. And he felt, as always, that Claire-Anne was by him, her dark understanding presence, her clear Greek face, her little smile.

"In a minute now we will come into the wind and lower a boat, Claire-Anne." And a shock of surprise came over him. She was not there. It was as though he had been talking with his back turned to some one, and turning around found they weren't there. For an instant he felt as if he had lost somebody overboard. And then it came to him that water, earth, material hazards were nothing to her any more. She had gone somewhere for a moment. And he turned to greet the pilot as he swung aboard.

"She will come back," he thought. . . . But she never came back. Once or twice or maybe three times, a month, six months, and ten months later, he felt her warm lover-like presence near him. "Claire-Anne! Is it you, Claire-Anne?" And she was gone again. Something that had hovered, fluttered, kissed, and flown away. Never again!

She had become to him in death much more real than she had ever been in life. In life she had been dynamic, a warm, multicoloured, perfumed cloud. In death she was static. All the tumult of material things gone, he had a vision of her clear as a line drawing. And he had come to depend on her so much. In difficulty of thought he would say: "Is this right, Claire-Anne?" And her answer would come: "Yes, Shane!" Or possibly when some matter of trade or conduct seemed dubious, not quite—whatever it was, her voice would come clear as a bell. "You mustn't, Shane. It isn't right. It isn't like you to be small." It might have been conscience, but it sounded like Claire-Anne. And oftentimes in problems, she would say: "I don't know, Shane. I don't quite know." And he would say, "We must do our best, Claire-Anne."

Well, she was gone. And he thought to himself: What do we know of the destiny of the dead. They, too, must have work, missions to perform. The God he believed in—the wise firm and kindly God—might have said: "Clare-Anne, he'll be all right now. At any rate he'll have to work out the rest for himself. Leave that. I want you to—" And she had gone.

That was one majestic explanation, but at times it seemed to him that no matter what happened in the world, or superworld, yet she must be in touch with him. "Set me, as a seal upon thy heart, as a seal upon thine arm," cried the prince's daughter, "for love is strong as death." If she loved him she must love him still.

It suddenly occurred to him that the fault was not occult, but a matter of spiritual deterioration in himself. To be in harmony with the lonely dead there must be no dross about the mind. The pre-occupations of routine, the occasional dislikes of some stupid ship's officer, or boatswain, the troubles about cargo—this, that, the other pettinesses might cloud his eye as a mist clouds a lens. There came to him the memory of a translation from some Chinese poet he had heard somewhere, in some connection:

How am I fallen from myself! For a long time now
I have not seen the prince of Chang in my dreams.

He decided he would clear and make ready the

quiet sweet place in his heart, the room of ghosts, so that she might come and dwell there. But induce the spiritual mood of the quiet October evening much as he could, yet she never came again.

From his mind now there faded the memory of her face, the memory of her hands, the memory of her voice even. With every week, with every month, with the year, she was gone. Like a lost thought, or a lost bar of music, she was gone. She had been there, but she was gone. The loss was a terrible one. To lose one who was alive was much. But to lose one who was dead was unbelievable, horrible . . . to lose the sun . . . forever . . .

He decided he could go back to the Prado of Marseilles, where first he had met her, where she would of all places have kept a tryst with him. There was no risk. The folk of the sea come and go so easily, so invisibly, and French law bothers itself little about the killing of a woman of evil repute. . . One of the risks of the trade, they would say. Even had there been a risk he would have gone. He went.

It was a dark night, a night of wind with the waves lashing the shore. A night of all nights to keep a tryst with a dead woman. Immense privacy of darkness and howling winds and lashing waves. With awe he went there, as a shaken Catholic might enter a cathedral, dubious of the mystery of the eucharist, expecting some silent word, some invisible sign from the tabernacle. . . . He went with bowed head. . .

She never came.

He concentrated until all faded away, even the night, the wind, the insistent waters. He might have been standing on a solitary rock in an infinite dark sea, to which there was no shore. Asking, pleading, willing for her . . . But she never came . . .

And it suddenly became inevitable to him that she would not come ; and slowly, as a man comes slowly out of a drug into consciousness, he came back into the world of lights and laughter and sodden things. And turning on his heel without a look, he went away. . . .

He never called to her again . . . He thought over her often enough, and she had never been real, he decided. His mother and his wife had been real. They were their own dimensions. But she was something he had made in his head, as an author may create a character. She was a hallucination. And she had never been with him after death ; that had been a mirage in the hinterland of the mind.

And he asked : Who was she, anyway ? She was a woman who said she loved him, might even have believed it. Women under stress believe so many things. A little anger, a little passion, a little melancholy, and things resolve themselves into so many differences of colour and line. And what standard of truth is there ? Suppose he were to tell any man of the world of the occurrence, and to ask who she was, what she was, and what he had been to her. They would have said it was simple. She was a harlot of Marseilles, and he was her *amant de cœur*. But the beauty of it ! he would have objected. All the beauty was in yourself. Or as they would have put it : All imagination !

What a snare it all was, and what was truth ?

How much better off a man was if he had never anything to do with them, and yet. . . .

A world of men, there would be something lacking! Friends he had in plenty, men would help him, as a ship stands by another ship at sea. Friends to talk to, of ships and sports, of ports and politics; but when one left them, one was left by one's self. And all the subtleties of mind came again like a cloud of wasps. To each man his own problem of living. To each man to decide his own escape from himself.

"And the Lord God said: It is not good that the man should be alone—" the Hebrew chronicler had imagined. No, it was not good. It was terrible. After the day's work was done, after the pleasant evenings of friends, then came the terror of the shadows. Unreal they might be, but they hurt more than real things did. Unless one sank into the undignified oblivion of drink, there was no escape. Shadows came. Acuter than the tick of a watch, they were there, the cold mother with the haunting eyes, the dead wife with the sullen mouth, visible as stars. And empty as air was the space Claire-Anne should have occupied, with her clear-cut beautiful features, her understanding eyes. Three ghosts, and the ghost that was missing was the most terrible ghost of all . . . He could not stand them any more . . . He must not be alone . . .

§ 7

He could not marry a Christian of the East, they were such an unspeakably treacherous race. He could not marry a Jewess, for about each one of the nation there seemed to be an awesome destiny, a terrible doom or an ultimate majesty blinding human eyes; a wall, so high that it was terrible . . . He could not marry a Moslem woman, for that would mean acceptance of Islam. And though Islam was very fine, very clean, and Campbell believed in resignation, and acknowledged there was no god but God, as the crypticism was, yet the Scots-Irish honesty of him would not accept Mohammed as the prophet of God. It would be like putting Bonaparte above the Lord Buddha. A faith is a very solemn thing and not to be approached lightly. To accept a faith publicly, the tongue in the cheek, was the sin of insincerity and rank dishonesty, having committed which no man should hold up his head. And moreover Moslem women were queer things. For centuries they had been held to be a little more beautiful than a flower, a little less valuable, less personal than a fine horse. Being told that for centuries they had come to believe it, and believing one's self to be particular leads one to become it. Moslem women, no!

He had become familiar with the Druses around Beirut. There was something in the hard independent tribesmen that reminded him of the Ulster Scot. Aloof, unafraid, inimical, independent, with a strain of mysticism in them, they were somehow like the glensmen of Antrim. Fairly friendly with the Moslems, contemptuous of the Latin Christians, impatient of dogma, they might have been the Orangemen of Syria. Their emirs had a great dignity and a great simplicity, like an old-time Highland chief. They acknowledged God, but after that their faith ran into esoteric subtleties of nature-worship, which they kept to the initiates among themselves . . . And the common run of them had strange legends, as that in a mountain bowl of China lived tribe on tribe of Druses, and that one day these of Syria and of China would be reunited and conquer the world. . . . They were very dignified men, and muscular. . . . Their women had the light feet of gazelles . . . One only saw their sweet low foreheads, their cinnamon hands . . . They claimed they were Christians sometimes, and other times they said they were Moslems, but the truth no stranger knew . . . A secret sect, like the ancient Assassins, who had the Old Man of the Mountain for their king. . . . With them dwelt beauty and terror and the glamour of hidden things. . . .

To Shane they were very kindly. They recognized him for a mountain man born, and for an honest man. They could not understand him as a Christian, seeing he took no part in Greek or Latin politics. They decided he must have some faith of his own . . . He did them some kindness of errands, and they were very hospitable to him . . .

In '61, after the massacres, when the tribesmen were preparing to retreat to the mountain of the Druses, he returned to find Syria occupied by the troops of Napoleon III and to hear that his friends Hamadj Beg of Deir el Kour was dead in the war . . . He went to condole with the family . . . Arif Bey, Hamadj's brother, was preparing to retreat towards Damascus. . . .

"Arif Bey," Campbell suddenly said, "also this, I seek a wife."

"Yes." The grizzled Druse scratched his head, and looked at him keenly.

"I am making Lebanon my home; therefore I don't want a wife of my country. There is no people sib to me here but the Druse people. . . . Would a Druse woman marry me?"

"I—I see nothing against it."

"Do you know a Druse woman who would have me?"

"Well, let me see," Arif said. "There is Hamdj's daughter, Fenzile."

"Is she young, Arif Bey?"

"Not so young, nineteen, but she is a mountain woman and lasts."

"Is she good-looking?"

"Yes, she is very good looking."

"Is she kindly?"

"Yes, yes, I think so."

"Is she wild?"

"No. She is very docile."

"You trust me a lot, Arif Bey."

"Yes, we trust you much."

"And I trust you, Arif Bey . . Will Fenzile marry me?"

"Yes," Arif Bey decided, "Fenzile will marry you."

§ 8

It seemed to him, at thirty-five, that only now had he discovered the secret of living. Not until now had his choice and destiny come together to make this perfect equation of life. The work he loved—— the bark *Queen Maeve*, with her beautiful sails like a racing yacht's, her white decks, her shining brass. The carrying of necessities from Britain to Syria, the land he loved next to Ulster, his mother. And the carrying from Syria into harsh plain Britain of cargoes of beauty like those of Sheba's queen—"camels that bare spices, and very much gold and precious stones." And the great ancient city where he lived; not even Damascus, the pride of the world, exceeded it for beauty. Forward of massed Lebanon, white with snow, it lay, a welter of red roots and green foliage—the blue water, the garlanded acacias, the roses, the sally branches. Beauty! Beauty! The Arab shepherds in abbas of dark magenta, the black Greek priests, the green of a pilgrim's turban, the veiled women smoking narghiles and daintily sipping sherbets, pink and yellow and white. The cry of the donkey-boy, and the cry of the cameleer, and the cry of the muezzin from the mosque. The quaint salutations as he passed along the staired streets: *Naharkum Sayeed!*—May your day be blessed. *Naharaka abyad!*—May your day be white. *Allah yahtikum el afiyeh!*—God give health to you. They were chanted like a refrain of a song.

Beauty! Riot and slashing of colour. Yet there was line here and massive proportion. The sparkling, magenta city had been the theatre of great marching hosts. The Phoenicians had built it: "the root of life, the nurse of cities, the primitive queen of the world," they had named her. And gone the Phoenicians, and came the slim subtle Egyptians. And the massive burly Assyrians came next: and now the memory of them was forgotten, also their love and their hatred and their envy was now perished. And then came the tramp of the Roman legions, Agrippa's men, and held the city for centuries. Justinian had one of his law schools there, until the earth quaked and the scholars dispersed. And then the Saracens held it until Baldwin, brother of Godfrey de Bouillon, clashed into it with mailed crusaders. Baldwin, overcome with the beauty of the land, took to him a Paynim queen. And then came the occult reign of the Druse. And then the Turk.

And St. George had killed the Dragon there, after the old monk's tale.

Shane Campbell was never weary of looking at the inscriptions on the great cliffs at the River of the Dog—the strange beauty of that name ! It was like the place-names of native Ulster—*Athbo,* the Ford of Cows, *Sraidcuacha,* the Cuckoo's Lane—one name sounded to the other like tuning-forks. And the sweet strange harmony of it filled his heart, so that he could understand the irresistible charm of Lebanon—the high clear note like a bird's song. Here was the sun and the dreams of mighty things, and the palpable proximity of God. Here was beauty native, to be picked like a nugget, not to be mined for in bitter hours of torment and distress.

High, clear, sustained, the note held. Arose the moon and the great stars like spangles. The slender acacias murmured. The pines *hush-hushed*. The *brouhaha* of the cafés was like a considered counterpoint. Everywhere was harmony ; beauty. And there would be no depression. It would last. There would be no ghosts. They were exorcised. For now there was Fenzile. How understandable everything was ! It must have been under a moon like this, under these Syrian stars, to the ***hush-hush-hush*** of the pine and the rustle of willow branches, that Solomon the king sang his love-song. And it must have been to one whose body was white as Fenzile's, to eyes as emerald, to velvety lips, to slim hands with orange-tinted finger nails that he sang. Surely the Shulamite was not fairer than Fenzile, daughter of Hamadj, a Druse emir !

How beautiful are thy feet with shoes, O prince's daughter !
The joints of thy thighs are like jewels,
The work of the hands of a cunning workman.
Thy navel is like a round goblet,
Which wanteth not liquor :
Thy belly is like an heap of wheat set about with lilies.
Thy two breasts are like two young roes that are twins.
Thy neck is like a tower of ivory :
Thine eyes like the fishpools in Heshbon,
By the gate of Bath-rabbim :
Thy nose is as the tower of Lebanon which looketh toward
Damascus.
Thine head upon thee is like Carmel,
And the hair upon thee is like purple,
The king is held in the galleries.
How fair and pleasant art thou,
O love, for delights !
This thy stature is like to a palm tree.
And thy breasts to clusters of grapes.

I said, I will go up to the palm tree.
I will take hold of the boughs thereof :
Now also thy breasts shall be as clusters of the vine,
And the smell of thy nose like apples ;
And the roof of thy mouth like the best wine for my
beloved,
That goeth down sweetly,
Causing the lips of those that are asleep to speak. . . .

§ 9

Where before he had made his mistake with women was allowing them to become spiritually important. His mother had been important; he had suffered from the sense of her lack of heart to him. His wife had been important; they had not understood life together, had made no attempt to . . . They were so young . . . And Claire-Anne had become spiritually important to him. So that when she was gone, it was hell.

If he had treated his mother causally, depending on his uncles, it would have been all right. If he had discerned—and he had discerned, though he knew not how to act—that his wife and he would forever be inharmonious, it would not have been a scar on his youth. If he had gone for instance to Alan Donn and said, " Uncle Alan, I'm afeared there's a mistake been made. And what are we going to do about this woman o' Louth ? " And Alan would have said: " I ken't well you were a damned young fool. Ah, well, gang off aboard your boatie, and I'll see to her." Alan would have ditched her and her mother mercilessly. There would have been no scar on his youth. . . .

And Claire-Anne, had he only taken her as he should have taken her, as a light love, easily gotten, to be taken easily, instead of tragedizing until his fingers were scarlet. . . . God ! . . . Yes, where before he had made his mistakes with women was allowing them to become spiritually important.

Well, he wouldn't do that with Fenzile. He knew better now. Keep the heart free. Let there be beauty and graciousness and kindliness, but keep the heart free, and ask for no heart. All tragedies were internal, all the outward deeds being only as symbols. Keep the heart free.

There were so many aspects to her. She was like a bird about the house, gaily coloured, of bright song. He loved to see her move here and there, with movements as of music. And she was like a child at times, as she solemnly made sherbets—very like a child she was, intense, simple. And she was like a young relative; there was emptiness in the house when she went, and when she came back it was like a bird singing.

And she was so beautiful about the place, with her eyes green of the sea, her dusky velvet lips, her slim cinnamon hands, with the dramatic orange tinting on the nails. Always was some new beauty in her, a tilt of the head, a sudden gracious pose. She was like some piece of warm statuary. From any angle came beauty, shining as the sun.

And in the dusk when his arms were about her, she was no longer child, relative, or statue. She was woman, vibrant woman. Tensed muscles and a little stifled moan. And an emotional sob, maybe, or a tear glistening on her cheek. Relaxation, and a strange, easy dignity. With her arms about her white knees, her little head upraised, thoughts seemed to be going and coming from her like bees in and out of their straw skep. And often he was tempted to ask her what she was thinking of. But he stopped himself in time. Of course she was thinking of nothing at all, barring possibly a new sherbet to be made, or whether, if they sold Fatima, the Abyssinian cook, who was becoming garrulous, would Fatima have a good home. Trifles ! What was the use of asking her ? And here was another possibility. She might—anything was possible—be in some deep subtle thought, into which, if he asked, he might get enmeshed, or be trapped emotionally. Better not ask. He wanted to know nothing of her heart, and to keep his.

He loved her in a happy, guarded way. And she loved him. When he came back after a voyage she looked at him with an amazed joy. " O *Zan !* Zan, dear ! Is it you ? Is it really you ? " She would rush and hold him. What amazing strength her little arms had ! And she would stand back and look at him again. " O Zan ! Zan ! " And she would bury her perfumed head in his shoulder to hide the glad tears. " O Zan ! "

" Do you know why I love you so much, Zan dear ? " she once said.

" Why, Fenzile ? "

" Because you are so big, and yet you are so gentle. And you wouldn't do a little thing, my Zan."

" Don't be foolish, Fenzile ! '"

" I am not foolish."

Only once she asked him how he loved her.

" I wonder—how much do you love me, my Zan ? "

" Oh, lots, Fenzile. A terrible lot." And he smiled.

" As much as you do your ship ? "

" Yes, as much as I do my ship."

" That is a lot, Zan . . . Zan, would you miss me if I should die ? "

" I should miss you terribly."

"If you died, I should die, too." Her voice quavered.

"Don't be silly. Of course you wouldn't."

"Don't you think I would?" And she laughed with him, one of her rare, rare laughs. And that was the way it all should end, in pretty laughter. Let there be none of this horrible emotionalism, this undignified welter of thought and feeling. Kindness of eyes, and pleasantness of body, but keep the heart away. Let them be—how? There wasn't a word in English, or in Gaidhlig to express it; in French there was—*des amis*, not *des amants*. Let them be that. Let there be no involution of thought and mind about it. Let there be this time no mistake. . . . Where before he had made his mistake with women was allowing them to become spiritually important. . . .

§ 10

Into this idyl of Beirut came now the wrestler from Aleppo, Ahmet Ali, and the occurrence irritated Campbell to a degree which he had not conceived possible. There he passed the door with his dreamy Syrian face, his red rose, his white burnoose, his straggling followers. And Fenzile smiled her quiet, aloof smile.

There might be amusement in it, a queer Eastern comedy of the mountebank who raised his eyes to a Druse princess, and wife of a Frank ship's master. It might be amusing to Fenzile to see this conqueror of men conquered by her presence, but it wasn't dignified. By God! it wasn't dignified.

But it wasn't dignified to talk about it. To show

Fenzile that it mattered a tinker's curse to him. So he said nothing, and the wrestler went by every day. It was becoming intolerable. It seemed to amuse Fenzile, but it didn't amuse him.

And suddenly a chill smote him. What did he know of these people of the East anyhow? In six years one could learn their language perfectly, know their customs, know themselves, but know only as much as they wanted to be known. The outer person, which is hallucination, one might know, but what of the inner, which is reality? A strange country, where the merchants spoke like princes and the princes like cameleers, and the *sakyeh*, the water-carrier, might quote some fancy of Hafiz, as the water gurgled from the skin. The obedience, the resignation in the women's eyes might cover intrigue, and what was behind the eyes of the men, soft as women's?

"Fenzile, you say you love me, because I am kind. Don't you love me because I am strong?"

"Anyway, anyhow, dear Zan."

"I am strong, you know. As strong as your friend, Ahmet Ali."

"Of course, dear Zan." But somehow her tone did not carry conviction. If she understood there was nothing this wrestler had he did not have better, it would have been all right. All attributes in the world would have been for her in him. But she thought the wrestler was strong. Damn women! Couldn't they understand the difference between the muscles of a hunting leopard and the bulk of a sea-cow? It was silly, but it irritated him.

And then a thought came to him that he felt degraded him, but of which he could not rid himself, try as he would. What did he know of Fenzile, barring that she was young and strong and beautiful ? Nothing. Of what was she thinking in those dreamy eyes, green of the sea ? And women always admired strength in a man. And he was away most of the time, half anyway. And the breath of the East was intrigue.

" Oh, don't be rotten," he told himself. But the occasional hot and searing pain remained, and the little black cloud was in his mind. When they were close in the soft gloom, shoulder to shoulder, her eyes closed, her slim cinnamon hands clenched, doubt rose blackly in him. And in the gay mornings, when she was arranging her flowers in vases of Persian blue, it made him silent as the grave. And in the evening when she was doing her subtle Syrian broideries, it aroused in him queer gusts of controlled fury . . . Could it be possible ? A mountebank . . . And the " Thousand and One Nights " began with *Shah Zamon's* queen and her love for the blackamoor slave . . .

If the wrestler would only go away, become tired of parading, and Fenzile would tire of smiling . . . And later on Campbell would laugh . . .

But the wrestler stayed, and many times Campbell met him in the streets, and each time was exaggerated, insulting courtesy from the Aleppo man, as he drew aside to let the Frank pass. There was hostility and contempt in his veiled eyes . . . There nonchalance in his smelling of the rose . . . Campbell passed by frigidly, as if the man weren't there, and all the time his blood was boiling . . . But what was one to do ? One could not make a scene before the riff-raff of

Syria. And besides, there was too much of a chance of a knife in the back . . . Franks were cheap these days, and it would be blamed on the war of the Druses . . .

Argue with himself as much as he could, it was intolerable. It was silly, but it was intolerable . . To think of another caressing that perfumed hair, of another kissing the palm of that slim hand, of another seeing those sleek, sweet shoulders . . .

Was he jealous . . . ? No, irritated, just, he told himself. Was he in love with her himself ? Of course not. She wasn't close enough to him for that . . . Then why . . . ?

Oh, damn it ! He didn't know why, but it was just intolerable . . .

§ II

The bark was in the open roadstead, cargo all ready, Levantine pilot on board. A reaching breeze from the north and all favourable. And when he would get home to Liverpool, he had a design to spend a few weeks in Ulster . . . The roads would be glistening with frost there, and the pleasant Ulster moon at the full . . . The turf would be nearly black, and bare as a board, and there would be coursing of hares . . . November mists, and the trees red and brown . . . Eh, hard Ulster, pleasant Ulster !

He should have been happy, as he made his way down the Beirut streets to go aboard, leaving the land of his adoption for the land of his birth, leaving pleasant Fenzile for the shrewd pleasantry of his own folk . . . A little while of Ulster and he would be coming back again . . . One's heart should lift at the glory of the world, the bold line of Ulster and the lavish colour of Syria ; the sincere, dour folk of Ulster and the warmth of Fenzile . . . He should have left so warmly. " In a little while, dearest, I'll be back and my heart will speak to your twin green eyes." " Yes, Zan. I'll be here." But he had left dourly. And Fenzile had watched him go with quivering lip . . . Oh, damn himself for his suspicions, for his annoyance, and damn the fatuous Arab fool for arousing them . . . Christ, if only he had that fellow on board ship! And suddenly he met him, with his attendants and hangers-on. The wrestler drew aside with his insolent smile. Campbell's temper broke loose.

" Listen, O certain person," he insulted the Aleppo man, " there is a street in Beirut down which it does not please me to see you go."

" Will the foreign gentleman tell me," the wrestler's voice drawled, and he smelled his rose, " who will stop a Moslem from going down a Moslem street ? "

" By God ! I would." The Syrians of Ahmet Ali's escort gathered around, smiling.

" The foreign gentleman forgets that I am the wrestler from Aleppo."

" Just so. I happen to be a bit of a wrestler myself."

" Some day perhaps the foreign gentleman will condescend to try a fall with me."

Syrians, Egyptians, Turks, were pouring from all quarters. Six French soldiers walking gapingly along the bazaars, stopped wonderingly.

" Dites, les soldats," Shane called. " Vous ne voulez pas voir quelque chose d'intéressant ? "

" Mais, si, Monsieur ! "

" Eh bien, je vais lutter contre l'homme avec la rose. C'est un lutteur arabe. Voulez-vous y assister? "

" Mais, pour bien sûr, Monsieur."

" All right, then, by God ! " Shane looked square at Ahmed Ali. " We'll wrestle right here and now."

" But the stones, the street," Ahmet Ali looked surprised. " You might get hurt."

" We'll wrestle here and now."

" Oh, all right." The Arab lifted an expressive shoulder. Carefully he removed the great white robe and handed it to an attendant. To another he gave the rose. Shane handed his coat and hat to a saturnine French corporal. Ahmet Ali took his shirt off. Kicked away his sandals. There was the dramatic appearance of an immense bronze torso. The Syrians smiled. The French soldiers looked judicially grave. Ahmet Ali stood talking for an instant with one of his men, a lean bilious-seeming Turk. The Turk was urging something with eagerness. The wrestler's soft girl's face had concentrated into a mask of distaste. He was shaking his head. He didn't like something.

" How much longer are you going to keep me waiting ? "

Ahmet turned. There was a smile on his face, as of amused, embarrassed toleration. He was like a great athlete about to box with a small boy. And the boy in earnest.

" Ready ? " he asked.

" Any time," Shane snapped.

" All right."

Very easily he came forward over the cobbled street. He was like some immense bronze come suddenly to life and shambling. Like the brazen servant Thomas Aquinas made under the influence of particular stars. His great brown shoulders, his barrelled chest, his upper arms like a man's leg, his packed forearms, his neck like a bull's, his shaven head. All seemed superhuman, and then came his shy embarrassed smile, his troubled eyes. One felt he hated to do this . . .

He dropped suddenly, easily into his wrestler's crouch. His shoulders swayed lightly. He pawed like a bear.

Campbell stood easily, left foot forward, like a boxer. His left arm shot out suddenly. The heel of his hand stopped, jolted Ahmet on the chin. The Syrian shook his head. Pawed again. Campbell slapped him on the forearms, jolted him again on the chin, broke away easily to the right. Ahmet's brown forehead frowned. "Don't be childish," he seemed to chide Campbell. The crowd pressed. The French soldiers rapped them back with the scabbard of their sidearms. *En arrière, les puants, en arrière!* " Back, sons of polecats, get back." The scabbards clacked like slapsticks.

Ahmet Ali stood up straighter. He wanted to get away from that annoying hand on his chin. His forearms moved faster now, like brown pistons. There was a slight frown on his face. He was becoming impatient. Shane broke again to the right. Ahmet followed, his immense hands poised. Campbell feinted for the chin again with his left hand. The wrestler's smile flickered. His right arm went out in guard. Campbell shifted, caught the brown wrist in his right hand, his left hand shot forward to the chin again. He brought forward all his forces to twisting that gigantic arm. He held the Syrian locked. The right arm began to give. If he could only shift his feet, get some sort of leverage. But how in God's name, how? How could he get behind. With an immense wrench of shoulders Ahmet got free. He stood for an instant, nursing his numbed wrist. He nodded and grinned. "That wasn't bad," he seemed to say. The lean bilious Turk on the edge of the crowd began talking viciously. The saturnine French corporal turned and smacked him terribly across the nose with the edge of the scabbard of his bayonet. "*Et ta sœur!*" He had the air of a school master reproving a refractory pupil. But his language was obscene and his blow broke the man's nose . . . He vouchsafed no further interest in the Turk, but turned to watch the wrestling, twirling an oiled mustache . . .

The Syrian closed his mouth, breathed heavily through his nostrils. His brow corrugated. His eyes became pinpoints. He was a workman out to do a job. He began to weave in, his brown arms describing slow arabesques. The crowd around became oppressively silent. They breathed hissingly.

Shane feinted, dodged, broke away. Doggedly Ahmet Ali followed. Faster than time, Shane's right hand shot out and gripped the wrestler's wrist. His right foot hooked around the Syrian's right ankle. He pulled downward with sudden, vicious effort. Ali crashed forward on his face, a great brown hulk like an overturned bronze statue. Shane stooped down for either the half-Nelson and hammer-lock, or full Nelson. . . . An instant too long of hesitation.

Light as a lightweight acrobat Ahmet Ali had rolled aside, put palm to ground, sprung to his feet. His face was bloody, his right knee shook. With the back of his hand he wiped the blood from his eyes. There was a twitter from the Syrians. The wrestler lumbered forward again. . . . A little quake of fear came into Campbell's being. There was an impersonal doggedness about the wrestler from Aleppo's eyes, a sense of inevitability. . . . Shane's eyes shifted, right and left. . . .

Then suddenly, the wrestler had him. . . .

He felt a twirl to his shoulder, and then he was pinioned by two immense brown arms. They caught him above the elbows around the chest. First they were like boys' arms, light. They became firm as calipers. They settled, snugged. Then they tightened slowly, with immense certainty. There was something about it like the rise of the tide. A gigantic cable around his chest. At his shoulder-blades the Syrian's pectoral muscles pressed like shollow knobs of steel. His arms began to hurt. His breathing began to be hard with every output of breath. The arms tightened. . . . All his vitality was flying through his opened mouth. . . . He hit futilely with his knuckles at the rope-like sinews of the brown forearms. . . . His head throbbed like drums. . . . In an instant he would be like a bag bound midways . . . his ribs giving like saplings in the wind. . . . Lights danced . . .

Stupidly he looked down at the clasped hands, and a sudden fury of fighting came on him. . . . Something terrible, sinister, cold. His free hands caught the Syrian's little finger, tugged, pulled, bent, tore.

. . . He wanted to shred it from its hand. . . . Rip it like silk. . . . He felt the great arms about him quiver, grow uncertain. . . . Tear, tear !

With a little whine like a dog's, the wrestler let go. . . . He nursed the finger for an instant like a hurt child. . . .

Opening and shutting the hand. . . . Looking worried. . . . Great waves of air came into Shane's chest. . . . His knees were weak. . . . The Syrian walked around an instant, thinking, worrying. . . . He was serious now. . . . Suddenly he plunged. . .

But swifter than Ahmet's plunge was thought and memory . . . of a day at Nagasaki . . . of a little brown smiling Japanese and a burly square-head sailorman. . . . Of the Japanese's courteous explanation in smiling Pidgin . . . With luck and timing he could do it. . . . Fast, but not too fast, and steady. . . . Handsomely, as the ship-word was. . . . There !

The hands trained to whipping lanyards caught Ahmet's wrists as he plunged. Shane's right leg went outward, foot sunk home. Backward he fell, leg taut, hands pulling. Above him Ahmet's great bulk soared, hurtled grotesquely. For an instant ; a flash. . . . The squeals of startled Syrians, the panic of feet. . . . Then a crash, an immense crash. . . .

A long, shuddering, frightened *eh* from the crowd. . . . . A French soldier mumbling . . . "*Cré nom de nom de nom de nom de Jésus Chri !*"

He staggered to his feet, put his hand to his face. . . . . It came away dripping. . . . His face was like the leeward deck of a flying yacht . . . swimming

. . . A few feet away Syrians and French soldiers were milling over . . . something. . . . The corporal wrenched Shane's arms into his coat. Pushed his hat into his hands.

"*Courez donc, le citoyen*. . . . Come on, get away. . . . Get . . ."

"Is he dead ?"

"No, not dead. . . . But get away. . . . He'll never wrestle again. . . . *Vite, alors !*"

He pushed him down the street.

"But——"

"Go on. We can take care of ourselves. . . ." He shoved him roughly forward. . . . Shane staggered, walked, ran a little. . . . Behind him a few blocks away, an ominous hum. He ran on. . . . Some one was shrieking . . .

"*Ma hala ya ma hala kobal en Nosara*. . . . How sweet, oh, how sweet, to kill the Christians. . . ." The crack of a gun . . . Tumult . . . The long Moslem war-song . . . Two rifles. "*A nous, les Français . . . A nous, la Légion !*"

A nausea, a great weakness, an utter contempt for himself, came over him in the boat pulling him toward his ship . . . God ! He had fought with and nearly killed—possibly killed—a man for personal hatred ! From irritation, and in a public place ! A spectacle for donkey-boys and riff-raff of French towns. . . . He tottered on the ship's ladder. . . . The sailors caught him. The mate ran up.

"Anything wrong, sir ? You look like a ghost."

"No. Nothing. All aboard ? Everything ready? Is she a-drawing ? Anchor a-peak ? All right. Get her up. . . ."

§ 12

" Arif Bey, where is my wife ? I come back to Beirut. I find my house deserted. My servants gone. Where is Fenzile ? Is she here ? "

" No, son."

" Is she dead ? "

" No, no, son. I wish she were . . . "

" Then where is she gone ? With whom ? "

" Trebizond. Stamboul. Cairo. I don't know where."

" With whom ? "

" With—oh, don't bother yourself, son. Forget her."

" With whom ? I must know."

" With—do you remember that wrestler you crippled, the wrestler from Aleppo ? "

" With Ahmet Ali ! Impossible ! I all but killed him."

" She went, though . . . "

" No, uncle, no. If he had been strong she might, but——"

The old Druse chief shook his head, smiled in his beard, a little, bitter, wise smile.

" You were never sick with her, never poor."

" No, never sick, never poor."

" Well, he was sick and poor, so she went with him."

" Then she loved him all along."

" No, son Zan, she loved you—until you threw him. She might have been amused at seeing him pass the house, laugh a little, be flattered . . . Such a big fool, and she a little woman . . . but she would never have left you. . . ."

"But she did."

"Well . . . after the fight, he had no friends . . . the Christians despised him, the Moslems hated him. . . . . There was no train to follow him . . . he went on crutches. . . . He passed her door and looked, and looked. . . . What could she do but come out. . . . It was her fault, after all. . . . And she was very tender-hearted. . . "

"Tender-hearted ? "

"Didn't you know ? "

"No, I never knew."

"She used to cry when the leaves fell from the trees. . . . You didn't know your wife well ? "

"No, sir, I did not."

"Well, she is gone, Zan. . . . Whither one doesn't know. . . . What will become of her, one doesn't know Destiny is like a blind camel. He doesn't know against what he stumbles. We do not see him come . . . only when the harm is done do we say: We might have listened for the tinkle of his bell. . . . Eh, one is young and does everything and sees nothing. One is old and sees everything and does nothing. There is no mystery . . . only ignorance . . . "

"You say she was very tender-hearted, my uncle. I didn't know . . . I thought of her as something else. . . ."

"Son Zan, you had better forget her in another woman. Listen, son, I will give you Aziyede in marriage, my own daughter. She is just as pretty, and younger and not so foolish as Fenzile."

"Oh, no, sir. No ! "

"Well, I don't blame you."

"It isn't that, Arif Bey. It isn't that. I'm very beholden to you . . . for your kindness . . . and your patience . . . I didn't know . . . And I thought I knew everything nearly, and am so ignorant. . . . Why until now I didn't know even this—the sun shone so brightly, and life was so pleasant, I thought that was the way of life. . . . But I was in love with Fenzile . . . and that was what made everything so wonderful . . . in love with the wife you gave me . . . head over heels, sir . . . just simply—head over heels. . . ."

BOOK FIVE

THE VALLEY OF THE BLACK PIG

THE VALLEY OF THE BLACK PIG

§ I

TO him, for a long time now, the sea had been only water. All the immense pelagic plain, dotted with ships; with bergs of ice, like cathedrals; with waves that curled or swept in huge rhythms; with currents defined in lines and whorls; with gulls that mewed and whales that blew like pretty fountains; with the little Portuguese men-of-war; with the cleaving of flying fish and the tumbling of dolphins, all this was water. All this joyous green, this laughing white, the deep, reflective blue, the sombre, exquisite gray, was water. An infinity of barrels of water, immense vats of water, wet water. . . .

To him, for a long time now, a ship had been a means of keeping afloat on water, of going from place to place. All its brave strakes, its plunging bows, its heeling beams, were wood, such as one makes a house of, or a tinker's cart. All the miracle of sails; the steady foresail; the sensitive jibs; the press canvas delicate as bubbles; the reliable main; the bluff topsails; top gallants like eager horses; the impertinent skysails; the jaunty moonraker, were just canvas stretched on poles. All the pyramidal wonder of them, fore, main, and mizzen, were not like a good rider's hands to a horse; compelling, coaxing, curbing the wind, they were utilities. The spinning wheel was a mechanical device. Port was left, and starboard only the right hand. The chiming of the ship's bell was not an old sweet ceremony, but a fallible thing, not exact as the ticking of a cheap watch. And "The lights are burning bright, sir," was not a pæan of comfort, but a mechanical artisans' phrase. . . .

To him, for a long time now, they who went down to the sea in ships were men only; men such as sell things in shops or scrub poorhouse floors, or dig tracks for a railroad. The slovenly Achill man, who would face death with a grin, the shambling Highlander who on occasion could spring to the shrouds like a cat; the old bo'sun who had been for years a castaway on Tierra del Fuego; the wizened chanteyman with his melodeon, who could put new vigour into tired backs, with his long-drag chanteys, like "Blow the Man Down," and "Dead Horse," and "Whisky Johnnie," and short-drags like "Paddy Doyle" and "Haul the Bowline," and capstans like "Homeward Bound" and "Wide Missouri," and pumping chanteys like "Storm Along"; the keen men at the wheel and the hawk-eyed look-out; the sailor swinging the lead in the bows, with a wrist and forearm of steel—all these were only men following the sea because they knew no better. And the mate who would wade into a mob of twenty with swinging fists, and the navigator who could calculate to a hair's-breadth where they were by observing the unimaginable stars—they were not of the craft of Noah, they were men who knew their job . . . just men . . . as a ticket-clerk on a railroad is a man. . . .

To him, for a long time now, ports were ports,—only places whither one went to get or deliver cargo. Baltimore, like some sweet old lady; Para, heavy, sinister with rain; Rio, like some sparkling jewel;

Belfast, dour, efficient, sincere; Hamburg, dignified, *gemütlich*; Libson, quiet as a cathedral—they were not entities, they were just collections of houses covering men and women. And men were either fools or crooks, and women were either ugly bores or pretty—bitches . . . Men and women, they were born crudely, as a calf is born of a cow, they lived foolishly or meanly, and they died . . . And they were hustled out of the house quickly. . . . They thought themselves so important, and they lacked the faithfulness of the dog, the cleanliness of wild animals, the strength of horses, the beauty of tropic birds, the mathematical science of the spider, the swiftness of fishes . . . And they grew old abominably, the women's breasts falling, the men getting bald. How the devil had they ever arrogated to themselves the lordship of created things?

To him, for a long time now, the world had been, was, one mean street . . .

§ 2

Of all cities, none was better calculated to foster this mood of his than the one to which his business now brought him—Buenos Aires on the Plate. Leaving Liverpool with steel and cotton, there was an immensity of ocean to be traversed, until one came to the river mouth. Then fifty leagues of hard sailing to the abominable anchorage . . .

Here now was a city growing rich, ungracefully—a city of arrogant Spanish colonists, of poverty-stricken immigrants, of down-trodden lower classes . . a city of riches . . . a city of blood . . . Here mud, here money . . .

Into a city half mud hovels, half marble-fronted houses, gauchos drove herd upon herd of cattle, baffled, afraid. Here Irish drove streams of gray bleating sheep. Here ungreased bullock carts screamed. From the blue-grass pampas they drove them, where the birds sang, and water rippled, where was the gentleness of summer rain, where was the majesty of great storms, clouds magnificently black and jagged lightning, where were great white moons and life-giving suns, where was the serpent in the grass, and the unique tree, where were swift horses . . . Beeves that had once been red awkward calves, and then sullen, stupid little bullocks, and then proud young bulls, with graceful horns . . . Such as earnest Christians believed had lowed at the manger of Christ born in Bethlehem . . . And stupid, suspicious sheep, that had once been white gamboling lambs, playful as pups, and so ridiculously innocent looking!—didn't they call their Lord *Agnus Dei*, Lamb of God? —and gentle ewes and young truculent rams, like red-headed schoolboys, eager for a fray, and shame-faced wethers . . . And by their thousands and their tens of thousands they drove them into Buenos Aires, and slew them for their hides . . .

But this was sentimental, Shane said. Bullocks and sheep must die, and the knife is merciful as any death. But oughtn't these things be done by night, privily as they should bury the dead? Must they drive down these infinities of creatures, and slaughter them openly and callously, until the air was salt with blood, until the carrion crows hovered over the city in battalions? Had they no feeling, had they no shame? Must the pitiful machinery of life be exposed so airily?

Of course it must, he knew. These things had to be done in bulk. Now weren't the Middle Ages when one killed a cow because one had to eat: one killed a sheep because the winter was coming when woollens were needed. All Europe needed shoes, saddles, combs, anti-macassars, afghans—what not? And Europe was a big place, so in bulk they must bellow and bleat and die, and have their hides torn from their pitiful bodies, salted, and chucked in the hold of a ship.

Of course it must. That was civilization.

§ 3

From long ago, from far away, came the chime of old romance, but very thin, like the note of a warm silver bell, that could not hold its own against this blatancy. Came ancient immortal names—Magellan, that hound of the world, whining fiercely, nosing for openings that he might encircle the globe, he had been up the silver river. Sebastian Cabot, too, the grim marauder, seeking to plunder the slender Indians, he had been here. It was he who had christened the great stream—Rio de la Plata, the river where silver is. And Pedro Gomez, who headed the greatest expedition the Argentine ever saw, and founded and named the city. And fighting Beresford, the British general who took it from Spain, and Whitelock who lost it again . . . Campbell could see his bluff grenadiers, their faces blackened with powder, their backs to the wall, a strange land, a strange enemy, and blessed England so far away . . . And the last of the Spanish viceroys, with a name like an organ peal, Baltazar

Hidalgo de Cisneros y Latorre—a great gentleman, he had been wounded fighting Nelson off Cape Trafalgar. Campbell could almost see his white Spanish face, his pointed fingers, his pointed beard, his pontifical walk . . . And of them nothing remained. Nothing of Magellan, nothing of Cabot, nothing of Gomez, nothing of staunch Beresford, or bluff John Whitelock, or of the great hidalgo . . . *Stat magni nominis umbra ?* . . . No, not even that. The shadows of the great names had gone. The dim chime of a silver bell drowned by the lowing of dying cattle, by the screech of bullock-carts, by the haggling of merchants over the price of hides . . .

But he could not remain on board ship in port. Ships, he had enough of them ! There was nothing to do but go ashore, landing at high tide at one of the two lugubrious piers, and make his way toward the squares . . . past the blazing water-front where the prostitutes chanted like demented savages, past the saloons where the sailors drank until they dropped or were knifed, or robbed, or crimped. Down the ill-lit streets, which must be trodden carefully, lest one should stumble into a heap of refuse. Down to the Plaza Victoria, with its dim arcades, or to the 25 de Mayo, with its cathedral, its stunted paradise trees. And from the houses came shafts of light, and the sound of voices, thump of guitars like little drums, high arguments, shuffle of cards. . . . Dark shadows and lonely immigrants, and the plea of some light woman's bully—" *cosa occulta* . . " A dim watery moon, the portico of the cathedral, a woman exaggerating her walk. . . . Pah ! . . . immigrants fearful of the coming snow . . . A vigilante strutting like a colonel . . . Mournful pampa winds . . .

The theatres? Sugary Italian opera; a stark Spanish drama, too intense for any but Latins, foreign; debauched vaudeville, incredibly vulgar; or at the concert-hall, sentimental Teutonic and Anglo-Saxon songs, with an audience of grave uncritical exiles—a little pathetic. No!

The clubs? Oh, damn the clubs! A blaze of light and raucous voices, ships' masters, ships' chandlers, merchants, discussing the riddle of local politics, and the simony of office; or the price of hides, and freight charges; how a ship's master could turn a pretty penny in bringing out shoddy clothes, or pianos —"Jesus! they were crazy for pianos here!" Rattle of glasses and striking of matches. Bluff, ceremonious salutations.

"Well, captain, what kind of a trip did you make out?"

"Pretty fair, captain."

"Will you have a little snifter, captain?"

"Well, captain, seeing that it's you——"

"Paddy, a little of what ails him for the captain—"

And after a while the whisky would dissolve the ceremony, and would come nauseating intimacies.

"We shipped a stewardess in Hull—" or "There was an Irish girl in the steerage, a raving beauty, and when I saw her, I said: Wait. So——"

They were all the same. Give them whisky and time and the talk would come around to easy money and easy women. All were the same, bluff, sentimental, animal, all but the one or two hawk-eyed, close-lipped men who came and went silently, who drank little and drank by themselves. These men made the really big money, but it wasn't easy; they took a chance with their lives, smuggling slaves from Africa for the Argentine plantations, or silver from Chile and Peru. But as for the rest, easy money, easy women!

Well, what was Campbell fussing about? Wasn't he too making easy money, bringing agricultural steel and cotton goods here and taking away his tally of hides?

And as to easy women, wasn't there Hedda Hagen?

§ 4

A ship's master had introduced him to her at a band concert in one of the public squares—a tall Amazonian woman with her hair white as corn, and eyes the strange light blue of ice. Her head was uplifted—a brave woman. The introduction had a smirking ceremony about it that defined Froken Hagen's position as though in so many words. Her bow was as distant to Shane as his salutation was curt to her. Shane was suddenly annoyed.

The captain of the American boat talked incessantly while the band blared on. Strolling Argentines eyed the woman's blond beauty at a respectful distance. They trotted to and fro. They loped. They postured. She paid no attention. To her they were non-existent. To the American skipper's conversation she replied only with a flicker of the eyelids, a fleeting smile of her lips. Shane she seemed to ignore. She was so clean, so cool, so damnably self-possessed.

"Froken Hagen," Campbell ventured, "aren't

you sick of all this? Captain Lincoln says you have been here for five years. Aren't you dead tired of it?"

"No." Her voice was a strong soprano timbre.

"Don't you want to get back to the North again?"

"Often." She had a quiet aloof smile. Somewhere was the impression of a gentlewoman. She did not mean to be abrupt. She was just immensely self-possessed.

It occurred to Shane suddenly that he liked this woman. He liked her dignity, her grave composure. He liked her coolness, her almost Viennese grace. He liked her features; but for the wideness of her mouth, and the little prominence of chin, she would have been immensely beautiful. Her corn-like hair, massively braided, must be like a mane when down, and beneath her Paris frock he could sense her deep bosom, great marble limbs. Her voice had the cool sweet beauty of Northern winds . . . Her eyes were steady, her chin up-tilted. Somewhere, some time, somehow she had mastered fate.

About, in the gas-lit square, escorted, guarded, went other women, reputable women. Great raw-boned women, daughters of Irish *porteños*, with the coarseness of the Irish peasant in their faces, the brogue of the Irish peasant on their Spanish, but punctiliously Castilian as to manners; gross Teutonic women; fluffy sentimental Englishwomen, bearing exile bravely, but thinking long for the Surrey downs; gravid Italian women, clumsy in the body, sweet and wistful in the face; Argentines, clouded with powder, liquid of eyes, on their lips a soft little down that would in a few years be an abomination unto the Lord; women of mixed breed, with the kink of Africa in their hair, or the golden tint of the Indian in their skin. Good women! And yet . . . for grace, for coolness, for cleanliness, the venal Swedish girl outshone them all. . . .

"Froken Hagen," Campbell said, "may I call on you some time?"

"If you like."

"Does that mean you don't want me to come?"

She smiled at him.

"Mr. Campbell," she laughed gently, "you know very well what I am. If you don't call on me it won't mean anything to me. If you do call I think I'll be rather glad. Because on first appearances I like you. But do whatever you like. I have no wiles."

"Thank God for that!"

Lincoln, master of the *Katurah Knapp*, listened in with a silent chuckle. She was a queer one, Hedda was. And Campbell, he was a queer one, too. Two queer ones together. Hedda was all right, but a man sickened of her quick. She wasn't what you might call warm. No affection; that's what a man missed far from home, affection. Yes, affection. Hedda had none. She was a fine woman, but she had no affection. He liked to see men get stung. In a few days Campbell would be down at the club with a face as long as to-day and to-morrow. He would call for a drink angrily.

"Well, captain, what's got into you? You don't look happy."

And Campbell, like the others, would grumble something about a God damned big Swede.

" Hey, what's wrong? Ain't Hedda treated you right?"

" Sure, she treated me right," he would say as the others said, " but God damn! that woman's not human. Take away that rot-gut and gi' me whisky. I got a touch o' chill."

Lincoln had seen it all before. He liked to see it all the time. He chuckled as Shane turned to him.

" Lincoln, are you seeing this lady home?"

" Not if you want to."

" I don't want to break up any arrangements of yours."

" Tell the truth," Lincoln said, " I've got a little party to-night. A party as is a party—Spanish girls, Spanish dancers . . . I wish I could take you, but it ain't my party . . . "

" Then I'll see Miss Hagen home."

Dog-gone, Lincoln would have to go down to the club and tell 'em how Campbell of the *Maid of the Isles* got stuck with the human iceberg!

§ 5

Without, the west wind had increased suddenly, a cold steady wind, coasting down the Argentine pampas, bending the sparse trees and giant thistle, ruffling the river, shallowing it, until to-morrow many a poor sailorman would regret his optimistic anchorage . . . Shane shivered . . . To-morrow October would be making a din in the streets . . . And the poor skippers fighting their way round the Horn, icy winds and head seas and immense gray dirty-bearded waves . . . To-morrow three men were to be shot in the 25 de

Mayo for a political offence, and Shane could see them in the bleak dawn, three frightened staunch figures; the soldiers would be blowing their fingers in the cold air, and their triggers would be like ice to the touch . . . the shoddy tragedy . . .

But within the room was warm, a little fire of coal in the unusual grate, and the soft and mellow lights of candles, and here and there gauchos' blankets on the wall, and here a comfortable chair and there a gleaming table, and brass things . . . clean and ascetic, and yet something womanly about the place, the grace and composition of things . . . And with her coming into her house, Hedda Hagen's manner had changed gently . . . She was no longer frigid, aloof . . . She unbent into calm smiles, and the grace of a hostess of the big world . . . the quiet masonic signal of a certain caste . . .

" I wonder," he said; " am I dreaming ? "

She paused suddenly. She had taken her hat off, and was touching things on the tables with her large fine hands. She turned her head towards him. There was a half smile in her eyes.

" Why ? "

" It doesn't seem right."

" That you never saw me before, that you are here in this house after meeting me half-an-hour ago, and that you can stay here the night ? "

" Yes."

" Well, it's true."

She was once more the hostess. It was as if some one had sprung nimbly from a little height to the ground.

" I can't give you any whisky. But I can make you tea. Or have my maid brew you some coffee."

" Is that a Russian samovar ? "

" Yes."

" Then I'll have tea."

So queer ! Without, the wind blustered and the little din of it crept into the room somehow, and within was warmth, and the stillness of still trees. And grace. Beauty moved like an actress on the stage. All her motions were harmonious, could have gone to some music on the violin. Now it was the easy dropping to her knees as she lit the quaint Russian teapot, now an unconscious movement of her hand to push back a braid of her hair, now the firm certain motion of her strong white unringed fingers. Now her large graceful body moved like some heroic statue that had become quick with life. The thought came into his head, somehow, that if he had had a sister he would have liked her to have been like this splendid blond woman. . . .

Yet into this house, where she had settled like some strange bird in an alien land, came ships' masters, reeking with drink, came merchants with their minds full of buying and selling and all the petty meannesses of trade, came dark Latins who hankered for blond women. . . .

" God ! I can't understand."

She came toward him frankly. . . .

" *Amigo mio*, have you a right to understand ? "

" I'm sorry."

" No, but—see ! You and I have often met. I mean : there is a plane of us, who must be loyal to one another. You understand. And to you, to one of us, I don't want to lie. Only certain persons have a right to ask. A father, a mother, a child, a sister or brother or husband. But our destinies touch only, hardly even that. Will never grip, bind. There is no right you have, beyond what—you buy, and there are things—I don't sell."

"I'm sorry," Shane turned aside. "I was just carried away. But I should go."

"Do you want to go?"

"No."

"Then stay. Others stay."

"But——"

"Are you better than the others? Think."

"No," he thought. "Of course not. Worse perhaps. I know better."

"You are nearly as honest as I am," she laughed. She put her hand out in a great frank gesture.

"If I can smile, surely you can." Her fingers beckoned. "Come, don't be silly."

He caught her hands and laughed with her. He had been acting like a boy in his twenties, and he a man of forty-two . . .

§ 6

He had thought somehow that in this affair of Hedda he would find—oh, something: that once more the moon would take on its rippling smile and the sun its sweet, low laughter, and the winds be no no longer a matter of physics, but strong entities. Quickly, unconsciously, the thought had come to him . . . With the wife of his young days had come the magic of romance, and with Claire-Anne of

Marseilles had come a sublime storm of passion, and with the Arab lady had come the scheme of an ordered life, good composition and rich colour. . . . They had lasted but little and gone as a rainbow goes. . . . With Hedda there was nothing . . . it was just abominably wrong . . .

Here he was, young—for his forty-two he was young—supple, successful in his way, rich if you wanted to put it in that word. And no heart for life ; listless. It was wrong. . . . All he could think of doing was to be intimate with an easy woman. No zest for her great noble frame, her surge of flaxen hair. The veneer of conventional good manners, conventional good taste, only made the actuality of it more appalling . . . . she with the gifts of life and grace, he with his, and all they could do was be physically intimate. . . . And she took money with a little smile, contemptuous of herself, contemptuous of him . . . They both knew better, yet there you were . . . God ! Even animals had the excuse of nature's indomitable will !

Yes, this made him face things he had been trying to pass casually by. Forty-two, a touch of gray at the temples, a body like a boy's, hooded eyes like a hawk's, and a feeling in him somehow that an organ—his heart maybe—was dead : not ailing—just unalive. Once he had zest, and he didn't even have despair now. If he could only have despair . . .

Despair was healthy. It meant revolt. A man might sob, gnash his teeth, batter walls with his bare fists, but that only meant he was alive in every fibre. He might curse the stars, but he was aware of their brilliance. He might curse the earth that would one day take his lifeless body, but he must know its immense fecundity. A man in revolt, in despair, was a healthy man.

But despair was so futile. Ah, there it was! Life's futility. It was the sense of that which had eaten him like a vile leprosy. Mental futility, spiritual futility. Of physical he did not know. All that was left him of his youth was a belief in God. At sea he was too close to the immense mechanism of the stars, on land too close to milling millions, not to believe, not to accept him as an incontrovertible fact.

But the God of degenerate peoples, the antagonistic furious, implacable God—that was a ridiculous conception. A cheap, a vain one. "As flies to wanton boys, are we to the gods." Wasn't that how Shakespeare's blind king had uttered it? "They kill us for their sport." How strangely flattering—to believe that the Immensity that had conceived and wrought the unbelievable universe should deign to consider man, so weak that a stone, a little slug of lead could kill him, an enemy worth bothering about. Man with his vanity, his broad fallibility, his poor natural functions!

And as to the God of the optimists, how ridiculous, too. "The Lord is my shepherd, I shall not want." So pathetic! They never saw that they did want. That for every well-filled body there were a hundred haggard men. They thought of him as benevolent, firm but benevolent, like Mr. Gladstone. To them he was an infinitely superior vestryman with a tremendous power for dispensing coal and food to the poor. And the poor devils were so patient, so loyal. And so stupid; they thought that much flattery, much fear, would move Him. Their conception never even rose to considering God as a gentleman, despising flattery and loathing fear. Poor, poor devils!

To Shane He existed, though how to think of Him was difficult. Why a man? Why not some strange thing of the air, as a cuttlefish is of the sea? Something tenuous, of immense brain power, of immense will. Something cold. But why even that? Why not, as the cabalists had it, a Figure, arithmetical or geometrical, a Sound. . . . A Formula of some great undiscoverable indefinable Thought . . . He was cold, He was efficient. He had so much brains. . . .

It seemed to Shane that this optimism, this despair, were strange mental drugs, going through the mental system as a depressant or a stimulant would go through the physical, creating illusions . . . illusions . . . and the sane man was one who had no illusions, not the meaning a man uses of the phrase when he has been jilted by a woman or wronged out of money by a friend, but actually, finitely, no illusions . . . He was sane, a few other men in the world must be sane, but the rest were drugged for their hell or their Fiddlers' Green . . .

Fiddlers' Green! Good God! Fiddlers' Green!

His mind flashed back a moment to the shining isle, the green sward, the singing waves, the sunlight on the green jalousies, but strangely his mind could see nothing. He could no longer make a picture for himself. Symbols were barren algebraic formulæ. Not enchanters' words. No light. No glamour. Only strange sounds reverberating in the gray caverns of his head . . . Once in the dead past he could see the Isle of Pipers—no more! It wasn't his past that was dead. The past lived. It was he was dead, he, his present, his future.

Out of the gray caverns of his head came a thin echo of a word he had known and he a boy. The Valley of the Black Pig. A phrase from some old folk-tale heard on a wintry Antrim coast. Some prophecy of old wives that when the Boar without Bristles would appear in the Valley of the Black Pig, then the end of all things was nigh. . . . He had a faint memory that somewhere in Roscommon was the Valley of the Black Pig . . . But that didn't matter; what mattered was the memory it evoked . . . Gray gray, gray . . . Gray hills, gray boulders, gray, barren trees, a gray mist sluggishly rising from the ground, and a gray drizzle of rain, falling, so slowly . . . And gray, rotting leaves beneath his feet . . . A little wind that moaned among the boulders, and the cawing of unseen, horrible birds . . . Neither was there direction, nor time, nor space . . . Everything gray like the grayness of old women's bodies. . . . There was no sun, and the moon abhorred the valley. In such a place as this wandered the souls of women who had killed their children, of monks who at dark of night had said the Black Mass . . . Here were masters who had deserted tall, gallant ships . . . Hither witches rode on the bleak east wind, to be flogged by their masters and horribly caressed . . . The Valley of the Black Pig . . . Here were those who had read the frightful inscription on the altar of the Unknown God . . . Gilles de Rais, marshal of France, and Avicenna; Nicolas Flamel and his wife Petronella; Lady Alice Kyteler of Kilkenny, and Gerald of Desmond, the Great Earl; and newer names, Dee and Edward Kelly . . . Degraded majesty with soiled beards . . . Gray, gray . . . And the faint ghosts in cerecloths, and the horrible shapes of the mist . . . The drizzle of the rain, and the rustle of the Feet of the Goat . . . The cawing of strange birds and the wind among the boulders and souls, weeping, weeping—unhoping, undespairing, weeping, weeping . . . The Valley of the Black Pig. . . .

What was it? In God's name what was it that had made him this way, his being suddenly lifeless, like a cow that goes dry, or a field that is mysteriously suddenly fallow . . . And weariness seemed immortal . . . What had led him into this dreadful cemetery of the mind? Had he gone too far in thought and emotion and come to a dreadful desert plane within himself . . . ? Had he eaten of the tree of which the cabalist wrote:

> Of every tree of the garden thou mayest freely eat;
> But of the tree of the knowledge of good and evil, thou shalt not eat of it; for in the day that thou eatest thereof thou shalt surely die.

Had he blundered on it unwittingly, eaten ignorantly and surely died . . . Or was he going mad? Good God! Could that be it? Was there something they hadn't told him—a strange taint in his blood, or his mother's blood . . . ? Would he end his days in a madhouse . . . ? What a fate, what a dreadful fate! A slavering, gray-headed man, wandering through the Valley of the Black Pig, for ever and for ever?

Better to end it now.

Yes, but would that end it? The material envelope of cells and fluids gone, might there not . . . ? Christ! Worse off yet, if anything were left . . . There might be something left; there was the trouble . . . One knew so little, so abominably little . . . Only material wisdom was certain, and that said: Don't chance it . . .

Drink? He had his men to think of, his ship . . . It might grip him.

But was he forever doomed to this mournful, weeping place, place of rain, place of mists, gray boulders, and moaning winds? Must he abide in the Valley of the Black Pig until the Boar without Bristles came lumbering out of the red west, and went grunting, eating ravenously, eating prey of souls, until he lay down in obscene sleep, and the stars one by one guttered like candles, and the sun shot into a vast explosion, and the moon was a handful of peat ashes, and the whole great universe snapped like a gunshot and the débris of all created things fell downward like a shattered wall, faster, faster, faster, to where, where, where?

§ 7

In the streets now the June snow fell, not the soft and flaky petals of the North, but a bitter steel-like snow, that whirled. And the winds of the pampas hurried like Furies through the sordid streets, and stopped to snarl, as a dog snarls, and now moaned, and now howled sharply, as a wolf howls. There was something cold, malignant, about it all . . . Old Irish writers said that hell was cold. *An Ait Fuar,* they called it, the Cold Place. *Ait gan chu, gan chat, gan leanbh, ait gan ghean, gan ghaire,* a place without a dog, or cat, or child, a place without affection or laughter . . . Had sainted Brendan come on Buenos Aires in winter on his voyage to Hy Brazil, and thought in his naïveté that here was hell . . . ? And was he wrong ?

Cold of wolves ! It must have been like this in ancient Paris when Villon thieved and sang, and the wolves came clamouring at the gates . . . and the crusaders off to warm Palestine . . . or in Russia—Siberia, a cold name . . . Here it was hell, but in Europe . . . oh, different there ! The heavy flakes, so solid, so wonderful, the laden trees, the great stretch of white. And in the houses the farmers blessing the snow, that would keep the ground warm and fertile for the coming year, that the blue flax might arise, and the fields of corn, with the great pleasance of the clover, and the golden-belted bees . . . and the turf fires of Ulster and Christmas coming, and after that Candlemas, and then March of the plowing, and glossy crows busy in the fields . . . always something to see ahead . . . Not in Ireland only, but England the jingle of bells and the people of ruddy faces . . . And in Germany too, the bluff important burghers having their houses heated by quaint porcelain stoves, huddling themselves in furs, and waddling obesely . . . very pleasant. . . . And in France, too, in the *assommoirs,* the tang of wine in the air and the blue hue of smoke, excited Latin voices. " *Encore un bock! T'es saoûl, mon vieux! Flûte! Je suis comme le Pont Neuf!"* A raucous voice singing a political skit:

> Cordieu, Madame! Que faites-vous ici?
> Cordieu, Madame! Que faites-vous ici!
> Je danse le polka avec tous mes amis!
> Je danse le polka avec tous mes amis!

Buenos Aires, hell!

And the worst was the strange inversion of time. Here winter was, cold streets, steely snow, garbage frozen to stone. . . . And in Europe was sane June. Purple flower of the heather in Ulster, and white flower of the bogs, and in the little bays of Antrim, men spearing flounders from boats in the long summer evenings. And the bairns hame from school with a' their wee games, fishing for sticky-backs wi' pins, and the cummers spinning. Eigh, Ulster! And in England, they punting on the Thames, among the water-lilies. Soft Norman days, and in Germany the young folks going to the woods . . . in Buenos Aires, hell!

Within the house a cold that the little fire could only gallantly fight against. Without, cold of wolves.

"Hedda, you come from a cold country. Tell me, is it like this in Sweden, any time?"

She was sitting in the candle-light, doing the needlework she took such quietness in. Her firm white hands moving rythmically, her body steady, her eyes a-dream. It was hard ever to think that she was—what she was. It was hard for him to think the word now, knowing her. She looked up and smiled.

"No, Shane, not like this. It's cold, very cold. But very beautiful. By day the countryside is quiet, white, ascetic, like some young nun. And at night there are lights and jollity. It is like a child's idea of fairyland. One wishes one were further north, where the reindeer are. One is not enemy to the cold, as you are here. One accepts it. It has dignity. Here it is naked, malevolent. That's the difference."

"Naked, with awful hands. . . . A cold that seizes . . ."

"Yes, Shane." She took up her work again. "Sometimes I think long until I get back to Sweden."

"You—you are going back?"

"Of course, Shane."

"When?"

"Five, six, seven years, unless I die, or am killed. Certainly I shall go back."

"Yes, but in five, six—hum!"

"But what, Shane?"

"I once knew a woman, Hedda. She was—as you are. Just having friends—And she was as handsome as you are, too, though she didn't have your head, your poise. She liked beauty, as you do. But this woman looked forward, as I don't think you do. She saw herself always going down. She saw herself in the end like the helmet-maker's daughter, in some archway of the city, seeking a couple of pence . . . And she was afraid, horribly afraid . . ."

"She was a silly woman."

"How, Hedda?"

"She didn't know two things. That luck changes; destiny is sometimes as kind as it is cruel. And also, when you are old, the money of the archway will bring you as much joy, a drink, a bed, a meal for the morrow, as do the diamonds of youth. The old don't need much, Shane. They haven't far to go."

"But you, Hedda. Aren't you afraid of—the archway, and the few pence——"

"No, Shane, that will not be my way." The broidery dropped to her lap. Her eyes, blue as winter, looked away, away. "I shall survive it all, barring death, of course, and in seven, eight, ten years, I shall drop all this and go back, and be a lady in the land of my birth, a quiet, soft-voiced woman in a little house that has glinting brass in winter and flowers around it in summer. And I shall be very kind to the poor, Shane. . . . And all young things that are baffled or hurt can come to me, and tell their troubles, and I shall understand. And oftentimes, sitting in the long Northern twilights, I shall think: Is this Froken Hagen, who is all the world's friend, the girl who was once despised in Buenos Aires? . . . And I shall choke a little and think: 'God is good!'"

"You are very sure of yourself, Hedda."

"Yes, Shane. I know my own capabilities. I know, too, my own limitations. I know I can always be of service. But I know, too, that there will be no love ever for me, nor any little children of my body, nor any big man to protect me and my house . . ."

"This other woman—I killed her to save her from the archway—she dreaded so much . . ."

"You were very silly, Shane," she snipped off a thread with the scissors. "People outgrow fear, and it may only have been a passing mood, that would have gone with the moon or the season. You know very little about women, Shane."

He laughed bitterly. "I have been married twice, and once I loved a woman greatly."

"From what you tell me," her voice was calm, "you have never been married. You made a mistake as a boy. And once again you bought a woman, as you might a fine dog, admired her, as you might admire a fine dog, and gave her a little passion, which comes and goes, knocks, passes on—but no trust. And once you were infatuated with a hysterical woman, and it all ended hysterically. No, Shane. I don't think you know much about women."

"You know so many things." He was irritated. "Perhaps you know what is wrong with me."

"Of course I do, Shane. Anybody would know. You are so important to yourself. All the world is in relation to you, not you in relation to the world. And people are not very important, Shane . . . I know. . . . You look for things. You don't make them. You want everything. You give nothing. You haven't a wife, a house. Your father gave poems. But you haven't a house, a child, a wife, a book. You only have a trading-ship."

"But I trade. I do my share of the world's work."

"Any shopkeeper !'"

"I handle my ship."

"Any mathematician . . . "

"I brave all the perils of the sea."

"Are you afraid of death ? "

"Of course not."

"Well ? "

"Hedda, I handle men."

'Any little braggadocio lieutenant . . . "

His anger rose in hot waves. "So I am not worth anything in life, Hedda. How much are you?"

"O Shane," she stood up and looked at him seriously, "my calling is the oldest in the world, they say, but to me it's not the least honourable. It is sordid or not, just as one makes it. I want you to think of men going to sea, and weary of the voyage, and from me somehow they get a glimpse of home. Are this house and myself more evil than the dram-shop and the gambling hell? And aren't there women in England and France who would rather have their menfolk with me than leaning on some sodden counter? They might hate the choice, but it's better . . . Shane, if you knew how many weary men have talked to me of families abroad, their hearts burdened. They cannot talk to men . . . and sometimes I exorcise devils, Shane, that young girls may walk safely in the dark. . . . And sometimes a man is athirst for a flash of beauty. . . . Think, Shane—you are not small . . . Even yourself, Shane, I have helped you. There were times this month when you were close to the river, terribly, terribly close. . . . I said nothing, but I knew. And I held you. I willed. I prayed even . . . Shane, Shane, *amigo*, when the time came that I had to work I chose this with my eyes open."

"I'm sorry," Campbell lowered his head. "I can only say I'm sorry I said—hinted . . . But Hedda, weren't there other things you could have done?"

"A sempstress, maybe. But I think it's more important to ease a man's mind than to cover his back."

"But children. You love children, Hedda. You

know so much. Couldn't you have been a governess in some great house?"

"O Shane, Shane *mío*, when will you understand?" Her calm voice had a note of distress in it. "None can judge of another's life. None can tell. None direct. What do you know of what passed before—I came to a mean house in a mean town? I once opened a door I shouldn't have, and left the lighted room . . . for a warm blue darkness . . . And I closed the door behind me . . . And daylight came. I am not of a breed that sues for mercy. So I went ahead . . . through the world. And I never look back, Shane. I am no Lot's wife, to become a pillar of her own salt tears . . ."

"But Hedda, you are good. And this life—"

"Of course I am good, Shane. There is no man can say I did him wrong in mind or body, or heart, either. And I am a comfort to many . . . All I have done is to outrage a convention of property in which I don't believe . . . Shane, do you know people cover greed with sentimentality and call it virtue?"

"But, Hedda, the women don't see. They scorn you—"

"Do they? Poor souls. Let them! *Amigo mío*, I have a life. I have to think, gage, act, concentrate. And when I want time of my own, Shane, I have it. The housewife with her frowsy duties, being kissed perfunctorily on the mat, the man who wears a stilted mask to the world, and before her—lets go . . . Ugh! And the *mondaine* with her boredom . . . the hatred in wide houses . . . Oh, I know. Sometimes I think it's so wonderful, being free. . . .

"O Shane, please don't be absurd, sentimental

. . . please, I know my way, and find yours . . . Tell me, do you know yet what day you sail ?"

§ 8

A sailor in a jersey and reefer caught his arm in the Avenida de Mayo . . .

"All filled up," Campbell uttered brusquely.

"It was no' that."

Campbell put his hand in his pocket looking for a coin.

"You'll be forgetting the Antrim glens, Shane Campbell." Shane flushed. The coin in his fingers burned him.

"How did I know you were fro' the Antrim glens?"

"You've seen me a few times, though you'd hardly know me. Simon Fraser of Ballycastle. You would no' recognize me, if you knew me, on account of my hair being white. I was lost on the coast of Borneo for four years. When I was lost my hair was black—maybe a wee sprinkle o' gray—but what you might call black; and when I was picked up, and saw myself in a looking-glass, it was white. They did no' know me when I got back to Ballycastle."

"Would you care for a drink, Simon ?"

"I don't care much either way, Shane Campbell. And if I wanted a drink bad, I always have the silver for 't. I would no' have you think I stopped you for to cadge a drink. I'm no' that kind of man. But I was wi' your uncle Alan when he died. Or to be exact, I saw him just before he died. I was visiting in Cushendun. I have a half-brither there you might know, Tamas McNeil, Red Tam they ca' him. And whiles I was there, I saw Alan Donn go down."

"My uncle Alan dead! Why, man, you're crazy—"

"You uncle Alan's a dead man."

"You're mistaken, man. It's someone else."

"Your uncle Alan's a dead man. And what's more: I have a word from him for ye."

"But I 'd have heard."

"I came out in steam. It went against the grain a bit, but I cam' out in steam. From Belfast . . . With a new boat out of Queen's Island . . . Alan Donn's a dead man. That's why I stopped you. For to tell you your uncle Alan's gone . . ."

"Come in, here," Shane said dazedly. He pulled the man into a bar, and sat down in a snug. "Tell me."

"It was about nine in the morning, and an awful gray day it was, wi' a heavy sea running and a nor'-easter, and this schooner was getting the timbers pounded out o' her. Her upper gear was gone entirely, and we could no' see how she was below, on account of the high seaway. She was a Frenchman, or a Portuguese. And she was gone. And we were all on shore, wondering why she had no' put into Greenock or Stranraer, or what kind of sailors they were at all, at all.

"Up comes your uncle Alan; and he says: 'Has anybody put out to give those poor bastards a hand?' says he.

"'There's no chance, Alan Donn,' says we.

"And he says: 'How the hell do you know?' says he.

"And we say: 'Can't you see for yourself Alan Donn, wi' the sea that's in it, and the wind that's in it, and the currents, there's no chance to help them ? '

" ' So you're not going,' says he."

" ' Och, Alan Donn, have sense,' says we.

" ' If you aren't, then by Jesus, I am.'

" He turned to one of the men there, a fisherman by the name of Rafferty, and he says : " Hughie, get ready that wee boat o' yours, wi' the spitfire foresail, and the wee trisail.'

" Then we said : ' You're not going, Alan Donn.'

" ' Who's to stop me ? ' says he. All this time we had to shout on account of the great wind was in it.

" ' We think too much of you, Alan Donn, to let you go.'

" ' If one o' you stinking badgers lays a finger on me to stop me, I'll break his God damned neck.'

" Says Hughie Rafferty to us—you know Hughie Rafferty, a silent man, a wise man—says he : ' He'll get out fifty yards, a hundred yards from shore and be stuck. And he'll say : " Well, I've done my best. Good-bye and to hell with ye, and die like men ! " And he'll come back. And if the boat turns over,' says Hughie Rafferty, ' he can swim like a rat, and he'll be back among us cursing, like his ain kind sel', within a wheen o' minutes.'

" Says Hughie Rafferty, says he : ' I'll go wi' your Honor's Lordship, Alan Donn.'

" ' You will like hell,' says Alan Donn. ' You'll stay here wi' your childer and the mother o' your childer.'

" Then a wee old man, that was a piper, speaks up. He was bent in two over an ash plant was in his right hand, and his left hand held his back.

" ' It's a foolish thing you are doing, Alan Donn,'

says he. 'How can you bring off the poor people?'"

"'I don't want to bring off the poor people, Shamus-a-Feeba, James of the Pipes. But there's not a rock, a wind, a current, a wave itself of Struth ña Maoile that I don't know. I'm figuring on rigging up some kind of sea-anchor,' says Alan Donn, says he, 'and getting the ignorant foreigners to chop their gear overboard, and riding the storm out. Don't worry yourself, Shamus-a-Feeba.'

"That was the way of your uncle, Alan Donn Campbell. He was very rough with the strong, but he was ay considerate of the old and over-young. He'd be rough with the king of England but he'd be awfu' polite to an ould man."

"God, is Alan Donn dead?" Shane was near tears. "Do people like Alan Donn die?"

"Aye, they die, too," said Simon Fraser. "And rogues live. It's queer.

"The boat was a'ready to be put into the sea, when your uncle sees mysel' on the edge o' the gathering. He comes straight to me. You mind how Alan Donn used to go through a crowd.

"'Are you the sailing man,' says he, 'wha's a half-brither to Red Tam McNeil of the Ten Acre?'

"'I am, sir, Alan Donn.'

"'Is it go wi' ye in the boat?' says I. 'I'll go.'

"'No, no,' quo' he. 'It's no' that. So'thin' different. You ken my brither's son, Shane Oge Campbell, wha's a master on the seas?"

"'I 've met him once or twice, and I've heard tell.'

"'If you see him, gi'e him a message. I'm sure you'll see him. I'm sure,' says Alan Donn, 'this morn I'm fey.'

" 'Tell him,' says Alan Donn, and he puts his hand on my shoulder. 'Tell him this: I've been intending to write him long this long time. There's a thought in my head,' says he, 'that all's not well with him.'

" 'Tell him this: I've been thinking and I've thought: There's great virtue to the place you're born in. Tell him he ought no' stay so long frae the braes o' Ulster. Tell him: The sea's not good for the head. A man's alone wi' himself too long, wi' his ain heid. Tell him that's not good.

" 'Tell him,' says he, 'there's great virtue and grand soothin' to the yellow whins and the purple heather. That's a deep fey thing. Tell him to try.'

" 'Is that all, sir, Alan Donn,' says I?

" 'You might tell him,' says he, 'aye, you might tell him: Your uncle Alan was not a coward, and he was a wise man.'

" At that I was puzzled—I tell you without offence meant—it sounded like boasting. And it was no' like Alan Donn to boast.

" 'Can I come along wi' you, sir, Alan Donn?' says I.

" With that he gi'es me a look would knock you down. 'Did na I tell you to do so'thin' for me?' says he.

" Then I kent he was na coming back.

" 'Aye, aye, sir,' said I.

" He goes to the boat on the edge of the water. You could hardly keep your footing with the wind, not hear your neighbour with the sea. And Alan Donn laughs: 'By Christ, 'tis myself that must be fond o' boating,' says he. 'And to-day is the grand day for it, surely. *Hi horo,* push her off,' says he. '*Horo eile! Horo,* heroes, *horo eile!*' We pushed with the water up to our waists. The keel ground. The sand sucked. We pushed with the water up to our shoulders. Then the trisail caught the wind. And Alan Donn was off.

"And Hughie Rafferty was wrong: Not at fifty, not at a hundred did he turn. Not at half-a-mile. He must have had the arms of Finn McCool, Alan Donn, and the hands of a woman. He'd take the high waves like a hunter taking a wall. Then you could nearly feel him easing her to the pitch. Apart from the waves themselves you could see the wee fountain of water when the bows slapped. Then he'd come up again. The trisail would belly and again he'd dive.

"And then he came to the ninth wave—*tonn a' bhaidhte,* the drowning wave. Even away off you could see it rise like a wall, and curl at the top. We were watching. There was the crippled schooner, and Alan Donn, and the great sea. And the wave curled and broke. And then was only the schooner and the great sea . . .

"And we waited for a minute, although we knew there was no call.

"And after a while an ould one falls to her knees and raises the keening cry:

"'*Mavrone!* my sorrow! *Mavrone dhu!* my black sorrow! *Mo chead vrone dhu!* my hundred black sorrows.

"'Is it gone you are, Alan Donn? Is it gone you are in the cruel sea? My black curse on it. It is between you and the people of your heart, between you and the land of your desire. Och, sea, isn't it cruel you are? Ruined Ireland is this day. The star of Ulster is out. And the little moon of Antrim shines no more. Och, *a'airrge!* My sorrow, O sea!

"'Who will be good to us, now, Alan Donn? You were good to the poor. God's gain and our loss. Who will make the young maids flush, and the young men throw back their shoulders, from pride at your having talked to them? *Avourneen dheelish, murn Alan Donn,* our Alan! Who will make the men of the South stand back, and you not striding through a gathering, ever, any more? And the dealing men of Scotland will miss you, you they could never get the better of in any fair, night, noon or morning. *Peader agas Pol, Muire, Padraig agas Brighid!* Peter and Paul, Mary, Patrick and St. Bride, let you be coming quickly now, and take up Alan Donn Campbell from the cold sea!

"'Your horse in the stable will miss you, Alan Donn. Poor beastie, he'll miss you sore. Your servant boys will miss you, they that would jump if you but dropped your pipe. The green fairways of Scotland will miss you when spring comes, and you not hitting the ball against the champions of the world. The lambs will miss you, wee lambs of the fields, and the colts. They'll be missing you, but 't will be nothing to our missing you. This night your dogs will be crying, and we'll be crying too.

"'Young women, look back of you, and see if the nine glens of Antrim are there. I wouldn't be surprised if they were gone, now Alan Donn's in the bitter sea.'

"Then up comes this woman, and she had a great cloak on——"

"What woman, Simon Fraser?"

"The woman there was talk of Alan Donn marrying. The woman from over the sea."

"'Has anybody seen Mr. Campbell?' And we don't understand.

"It's Alan Donn she means,' says Hughie Rafferty.

"Then the ould one on her knees takes up her keening. And this woman understands. Her face goes white. She sees the schooner being battered by the Moyle.

"'Did he go out to that?' she asks.

"'Yes, ma'am, your Ladyship's Honour.'

"'He didn't get there?'

"'The drowning wave caught Alan Donn,' says Hughie Rafferty.

"For a moment you'd think she hadn't heard. Then—a strange thing—a wee smile came on her face, and suddenly it changed to a queer twist, all over the face of her. Then she stood up proudly and looked out to sea. . . . and two tears came to the eyes of her and she raised her head higher still . . . The tears came in spite of her . . . and suddenly she gave a wee gulp like a person who's sick . . . And she turned and began to stumble away in the sand . . . A couple of the young ones went as if to help her, but she turned.

"'Please,' was all she said. And she went off on her lee lone.

"And then says Hughie Rafferty: 'The tide will bring him to Cushendall.'

"And at Cushendall next day we found the corp.

There wasn't a mark on him. Even the things of the deep water had respect for Alan Donn."

"What was this woman like, Simon Fraser? This women there was talk of Alan Donn marrying?"

"This woman was not a woman of Alan Donn's age. An' she was not a young woman. Her face was showing not the face of a girl but the face of herself. She had a proud face and a brave face. This woman would be around twenty-five.

"She was a brown woman: she had brown eyes and brown hair. She was not an Irishwoman. She was an Englishwoman. She had no Gaelic. And her English was not our English. This woman could ride a horse, though not too well. She would put a horse at a jump, though she was afeared of it.

"This woman had money. She was a niece of the admiral's, and she was on a long visit to the admiral's house.

"I've heard tell a queer thing about this woman. She would play at the piano for hours on a stretch, reading from a book. For hours she would play, all by herself. The people passing the road and the servant girls of the house couldn't make head or tail of her music. But our folk ken nothing of the piano. The pipes, the melodeon, the fiddle, they know that—and a few ould ones have heard the harp. They couldn't tell whether it was good music or bad music was in it.

"There's another queer thing about this woman. When she walked you'd think she was dancing. Not our reels or hornpipes, but queer ould dances you'd be walking to, not stepping. She had wee feet, though she was not a small woman.

"Your uncle Alan's dogs took to this woman, and you ken how Alan's terriers had little liking for any but his ain sel'. I was told also to tell you that she had the dogs, and that they were comfortable, and would be well looked after. So that you need not be worritin' about your uncle Alan's dogs . . .

"I'm afeared I've given you a poor picture of this woman, Shane Campbell: but it's a queer thing, you'd feel this woman more nor you'd see her. In a great deal of people, you wouldn't note her at all. But were you coming along the road, and a fey feeling come over you, and you say: Around the next corner is something kindly, something brave, something fine; as you turned the corner you'd meet this woman.

"Your uncle Alan liked this woman, liked her fine, but this woman was sick with love for your Uncle Alan.

"You'll blame me sore, Shane Campbell, and rightly too; it was very careless of me, me who's got a careful name—it didn't seem to matter, though! The name of this woman is not at me . . ."

All the tears in Shane's eyes, all the emptiness in his heart was gone now. A sudden elation seized him. He understood. Alan Donn had done a fine brave thing; Alan Donn had done the strong thing, the right thing, as Alan always did.

He thought: Alan was in love with this woman and this woman with Alan, and Alan had looked ahead sanely, seen, decided. Many years difference of age. Dignified strong wisdom and beautiful brave youth, one firm as a great firm rock, the other with the light wings of birds; spiritually never could they mate. Youth spiritual is like a gosling of yellow down, age spiritual is an eagle of great wings. . . . If the spirit has not died . . . Alan would never be an irritated, jealous, paretic old man, nor would he see " this woman " grow stern with repression and ache, and loneliness of heart and spirit . . .

Ah, he had done it well ! A line of Froissart's came to Shane : " They were very noble ; they cared nothing for their lives ! " He had given her no shattered marriage, no empty explanation that breeds only bitterness and perhaps contempt. He had given her a very gallant memory that would exalt her in the coming days . . . The world, the flesh, and the devil had played at cards with Alan Donn, and Alan had won . . .

He thought : Were it I now, I should have drifted into this, and come to ancient tortured days, and not having strength maybe, should have ended, not before as Alan Donn did, gallantly, but afterward meanly, leaving bitterness and desolation . . . Ah, wise Alan.

And it occurred to him suddenly, wise Alan, fey on the threshold of death, remembering him : There is virtue in the yellow gorse of Ulster, in the purple Ulster heather. Come back to where you were born, and rest, and get strength . . . This is a deep thing . . . Alan knew something. . . . The rain and the mist and the wind among the rushes had taught him natural secrets . . . maybe from the ground man drew strength, and maybe strange ground was alien to other than its own . . . a motherland—why did they call a place a motherland . . . ? Antæus, the Libyan wrestler, was invincible so long as his feet were on mother earth, and Heracles had lifted him into the air and the air had crushed him . . . What did the Greek parable mean . . . ? It meant something . . . the purple hills . . . the purple heather . . The Moyle purple in the setting sun . . .

"I'll go back," he decided. Scots superstition welled up in him. "A man seeing death sees more than death. Sees life. The Keepers of the Door maybe anoint his eyes, and if he looks back for an instant, God knows what he sees . . . . I'll go."

"Can I give you a lift back to Ballycastle, Simon Fraser? Or a lift anywhere you want. It's the least I can do and you coming this long way to tell me news."

"I'm very thankful to you, Shane Campbell very thankful indeed. It's just the way of you to ask a poor sailor man does he want a lift half-way across the world. But I'll never again see Ballycastle with living eyes."

"And why not, man Simon?"

"It's this way, Shane Campbell. It's this way. When I came back after six years—four years lost on the coast of Borneo—my three fine sons were gone—twenty and nineteen and seventeen they were. Gone they were following the trade of the sea. And herself the woman of the house was gone, too. I didn't mind the childer, for 'tis the way of the young to be roving. But herself went off with another man. A great gift of making a home she had, so there was many would have her in spite of her forty year. Into the dim City of Glasgow she went, and there was no word of her. And she might have waited, Shane Campbell; she might so. Four years lost on the coast of Borneo to come and find your childer scattered and your wife putting shame on you. That's a hard thing."

"You're a young man, Simon Fraser. You're as young as I am, forty-two. There's a quarter-century ahead of you. Put the past by and begin again. There'd be love at many a young woman for you. And a house, and new bairns."

"I'm a back-thinking man, Alan's kinsman, a long, back-thinking man. And I'd always be putting the new beside the old and the new would not seem good to me. The new bairns would never be like the old bairns, and it would na be fair. And as for women, I've had my bellyful of women after her I was kind to, and was true to for one-and-twenty years, going off with some sweating landsman to a dingy town . . . I was ay a good sailor, Shane Oge . . .

"It's by now, nearly by. . . . So I'll be going up and down the sea on the chance of meeting one of my three braw bairns. And maybe I'll come across one of them on the waterfront, and him needing me most. . . . And maybe I'll sign articles wi' the one aboard the same ship, and it's the grand cracks we'll have in the horse latitudes . . . Or maybe I'll find one of them a young buck officer aboard a ship I'm on ; and he'll come for'a'd and say : 'Lay aloft, old-timer, with the rest and be pretty God damned quick about it.' And I'll say : 'Aye, aye, sir.' And thinks : Wait till you get ashore, and I'll tell you who I am, and give you a tip about your seamanship, too, my grand young fello' . . . Life has queerer things nor that, Shane Oge, as may be you know . . .

The only thing that bothers me is that I'll never see Ballycastle any more."

"Is there nothing I can do for you, Simon Fraser?"

"There's a wee thing, Shane Campbell; just a wee thing?"

"What is it, man Simon?"

"Maybe you'd think me crazy——"

"Of course not, Simon."

"Well, then, when you're home, and looking around you at the whins and purple heather, and the wee gray towns, maybe you'll say: 'Glens of Antrim, I ken a man of Antrim, and he'll never see you again, but he'll never forget you.' Will you do that?"

"I'll do that."

"Maybe you'll be looking at Ballycastle, the town where I was born in."

"Yes, Simon."

"You don't have to say it out loud. You can stop and say it low in yourself, so as nobody'll hear you, barring the gray stones of the town. Just remember: 'Ballycastle, Simon Fraser's thinking long . . .'"

§ 9

A cold, southerly drove northward from the pole, chopping the muddy waves of the river. Around the floating *camelotes*, islands of weeds, were little swirls. The poplars and willows of the banks grew more distant, as *Maid of the Isles* cut eastward under all sail. As he tramped fore and aft, Buenos Aires dropped, dropped, dropped behind her counter, dropped . . . became a blur. . . .

Maid of the Isles was only going home, as she had

gone home a hundred times before, from different ports, as she had gone home a dozen times from this one. But never before had it seemed significant to Shane . . . Back, back the city faded. . . . If the wind lasted, and Shane thought it would last, by to-morrow they would have left the Plate and be in the open sea. Back, back the city dropped. . . . It couldn't drop too fast . . . it was like a prison from which he was escaping, fleeing. . . . A great yearning came on him to have it out of sight . . . definitely, for ever. Once it was gone, he would know for a certain thing, he was free. . . . Free from the Valley of the Black Pig. . . .

He was surprised to be free. As surprised as an all but beaten wrestler is when his opponent's lock weakens unexpectedly, and dazedly he knows he can get up again and spar. A fog had lifted suddenly, as at sea. And he had thought the mist of the Valley of the Black Pig could never lift, would remain, dank and cold and hollow, covering all things like a cere-cloth, binding all as chains bind . . . and that he must remain with the weeping population, until the Boar without Bristles came . . . for ever and for ever and for ever. . . .

But the nearest and dearest had died gallantly, and somehow the fog had lifted. And then he was dazed and weak, but free. Where was he going? What to do? He didn't know, but hope, life itself had come again, like a long awaited moon.

Buenos Aires faded . . . Faded the Valley of the Black Pig . . . Buenos Aires its symbol . . . Buenos Aires with bleak squares, its hovels, its painted trees —*timbo* and *tipa* and *palo barracho*.

He stood aft of the steersman, and suddenly raised his head.

Mo mhallacht go deo leat, a bhaile nan gcrann !
'S mo shlan do gach baile raibh mi riamh ann.

" My curse for ever on you, O town of the trees," an old song came to him, " and my farewell to every town I was ever in——"

A great nostalgia for Ulster, for the whins and heather, choked him :

" *S iomadh bealach fliuch salach agas boithrin cam*——

" There's many a wet, muddy highways and crooked half-road, *eader mise*, between me, *eader mise, eader mise*——" He had forgotten.

" Between me and the townland that my desire is in," the Oran steersman prompted. " *Eader mise agas an baile bhfuil mo dhuil ann !* "

" Mind your damned wheel," Shane warned. " This is a ship, not a poetry society. Look at the way you're letting her come up, you Highland bastard. Keep her off—and lam her ! "

" Lam her it is, sir," the steersman grinned. . . .

BOOK SIX

THE BOLD FENIAN MEN

THE BOLD FENIAN MEN

§ 1

THE worst of it all, Campbell smiled, was this: that life was so immensely healthy now, immensely peaceful, immensely sane. Here he was in the house of his fathers, built from the angle of a turret of King John's time. Here he was by the purple hills, by the purple Moyle. Five springs had come since he had given up the sea. Five times he had seen the little mountain streams swell with the import of the season, hurrying from the summit of the eagles, carrying water on nature's business. Five times had the primrose come, and the cuckoo. The faint delicate blue of early grass turned to green. The heat haze of summer on the silent glens. The Moyle thick with fish. Then autumn, a deep-bosomed, grave woman moving through the reddening woods, the turf-cutters with their spades, the pillars of blue smoke from the cottages in the stilly September sky. And the three great moons of autumn, silver as sixpence. Five times the distant trumpeting of the wild swans and winter came, in great galloping winds, and sweeping sheets of sea-rain. And Moyle tossed like a giant troubled in his sleep. And on the mountain sides the rowan stood up like a proud enemy, and the ash bent humbly, and the dwarf oak crouched under fury. And the wind whistled in the frozen reeds. And with the snow came out the hunted ones unafraid, the red fox, and the badger of dark ways, and the cantering hare.

Without, the wind might roar like cannon, and the

sea rise in great engulfing waves. Within the old house, with its corner dating from King John's time —so long ago!—was comfort. Here was the library where Robin More—God rest his soul!—had puzzled over the round towers of Ireland and written his monograph on the Phœnician colony of the County Down, and bothered about strange, quaint old things, comparing the Celtic cross to the sistrum of Egypt, and wondering whether the round towers of Ireland had aught to do with worship of the sun, and writing of Gaelic occultism to Bulwer Lytton, and dreaming of the friend of his youth, Goethe, in the dusk. And down in the gun-room were the cups of Alan Donn, cups for sailing and cups for golf, and ribbons that horses won. And in the drawing-room was the needlework of his mother, the precise, beautiful broidery . . . so like herself, minute, mathematical, not significant . . . And in the kitchen was the red turf, and the flitches of bacon in the eaves, and the thick servant girls hustling impatiently, and the servant boys in their corduroy trousers bound with rushes at the knee . . . their heavy brogues, their honest jests of Rabelais . . . and in the fold the silent sheep, and great solemn cows warm in their manger. . . .

Five years, going on six now, since he had left the sea, and invested his fortune in a Belfast shipyard, and taken over the homestead of Clan Campbell to run as it had always been run, wisely, sanely, healthily . . . There were the servant boys and girls, with a comfortable roof above them. There were the cotter tenants, satisfied, certain of justice. At the shows his shorthorns took ribbons. For local charities, his duty was done . . . But there was something, something lacking. . . .

It wasn't peace. Peace he had in plenty. The spring of the heather, the tang of the sea brought peace. The bats of twilight, and the sally branches, and the trout leaping in the river at the close of day. And the twilight itself, like some shy girl. . . . Out of all these came an emanation, a cradle-song, that lulled like the song of little waves. . . . And as for pleasure, there was pleasure in listening to the birds among the trees, to seeing the stooking of barley, to watching the blue banner of the flax, to walking on frosty roads on great nights of stars. . . . To riding with the hunt, clumsily, as a sailor does, but getting in at the death, as pleased as the huntsman, or the master himself. . . . To the whir of the reel as the great blue salmon rushed . . . Pleasure, and peace, and yet not satisfaction.

He thought, for a while, that what he missed was the ships, and that, subconsciously, there was some nostalgia for the sea on him. He had gone to Belfast thinking that with live timbers beneath his feet, that the—the vacuum within him would be filled, but the thought of a ship somehow, when he was there, failed to exalt him. He loved them always, the long, live ships, the canvas white as a gull, the delicacy of spars —all the beautiful economy. . . . But to command one again, to go about the world, aimlessly, but for the bartering of cargo, and to return at the voyage's end, with a sum of money—no ! no ! not enough !

And so he came back to the peace and pleasure of the glens, the purple heather, and the red berries, the chink of pebbles on the strand. To the hunts on frosty mornings, to the salmon-fishing, to the showing of cattle. To peace: to pleasure. . . .

And he suddenly asked himself what had he done to deserve this peace, these pleasant days? What right had he to them? What had he given to life, what achieved for the world, that he should have sanctuary?

The answer put him in a shiver of panic. Nothing! He had no right, no title to it. Here he was drawing on to fifty, close on forty-eight; and he had done, achieved, nothing. He had no wife, no child; had achieved no valorous unselfish deed. Had not—not even—not even a little song.

§ 2

Strange thing—it hadn't occurred to him at first; but it did now when he thought over it in the winter evenings—was this: that Alan Donn Campbell, for all that he was dead these six years and more, existed still, was bigger now than he had ever been in life. . . .

Because Shane had hated to see the fine boat drawn up, he had put *Righ nam Bradan*, the *Salmon King*, Alan Donn's great thirty-footer, into commission, and raced her at Ballycastle and Kingstown, losing both times. He had ascribed it to sailing luck, the dying of a breeze, the setting of a tide, a lucky tack of an opposing boat. But at Cowes he should have won. Everything was with him. He came in fifth.

"I can't understand," he told one of Alan's old crew.

"Man," the Antrim sailor told him bluntly, "ye have na' the gift"

"But, Feardoracha, I'm a sailor."

"Aye, Shane Campbell, you're that. For five times seven years you've sailed the seven seas. But for racing ye have na' the gift. Alan Donn had it. And 't was Alan Donn had the gift for the golf, and the gift for the horses. Just the gift. You must not blame yourself, *Shane na fairrge*, there's few Alan Donns."

And thinking to himself in the lamp-lit room, Shane found what the old man meant. Beneath the bronzed face, the roaring manner of Alan Donn, there was a secret of alchemy. Rhythm, and concentration like white fire. To the most acute tick of the stars he could get a boat over the line with the gun. Something told him where breezes were. By will-power he forced out the knowledge of a better tack. As to horses, where was his equal at putting one over a jump. At the exact hair's-breadth of time, he had changed from human being to spirit. It was no longer Alan Donn and his horse when he dropped his hands on the neck. There was fusion. A centaur sprang. . . . On the links he remembered him, the smiling mask, the stance, the waggle, the white ball. The face set, the eyes gleamed . . . the terrific, exact explosion. . . . Not a man and a stick and a piece of guttapercha, but the mind and will performing a miracle with matter. . . . And Alan Donn was dead six years . . . and yet he lived. . . .

He lived because he had been of great use. He was a standard, a great ideal. Children who had seen him would remember him for ever, and seek to emulate the fire and strength of him, having him to measure by as the mariner has the star. . . . In foreign countries they would tell tales of him: There was once a great sportsman in the North of Ireland, Alan Donn Campbell by name. . . .

His father, too, who had been dead so long—mortality had not conquered him. Once in Ballycastle Shane had seen a shawled girl look out to sea with great staring eyes and a wry mouth, and, half whispered, staccato, not quite sung, her fingers twisting her shawl, came a song from her white mouth:

Tiocfaidh an samhradh agas fasfaidh an fear;
Agus tiocfaidh an duilleabhar glas do bharr nan gcraobh.
Tiocfaidh mo chead gradhale banaghadh an lae,
Agas bvailfidh se port ciuin le cumhaidh 'mo dhiaidh.

The summer will come, and the little grass will grow;
And there will come a green thickness to the tops of the trees.
And my hundred loves will arise with the dawning of the day,
And he will strike a soft tune out of loneliness after me.

A queer stitch came in Shane's heart—a song his father made! And following the stitch came a surge of pride. Those songs of his father! The light minor he had heard, and the others—the surge of *An Oig-bhean Ruadh*, the Pretty Red Maiden:

"*Se do bheatha is an tir seo.* . . . A welcome before you into this country, O sea-gull, more lovely than the queen, than the woman of the West, whom Naesi, son of Usnach, held in the harbour. I could destroy all Ireland, as far as the Southern sea, but in the end I would be destroyed myself, when my eyes would alight on the white swan with the golden crown. . . .

Or the despairing cry of his poem, *Ig Cathair nan g Ceo*: "In the City of Fogs"—he meant London—

"*A athair nan gras tabhair spas o'n eag domh*—O Father of the Graces, give me a little respite from death. Let the axe not yet strike my forehead, the way a goat or a pig or a sheep is slain, until I make my humility and my last repentance."

Shane wished to God he had known his father, that the man had been spared a little until he could have loved him. . . . He had only the picture of him left. . . . Great throat and pale, liquor-harried face, burning eyes, and black tossing hair. . . . The bald-headed bankers might shake their heads and say: He was no good . . . he was a rake . . . he drank . . . his relations with women were not reputable. . . . And old maids purse their thin-blooded lips. . . . But when the little money of the bankers was scattered through the world, and even their little chapels had forgotten them, and the stiff bones of old maids were crumbling into an unnecessary dust, his father's songs would be sung in Ireland, in Man, in the Scottish Highlands, in the battered Hebrides. So long as sweet Gaelic was spoken and men's hearts surged with feeling, there would be a song of his father's to translate the effervescence into words of cadenced beauty . . . he had an irreverent vision of God smiling and talking comfortably to his father while the bald-headed bankers cooled their fat heels and glared at one another outside the picket-gates of heaven. . . . The world had gained something with the last Gaelic bard. . . .

And he had found out too, that his other uncle, Robin More, had a great importance in a certain circle.

In Dublin he met an old professor, a Jesuit priest, who seemed intensely excited that a nephew of Robin More Campbell's should be present.

"Do you know, by any chance, what your uncle was working on when he died?"

"I'm afraid I do not, sir."

"You know his manuscripts."

"Just casually, sentimentally."

"You don't know much about your uncle's work, then?"

"Not very much."

"Did you know," the old priest said—and his urbanity disappeared; there was pique in his tones—"that your uncle was the man who definitely decided for us that the Highlanders of Scotland migrated from Ireland to Scotland? Did you know that?"

"No, sir, I did not."

"I don't suppose," the old man was sarcastic, "that seems important to you."

"To confess, Dr. Hegan, it does not. Is it?"

"My child," the old priest smiled—it was so queer to be called "my child" at forty-seven—"all knowledge is important. All details of knowledge. We come we know not whence, and we go we hope we know whither. Our history, our motives, our all, is vague. All we have is faith, a great broad river, but knowledge is the little piers. . . ."

They had all been significant: Alan Donn, his father, even Uncle Robin, whom he had thought only a bookworm in the fading sunshine. The world was better, more mature, for their having lived. . . .

And he had nothing. Here he was, drawing on to fifty, close on forty-eight. And he had done, achieved nothing. He had no wife, no child; had achieved no valorous, unselfish deed. Had not—not even—not even a little song. . . .

§ 3

And then he said to himself: "I am too sensitive. I have always been too sensitive. The stature of my family has dwarfed me in my own esteem. Have not I got as much right as others to the quiet of the glens?" And again he said: "I sit here and I think. And my thoughts grow into a maze. And I wander in it, as a man might wander through some old gardener's fancy, having stumbled on it inadvertently, and now being in it, now knowing the secret of exit." But a maze was non-existent, did a person regard it so, and if one were to walk on nonchalantly a little turn would come, and he find himself in the wide sunshine and smiling flowers. And he said: "Damn the subtleties! A person is born, lives, dies. And what he does is a matter for himself alone." But some inner antagonist said: "You are wrong."

And he said: "Look at the people around me. What more right have they than I to this quiet Ulster dusk?" And the antagonist smiled: "Well look."

First were the farmers and the fisherfolk. Well, they didn't count. They were natural to the soil, as grass was. They grew there, as the white bog flower grew. An institution of God, like rain. And then there were the summer visitors, honest folk from the cities. Well, they had a right. They spent their winters and autumns and springs in mills and count-ing-houses, clearing away the commercial garbage of the world. And when the graciousness of summer came, they emerged, blind as moles, peak-faced. And before them stretched the Moyle, a blue miracle. The crisp heather, the thick rushes, the yellow of the buttercups, the black bog waters. And when clouds came before the sun the mountains drew great purple cloths over them. And in the twilight the cricket chirruped. And at night the plover cried out against the vast silence of the moon. And the hearts of the selling people turned from thoughts of who owed them money and who was harrying them for money. And the tight souls opened, just a little perhaps, but even that—Poor garbage men of the world, who would begrudge them a little beauty?

Then there were the country people, the landlords, the owners of the soil. Red-faced, sportsmen, connoisseurs of cattle, a sort of super-farmer, they were as natural to the soil as the fisher-folk or the tillers. Their stock remained from ancient tides of battle, centuries before. The founders of the families had been Norman barons, Highland chiefs, English squires; but the blood had adapted itself, as a plant adapts itself in a strange country. And now they were Ulster squires. Smiling, shy, independent. They had a great feeling for a horse, and a powerful sense of fair play. They were very honest folk. A station had been set them and they lived in it, honestly, uncomplainingly, quite happily. But a meadow was a piece of land to them and a river a place where trout could be caught, and snow was a good thing, because it kept the ground warm. They were a folk whom

Shane respected a great deal, and who respected him —but they weren't his folk.

Above all these of his neighbours towered three figures, and the first of these was the admiral.

He had a name. He had a title, too—Baron Fraser of Onabega. But to everybody he was the admiral, and in speech plain "sir." A purple-faced and terrible old man, with bushy white eyebrows and eagle's eyes. Very tall, four inches over six feet, very erect for all his ninety years, with his presence there thundered the guns of Drake, there came to the mind the slash of old Benbow . . . He had been a midshipman with Nelson at Cape Trafalgar.

Silent and fierce, about his head clouds of majesty, all his life had been spent with pursed lips and hooded eyes, keeping watch for England . . . And never a great battle where he could prove himself the peer of Benbow and Drake and Nelson . . . Never a dawn when the fleet rolled down to battle with polished guns and whipping flags . . . And a day came when he was too old . . . So here he was in the Antrim glens . . .

A great life, his, a great and serviceable life, frustrated of glory . . . And well he deserved the quiet of Ulster, where he sat and wrote his long letters to archæological papers, proving, he thought, that the Irish were a lost tribe of Israel and that the Ark of the Covenant was buried on Tara Hill . . . And there were none to laugh at him . . . All spirit he was ; watchful, dogged, indomitable spirit with a little husk of body . . . Soon, as he had directed, his old bearded sailormen would take his flag-covered casket out to sea in the night, and the guns would thunder: A British admiral sails by . . .

And there was Simon Fowler in his little cottage, who was dying by inches from some tropical malady . . . A small chunky man with white hair and wide blue eyes . . . He had been a missionary in Africa, in China, in India—not the missionary of sentimental books, but a prophet whose calm voice, whose intrepid eyes, had gained him a hearing everywhere . . . "Put fear away," he had preached in Africa; "let darkness flee. I come to tell of the light of the world . . . After me will come the sellers of gin and of guns. But I shall give you a great magic against them . . . Little children, love one another . . ." In China his fire had shamed philosophers: "I know your almsgiving. I know your benevolence. It is selfishness. Though I bestow all my goods to feed the poor, and though I deliver my body to be burned, and have not charity, it profiteth me nothing. Unless ye become as little children . . ." And in the sensuous Indian lands, his voice rose in a great shout: "Subtle Greece is dead," he proclaimed, "and razed are the fanes of Ephesus. And the Unknown God slinks only through the midnight streets . . . 'Blessed are the pure in heart' . . ." He had gone like a flame through the pagan places of the world, and here he was dying in the Antrim glens, with the quiet of Christ about him, the droning of God's little bees, and the lowing of the cattle of Bethlehem . . . He was a great man. He had only one contempt: for hired clergymen.

There were three folk of heroic stature around him: the admiral, and Simon Fowler, and the woman of Tusa hErin.

§ 4

A very small townland is Tusa hErin, the smallest in Ireland, it is said. And a very strange name on it: Tusa hErin, the beginning of Ireland. Why it is so called, none know. Possibly because some Highlanders named it this on landing there. Probably because it was a division between the Scottish and Irish clans. So it was called when the Bruce fled to Ireland. So it is called to this day.

Twenty acres or so are in it—a wind and sea lashed little estate, a great gray house and a garden of yew-trees. For ten years it had been untenanted, until a Miss O'Malley had bought it, and opened the great oak doors, and let the sea-air blow through the windows of it, and clipped the garden of the yews. The country people knew little of her, except that she had a great reserve. To the glensmen she was *Bean Tusig Erin*, the woman of Tusa hErin.

"What kind of a person is she?" Shane asked.

"A strange woman is in it, your Honour; a strange and dark woman."

"An old lady?"

"If she was one of us, she would be an old woman, your Honour, what with the bitter work and the hard ways. But being what she is, she is a young woman, your Honour. I heard tell she said she was thirty-four."

"Is she good-looking?"

"Well, now, your Honour, that would surely be a hard thing to say. A great dark face she has on her, and her head high, the like of a grand horse. Barring her eyes, you might call her a fine woman."

" What's wrong with her eyes ? "

" Hard eyes she has, your Honour, hating eyes. She's always looking at you to see if it is an enemy is in it. A queer woman, your Honour ; the like of her was never known."

" But how ? "

" The talk that's at her, your Honour. The great hatred she bes having of England, and the talk of old Irish times."

" And she a lady ? "

" You'd think it was a queen was in it, with the high head of her, and the proud step of a racing horse. You would, your Honour, you would so."

He asked the admiral about her.

" Do you know this Miss O'Malley, sir, of Tusa hErin ? "

" I had the honour to meet her twice, Campbell. A very great woman. A great loss, Campbell, a great loss."

" Who is she, sir ? "

" Good God ! Do you mean to tell me you don't know who Miss Grace O'Malley is ? "

" No, sir, I don't."

" One of the greatest Shakespearian actresses the English stage ever knew—and you never heard of her. Good God ! How abominably ignorant you merchant marine men are ! "

" Abominably so, sir. . . . But please tell me, sir why does she hate England so much ? "

" Oh, these geniuses, Campbell ! They must hate something, or love something, to excess. . . . Depths of feeling, I suppose . . . Campbell, do you know anything about Ogham writing ? "

"Only that it's straight lines on the corners of stones, sir!"

"Well, now, I think I've discovered something important, most terribly important . . . You may have heard of the Babylonian cuneiform script . . ." And the old gentleman was off full gallop on his hobby. . . .

From Simon Fowler he extracted a little more information.

"Fowler, do you know Miss O'Malley of Tusa hErin?"

"I do, poor lady."

"Why poor lady?"

"Wouldn't you call anyone poor lady who had just been widowed, then lost her two children? Poor lady, I wish I could say something to comfort her."

"You! Fowler! You couldn't say anything?"

"The wisdom of God, Shane, is sometimes very hard to see. Our physical eyes can only see a little horizon, and yet the whole world is behind it. Miss O'Malley is not a case for any of the ministers of God . . . . but for Himself. . . ."

"You exaggerate, Fowler. Surely you are wrong. . . . . They say she is young and proud and beautiful."

"I don't know. I never noticed. . . . She may be young and proud and beautiful . . . I only thought of the dark harassed thing—inside all the youth and pride and beauty. . . ."

§ 5

He met her for the first time at a neighbouring fair . . .

Eleven on a hot June morning, and the little town was crowded, like some old-time immigrant ship. Women in plaid shawls and frilled caps, men in sombre black as befitted a monthly occasion. Squawking of ducks and hens, trudging of donkeys, creaking of carts, unbelievably stubborn bullocks and heifers being whacked with ash-plants, colts frisking. Girls with baskets of eggs and butter ; great carts of hay and straw. Apple women with bonnets of cabbage-leaves against the sun. Herring men bawling like auctioneers. Squealing of young pigs. An old clothes dealer hoarse with effort. A ballad singer split the air with an English translation of *Bean añ Fhir Ruaidh*, " The Red-haired Man's Wife."

Ye Muses Nine,
    Combine, and lend me your aid,
Until I raise
    the praise of a beautiful maid—

The crash of a drover driving home a bargain :

" Hold out your hand now, by God ! till I be after making you an offer. Seven pounds ten, now. Hell to my soul if I give you another ha'penny. Wait now. I'll make it seven pound fifteen."

" Is it insulting the fine decent beast you are ? "

" Eight pounds five and ten shillings back for a luck-penny ? "

" Is it crazy you've gone all of a sudden, dealing man. If the gentle creature was in Dublin town, sure they'd be hanging blue ribbons around her neck until she wilted with the weight of them."

Patrick Sarsfield, Ireland's wonder !
Fought in the field like bolts of thunder !
One of Ireland's best commanders !
Now is food for the crows of Flanders !
Och ! Ochone !

A knot of older people had gathered around him, white-headed farmers, bent turf-cutters of the glens, a girl-child with eyes like saucers. A priest stopped to listen . . . The crude English of the ballad faded out, until there was nothing but disheveled agony . . . rhythm . . . a wail . . . Somewhere a leaping current of feeling . . . There was a woman on the edge of the crowd, a lady . . . She came nearer, as though hypnotized . . .

The country bard stopped suddenly, exalted, and swung dramatically into Gaelic . . . Dropping the alien tongue he seemed to have dropped fetters . . . His voice rose to a pæan . . . he took on stature he looked straight in the eye of the sun . . . And for Shane the clamour of the drovers ceased . . . And there was the plucked note of harpers . . . And fires of ancient oak . . . and wolf-dogs sleeping on skins of elk . . . And there was a wasted place in the twilight, and grass through a split hearthstone . . . And a warrior-poet, beaten, thinking bitter under the stars . . .

Do threasgar an saoghal agas do thainic an gaoth mar smal—
Alastrom, Cæsar, 's an mead do bhi da bpairt ;
Ta an Teamhair na fear agas feach an Traoi mar ta !
'S na Sasanaigh fein, do b' fheidir go bhfaighidis bas !

A voice spoke excitedly, imperiously to Shane : " What is he saying ? Do you know Gaelic ? "

"I'm afraid I've forgotten my Gaelic, but I know this song."

"Then what is it? Please tell me. I must know."

"He says:

"The world conquers them all. The wind whirls like dust.
Alexander, Cæsar, and the companies whom they led.
Tara is grass, and see how Troy is now!
And the English themselves, even they may die."

"How great!" she said. "How very great!"

She turned to Shane, and as he saw the dark, imperious face, he knew intuitively he was speaking to the Woman of Tusa hErin. She seemed puzzled for an instant. Something in Shane's clothes, his carriage. . . .

"You don't look as if you understood Gaelic? How is it you can translate this poem?"

"I knew it as a boy. My father was a Gaelic poet?"

"Then you are Shane Campbell."

"And you are the woman of Tusa hErin!"

"You know Tusa hErin?"

"I know every blade of grass in the glens."

"If you are ever near Tusa hErin, come and see me."

"I should like to."

"Will you really?"

"Yes."

She left him as abruptly as she spoke to him, going over to the ballad-monger. She left him a little dazed. . . . He was aware of vitality. . . . He was like a man on a wintry day who experiences a sudden shaft of warm sun, or somebody in quiet darkness whose eye is caught by the rising of the moon.

§ 6

As in a story from some old unsubtle book, in passing the gates of Tusa hErin, he had gone into another world, a grave and courteous world, not antique—that was not the word, but just older. . . . A change of tempo. . . . A change of atmosphere. . . . . The *Bois Dormant*, the Sleeping Wood of the French fairy-tale? . . . Not that, for the Sleeping Wood should be a gray wood, a wood of twilight, with the birds a-drowse in their nests. . . . And here were clipped rich yew-trees, and turf firm as a putting-green's, and rows of dignified flowers, like pretty gracious ladies; and a little lake where a swan moved, as to music; and the sunshine was rich as wine here . . . all golden and green. . . . But the atmosphere? He thought of the cave of Gearod Oge, the Wizard Earl in the Rath of Mullaghmast, and the story of it. . . . A farmer man had noticed a light from the old fort, and creeping in he had seen men in armour sleeping with their horses beside them. . . . . And he examined the armour and the saddlery and cautiously half drew a sword from its sheath . . .. And the soldier's head rose and: "*Bhfuil an trath ann?*" his voice cried. . . . "Has the time come?" "It has not, your Honour," the farmer said in terror, and shoved the sword back and fled. . . . An old man said for a surety that had the farmer drawn the blade from the scabbard, the Wizard Earl would have awakened, and Ireland been free. . . . There was great beauty and great Irishness to that story, but there was terror to it, and there was no terror on this sweet place. . . .

He said: It is a trick of my head, an illusion that this is different. Some shading that comes from the yews, some phenomenon of cliff and water. . . . But even that did not quite explain the rich grave look of grounds and house. A song from "The Tempest" came to him:

> Full fathom five thy father lies;
>   Of his bones are coral made;
> Those are pearls that were his eyes:
>   Nothing of him that doth fade
> But doth suffer a sea-change
> Into something rich and strange . . .

That was it, something rich and strange, like some old cloister into which one might turn from an inquiet and hubbubby street. . . . A knock at an oaken wicket; a peering shy brother, and one was on green lawns and the shadows of a gabled monastery. Cowled, meditative friars, and the quiet of Christ like spread wings. . . . But there was a reason for the cloister's glamour: cool thoughts and the rhythm of quiet praying, and the ringing of the little bell of mass, and the cadenced sacramental. All these were sympathetic magic. . . . But whence came the glamour of Tusa hErin?

§ 7

And she said: "I am glad you came. I knew somehow you would."

"I am glad, too. I knew Tusa hErin as a boy.

It was then a weird old place. The yew trees were unclipped, the turf riotous, the little lake ungravelled. . . . . It had an eeriness. But now—it is very different."

"Any place is different for being loved, tended."

"I suppose so. One loves but one gets careless toward . . . I know Antrim has always had an immense attraction for me. . . ."

"Antrim—alone?"

"Yes, of course, Antrim."

"Not all Ireland, then?"

"I never thought of Ireland as all Ireland."

"O Shane Campbell, you've sailed so much and seen so much—China, they tell me, and South America, and the Levant. And in the North, Archangel. I'll warrant you don't know Ireland."

"I never saw much, though, in any place outside Antrim."

"You never saw much in the little towns of the Pale, or gray Dublin, with the Parliament where Grattan spoke now a money-changer's business house, and the bulk of Trinity of Goldsmith and Burke—or the great wide streets where four-in-hands used to go. And Three-Rock Mountain. And Bray. And the beauty of the Boyne Valley. And the little safe harbours of the South. And the mountains of Kerry. And all the kingdom of Connacht. And the great winds of Donegal."

"But it's so eery, deserted, a dead country. All like Tusa hErin was before you took it."

"If one could take it all, and do to it as I've done to Tusa hErin. By the way," she asked suddenly, "is Tusa hErin haunted?"

"No, I never heard. Did you see anything?"

"I think I heard something a few times. A piper piping when the storms rose. A queer little tune—like that thing about McCrimmon."

"*Cha till, cha till, cha till McCrimmon.*"

"Are there words to it?"

"*Le cogadh mo sidhe cha till McCrimmon.*"
Never, never, never, will return McCrimmon.
With war or peace never will come McCrimmon.
For money or spoil never will return McCrimmon.
He will come no more till the day of the Gathering."

"A lamenting tune like that, I heard."

"The drone was just the grinding of the waves, the air the wind among the yews."

"That's possible. But isn't a phantom piper possible, too, in a land of ghosts?"

§ 8

"A land of ghosts"; the phrase remained with him. And the lighted lamp and the burning peat fire seemed to invoke like some necromantic ritual. How often, and he a young boy, had the names trumpeted through his being. Brian Boru at Clontarf, and the routed red Danes. And with the routing of the Danes, Ireland had come to peaceful days, and gentle white-clothed saints arose and monasteries with tolling bells, and great Celtic crosses . . . And gone were the Druids, their cursing stones, their Ogham script . . . Gone old Celtic divinities, Angus of the Boyne, and Manannan, son of Lir, god of the sea . . . and the peace of Galilee came over the joyous hunting land . . . The little people of the hills, with their pygmy horses, their pygmy pipes, cowered, went into exile, under the thunder of Rome . . . And the land was meek that it might inherit the kingdom of heaven . . . And the English came . . . The Earls of Ulster fled into Spain . . . And only here and there was a memory of old-time heroes, of Cuchulain of the Red Branch ; of Maeve, queen of Connacht, in her fighting chariot, her great red cloak ; of Dermot, who abducted Grania from the king of Ireland's camp, and knew nine ways of throwing the spear . . . The O'Neils remembered Shane, who brought Queen Elizabeth to her knees with love and terror . . . And Owen Roe, the Red . . . And the younger Hugh O'Neil, with his hard-bitten Ulstermen at Benburb. . . . They had to bring the greatest general of Europe, Cromwell, the lord protector, to subdue the Ulster clans. . . Sullen peace, and the Stuarts came back, and again Ireland was lulled with their suave manners, the scent of the white rose . . . The crash of the Boyne Water, the King James running for his life . . . And Limerick's siege, and the Treaty, and Patrick Sarsfield and the Wild Geese setting wing for France . . . France knew them, Germany, Sweden, even Russia . . . Ramillies and the Spaniard knew Lord Clare's Dragoons. . . . And Fontenoy and the thunder of the Irish Brigade . . . And Patrick Sarsfield, Earl of Lucan, dead at the end of the day . . . Even to-day Europe knew them : O'Donnel, Duke of Tetuan and grandee of Spain ; and Patrice McMahon, Duke of Magenta, who had been made president of the Republic of France—they were of the strain of Lucan's wild Geese . . .

And again a sullen peace, and Ulster rang to the trumpet of American freedom, and the United Irishmen arose in Belfast . . . And Napper Tandy at Napoleon's court, and Hoche with his ships in Bantry Bay. . . . Wolfe Tone's mangled throat, and Lord Edward Fitzgerald murdered by his captors. . . .

What had made these men, sane men—Ulstermen mostly—risk life and face death so gallantly ? What brought out the men of '48 and the men of '67 ? What was making little Bigger fight so savagely in Parliament, blocking the legislation of the empire ? What had got under their skins, into their blood ? Surely not for a gray half-deserted city ? Surely not for little bays and purple mountains ? Surely not for an illiterate peasantry, half crazed by the fear of hell ?

He tried to see Ireland as a personality, as one sees England, like the great Britannia on a copper penny, helmeted, full-breasted, great-hipped, with sword and shield, a bourgeois concept of majesty, a ponderous, self-conscious personality :

> When Britain first, at Heaven's command
> Arose from out the azure main,—

Just like that !

And Scotland he could see as a young woman, in kilt and plaid and Glengarry cap, a shrewd young woman though, with a very decisive personality, clinching a bargain as the best of dealers might, a little forward. He could think of her as the young girl whose hand Charles the Young Pretender kissed, and who had said to him directly : " I'd liefer hae a buss for my mou'." " I'd rather have a kiss on my mouth." Scotland knew what she wanted and got it, a pert, a solid, a likable girl.

But Ireland, Ireland of the gray mists, the gray towns. How to see her? The country ballad came to him. The "Shan Van Vocht," the poor old woman gray, shawled, pitiable, whom her children were seeking to reinstate in her home of many fields:

And where will they have their camp?
Says the Shan Van Vocht.
And where will they have their camp?
Says the Shan Van Vocht.
In the Curragh of Kildare.
The boys will all be there,
With their pikes in good repair,
Says the Shan Van Vocht.
To the Curragh of Kildare
The boys they will repair,
And Lord Edward will be there,
Says the Shan Van Vocht.

No! Not enough. One might work, sacrifice money, for the Shan Van Vocht—but life, no! He thought again. Poor Mangan's poem flashed into his mind and heart . .

O my Dark Rosaleen,
Do not sigh, do not weep!
The priests are on the ocean green
They march along the deep.
There's wine from the royal pope
Upon the ocean green.
And Spanish ale shall give you hope,
My dark Rosaleen!
My own Rosaleen!
Shall glad your heart, shall give you hope,
Shall give you health, and help, and hope,
My dark Rosaleen!

Ah, that was it ! Not pity, but gallant, fiery love. Modern ideals and ancient chivalry. . . . A young dark woman with a quivering mouth, with eyes bright in tears . . . There was an old favourite print that portrayed her, a slim wistful figure resting a pale hand on a mute harp, a great elk-hound at her feet on guard, and back of her the rising sun shone on the antique round tower. . . . A pretty picture, but was it enough ? He tried to envisage her close, concentrated. . . . There the dog, there the harp, there the slim form . . . But the face . . . It seemed to elude him. And suddenly it flashed at him with abrupt dark beauty . . . the face of the woman of Tusa hErin . . .

§ 9

The long Ulster twilight had set in, the twilight of bats, gray-blue, utterly peaceful . . . the little chiming of the sea. . . . Even the wind was still. . . . All things drowsed, like a dog before the fire, relaxed but not asleep. . . . Beneath the feet the turf was firm . . . beneath that the husheen-husho of the purple Moyle . . . Soon there would be a moon and her servants would saddle Shane's horse for him and he would ride home in the Antrim moonlight, eleven miles of firm road with the friendly moon above him, and the singing Moyle on his left hand, and on his right the purple glens . . . And the shadows . . . the delicate tracery of the ash-tree, and the tall rowans, and the massive blue shadows of the cliffs . . . a golden and silver land . . . A very sweet silence had fallen between them, as if music had ceased and become restful colour. . . . They watched the quiet swan. . . .

"I am a little afraid to leave Tusa hErin," she said suddenly and softly, as though thinking aloud. . . . "I am like a nun who has been in a convent . . . She is lost in the open world. . . . Will I ever again find a place like Tusa hErin ?"

"Granya, are you selling Tusa hErin ?"

"I have sold it, Shane."

"I am sorry," was all he could say. A little silence, and he could feel her smiling through the dusk.

"You never ask any questions, Shane ?"

"It never occurs to me to ask them, Granya. If any one wants to tell me a thing, I know they will, and if they don't why should I intrude ?"

"I should like to tell you why I sold Tusa hErin. But I cannot. It is not my own secret."

He nodded in the dusk : "I understand."

She turned to him slowly. Her sweet dark head was like some fragrant shrub . . . Her low soft voice had so much life to it . . .

"I wonder if you know what a friend you are, Shane ? If you understand how peaceful it is to have you here ? You are such a sweet fact, Shane, like the moon."

"I am a friend, Granya . . ."

"You are, yes . . . And you know so little about me, Shane. And I know all about you . . . I know the adventures of your youth . . . And of the hard girl of Louth, and the poor harassed woman of Marseilles. . . . And of the little Syrian wife whom you didn't know you loved until you lost her . . . and the gray voyages to the cruel country. . . . At times I see you like a little boy hunting the leprechawn. . . . And then I see your face, your eyes, and understand how you commanded men in ships. . . . You are like some beautiful play, Shane. . . . I wonder what is the ending ?"

"It is already ended, Granya."

"No, Shane. I know, the end hasn't come. . . I know you, Shane," she asked abruptly; "what do you know about me ?"

"Nothing much, Granya, except that you are you. I heard you were a great actress . . . and that you had two babies . . . who died . . ."'

"Not a great actress, Shane, a very good one, perhaps. I might have been great one day . . . and again, I mightn't. I shall never know . . . And I had two babies. . . . They were very nice little people, Shane. I was very fond of them. . . . But a physical life is a little thing, I have come to believe; and there is another life, a life of thought and emotion. And that one is so long . . . It seems ages since I was an actress and had two pretty babies. It seems in another life . . . Shane, I don't think I was alive until my babies died. . . ."

"I don't understand, Granya."

"I mean this, Shane, that things were so casual to me. They came and they went, and I was what I was, and that was all. . . . When you were a boy, Shane, you had what I never had—wonder. I was the child of actors, Shane, brought up to a mechanical tradition, knowing the business thoroughly—a part was words and directions, and a salary. . . . That things were mimic meant nothing . . . do you see? That there was a life that was unreal, and another life that was real, and then a further life, too subtle, too profound for the value of words . . . one sees glimpses . . . one feels . . . and when you try to fix it, it eludes you. Do you understand? Like your mirage, a little . . . That is only a symbol. . . . Am I talking nonsense, Shane? Anyway, I took things, well, just casually. . . .

"See the moon rising, Shane?" she paused. She turned again.

"I got married, just got married; he was a good man, Shane. But I didn't love him. I loved nobody. I got married because he was suitable, and every one got married. And just the same way I accepted marriage . . . And when he died, I was very sorry, but impersonally sorry . . . as if something nice in the world had been gone . . . a swan shot . . .

"And my little people, Shane, they were very nice little people . . . I was fond of them, but as I might be fond of some terrier dogs . . . I was good to them. . . . Often I sit here and wonder: Was I good enough? And, Shane, God is my witness and this garden, and the moon above, there is nothing I could give them I held back . . .

"You know how they died, Shane? . . . I was playing and my house went on fire, and the servants fled . . . When I came back from the theatre a policeman said: 'We got everything all right, Miss O'Malley. Your dogs, your piano.' . . . 'Where did you put the babies?' I asked . . . They said: 'What babies?'

"Shane, I knew after a little while that I cried too easily . . . a little sweet rain of affection . . . . April. . . . I didn't forget them. . . . I wouldn't let myself. . . . And then I thought: God!

if I had loved my husband my heart would have been like a cracked cup when he died. . . . And when my babies died, I could not have lived. . . . And all I shed of tears was a little shower of April. . . . O Shane, one isn't like that when one is hurt. . . . Do you remember David, Shane, when he went up to the chamber over the gate . . . and as he went thus he said, 'O my son Absalom, my son Absalom! Would God I had died for thee, O Absalom, my son, my son!' . . . . And he was only a man, Shane. . . .

"Am I bothering you, Shane? No? I am just thinking aloud, with you there. . . . I never thought I could, with any human being. . . .

"And then I knew, Shane. . . . Part of me was not alive. . . . That was terrible to know, like finding out a horrible deformity, or knowing you are insane. . . . And I began to watch people. . . . I could say: There is a woman who knows she is loved, Shane. . . . There is a radiance in her face, an indescribable something. . . . You remember the Bible word 'Shekinah,' the Glory of the Lord! . . . And there were women with children . . . that had lost themselves in the joy of giving . . . would always have that joy of giving. . . . And it made me feel strange, shameful . . . as though I had no breasts. . . .

"I must have been a little insane then, Shane. I would go along the streets, looking at people, and saying: 'That person looks as if they would understand,' and thinking of stopping them with: 'Please a moment, there is something wrong with me!' But I knew they wouldn't understand . . . wouldn't believe it real. . . . Even if they were kind, all they would say was: 'It's all imagination . . .' as if imagination were not the most terrible thing in the world. . . . All that is wrong with the poor mad people is imagination. . . . Shane, I was like some poor cripple holding out his deformity to the passers-by, asking for help. . . . All he would want was money, but I wanted . . . oh, I don't know what I wanted. . . .

" And then, Shane, I would go into a church, and pray, and wait, kneeling there, for something to happen. . . . It never happened. . . . Then I would laugh. People used to turn and look at me. . . . . I began to hate them. I grew proud. I hated them more and more. . . .

" I said I'd get back to work, and forget it all. . . . I was made as I was made. . . . Accept it. . . . I thought I could. . . . I was to play *Lady Macbeth* in Nottingham.

" You know hows he enters, Shane. She comes in reading a letter. She is alone on the stage, in Macbeth's castle of Inverness : ' " They met me in the day of success," ' she reads—Macbeth is writing of the witches in the desert place : ' "and I have learned by the perfectest report, they have more in them than mortal knowledge." ' I came on as I always came on. . . . And the moment I left the wings, Shane, saw the audience, a strange thing happened. . . . . Illusion died; not died . . . but was dead. . . . . And there I was supposed to be reading a letter that had never been written by people who had never possibly an existence, before an audience who had paid a little money to be amused. . . . I couldn't read it. I just couldn't. . . .

" Behind me in the wings they were prompting,

whispering fiercely. . . . But I couldn't. . . . I stood there. . . . Then I said: I'll go off the stage. But I couldn't do that even. . . . My feet were shackled to the ground. . . . I seemed to have been charmed. . . . My hand fell to my side. . . . And then a panic came. My knees hit one another. My teeth chattered . . . awful, awful. . . .

"There was such a silence. The audience stirred, whispered. . . . Then some laughed. . . . Never laugh, Shane, suddenly, with me. . . . I crumpled up. They rang the curtain down. . . . I stole away to Ireland. . . . Whenever I am not hating—enough, the thought of that laugh comes to me. . . ." She shivered on her seat.

"That was only nervousness, Granya. Somebody got nervous and laughed."

"No, Shane, no."

"They talk of people laughing in the face of death. It's just a nervous action, Granya."

"I tell you, no, Shane." She grew vehement. "It's a cruel country, England. And, Shane, they hate us Irish. As long as we are pleasant, witty, as long as we are buffoons . . . but let us be human beings, Shane, and they hate us."

"Don't be silly, Granya!'

"I'm not silly, Shane. I know. They hate us because we have something they have not. The starved Irish peasant is higher than the English peer. He has a song in his heart, a gay song or a sad song, and his eyes see wonders. . . ."

"But, Granya, we are only a little people, and they all but rule the world. . . You are wrong. They don't hate us."

"Do you remember Haman, Shane; Haman who had everything:

"'And Haman told them of . . . all the things wherein the king had promoted him; and he said: 'Yet all this availeth me nothing so long as I see Mordecai the Jew sitting in the king's gate.'"

"Shane, do you remember how Haman died?"

"Granya!"

She rose. Her hands stretched out to the Irish hills. Her voice took on the throbbing of drums:

"Oh! the Erne shall run red
With redundance of blood,
The earth shall rock beneath our tread,
And flames warp hill and wood,
And gun-peal and slogan-cry
Wake many a glen serene,
Ere you shall fade, ere you shall die,
My dark Rosaleen!
My own Rosaleen!"

"Poor Granya!" he said. He caught and kissed her hand.

She let her other fall on his shoulder for an instant.

"Good-night, Shane!" she said abruptly. She moved swiftly toward the house through the yew-trees. In her pale dress against the moonlit turf, between the dark trees, she was like some old, heart-wringing ghost. . .

§ 10

He brought back from Tusa hErin that night a sense of dread. What in God's name had Granya done? To what committed herself? There were rumours abroad that the men of '67 were not dead yet. . . . In America, in the hills of Kerry, in Galway, there was plotting . . . not glorious, but sinister plotting. . . . God! had they enmeshed her?

He had three times heard her sing the old Ulster ballad of General Munro:

Up came Munro's sister, she was well dressed in green,
And his sword by her side that was once bright and keen
And she said to the brave men who with her did go,
"Come, we'll have revenge for my brother Munro!"

He had looked on that as only a queer romantic gesture, but with what she said last night, it occurred to him that there was a deeper motif to it all. . . . She was often in Dublin these days. . . . Did they? Had they? . . .

If it had been the Jacobite times, or '98 or even '48, he would not have minded. The Irish might call these Irish rebellions, but in reality they were world affairs. James and the Prince of Orange were the clash of the ideal of courtliness and tradition worn to a thin blade and of the stubborn progress of pulsing thought. And '98 was the echo of the surge for liberty—the frenzy of France and the stubborn Yankee steel. . . . And '48 was another breathing of the world. . . . Even '67 he would not have minded. Sixty-seven was a gallant romantic rally, a dream of pikes amid green banners, and men drilling by moonlit rivers. . . .

But to-day was different. . . . Revenge was in the air, and revenge was no wild justice, as an old writer had said. Revenge was an evil possession. . . .

An exhausting, sinister mood. . . . The men who would fight this modern battle, if battle there was to be one, were dark, scowling men. . . . The amenities of battle, the gallantry of flags meant nothing to them. They would shoot from behind ditches in the dark. . . . In America was talk of dynamite—an idealist using a burglar's trick. . . . There was no gallantry that way. . . .

And besides, it wasn't an Irish war. It was a matter of agriculture. . . . A war of peasants against careless landlords, Irish themselves in the main, who had fled to England to avoid the suicidal monotony of Irish country life, and lost their money in the pot-houses and gambling-dens of London, and turned to their tenants for more forgetting in the glamour of London the poverty of the Irish bogs. . . . It was contemptible to squeeze the peasants as a money-lender squeezes his victims, but the peasants' redress, the furtive musket and horrible dynamite, that was terrible. God, what a mess . . . And had Granya been caught into that evil problem, a kingfisher among cormorants?

And if she had, what was he going to do about it? What could he do? What right had he to meddle with her destiny? Friendly they had become, close sweet friends—the thought of her was like the thought of the hills purple with heather—but friendship and destiny are a sweet curling wave and a gaunt cliff. They were two different people, independent. Shane Campbell and the Woman of Tusa hErin.

§ II

She had been distraught all the evening. Merry, feverishly merry at times, and again silent, her eyes far off, her mouth set. She rose suddenly from the piano she was playing, and looked at him. Standing, above the light of the candles, her face and head were like some dark, soft flower.

"Shane, you are a very true friend of mine, aren't you?"

"Yes, Granya."

"If I wanted a very great favour, would you consider it?"

"Not consider, but do it."

"Yes, but the risk," she faltered. "I hardly dare——"

"What risk? What are you talking about, Granya?" A thought struck him. "Is it money? Don't be silly and talk about risk! Anything I can give you is yours, and welcome!"

"It's not money, Shane. And thank you! It's—it's this——"

"Yes, Granya."

"It's this, Shane. Would you—would you bring a ship for me from St. Petersburg to Lough Foyle, very quietly?"

"What kind of ship?"

"A ship, just a ship, a sailing-ship."

"What's in the ship?"

She paused. "Guns, Shane."

"No, Granya, I won't."

"Oh, well," she sat down, "I shouldn't have asked."

"Granya," he walked over and caught her shoulder, "don't be foolish."

"I'm not foolish, Shane. If I am, it's done now." She smiled. . . . The air crashed out beneath her fingers. Her voice rang:

In came the captain's daughter—the captain of the Yeos—
Saying, "Brave United Irishmen, we'll ne'er again be foes.
One thousand pounds I'll give to you, and go across the sea;
And dress myself in man's attire and fight for liberty!"

"You'll not move one foot from Tusa hErin!"

"O Shane, Tusa hErin's no longer mine, and I've got to go."

"Because the ship and the guns are mine, Shane," she smiled quietly; "my present."

With a terrific smash of the fist he broke in the top of the piano. The wires jangled in pandemonium. The candles fell to the floor.

"Hell's fire and God's damnation!" He swore at her. "You fool!"

She rose, her breasts heaving. Her eyes flashed.

"You've no right to speak to me like that, Shane Campbell."

"Oh, yes, I have. Every damned right! Do you think I'd let any woman go cruising around the North Seas, with a crew of foreigners, and a shipmaster she doesn't know . . . I'll bring the damned boat in . . ."

§ 12

They left the city of strange ugly women, with great spirit in their faces, and great bearing to the body of them, and of slim cat-like men, who had great power in their eyes . . . A very beautiful city of churches and hammered brass . . . a place of high rarefied thinking and savage animal passion. . . . They left it on a July morning with the sun high. . . . And they sailed west, sou'-west down the Gulf of Finland, until Dago Island was on their port quarter. . . .

And they rolled down the Baltic Sea, sailing sou'-sou'-west, until they passed Gotland, and, they edged west again, leaving Bornholm to port. . . . And they sailed past Malmö into the Sound, heading north for the Cattegat . . . They turned the Skaw and swung her into the Skage-Rack. . . . And the wind held . . . .

And once out of there, they pointed her nose nor-'west by nor' as though Iceland were only a buoy in a yacht-race . . . And the wind held. . . . The summer nights of the North were on them, the unearthly beauty of the light. . . . There was no world. . . . They were sailing on the Milky Way. . . . Only the gurgle of the water at the bows, the whush of the wake beneath the counter, held them as by a thin umbilical cord to the world of men. . . . The whap-whap-whap of the cordage. . . . The ting-ting-ting of the helmsman's bell. . . . The cry for'a'd : " The lights are burning bright, sir ! " . . .

§ 13

The gaunt Shetlands were on their starboard beam now, the dun Orkneys off the port bow. Sumburgh Head dropped away, and they headed due west. . . . The waves were laughing, the sun rose in a great explosion abaft of them . . . The world was a very small place . . . The universe so large. . . . At dawn the gulls chattered and whined, and screamed until they felt immense loneliness. . . . One seemed to be intruding in a world of white feathers and cold inimical eyes, and complaints in a language one could not understand. . . . So lonely . . . so undefiled . . . the home of the great whale . . . Here was the world as God first made it . . . clean and beautiful and absolute. . . . Up here steam engines seemed ridiculous toys. . . . In winter the sleek seal and the great white bear. . . . And the great crying of the gulls. . . . One thought of Adelina Patti's great singing and wondered did it matter a lot.

And they swung sou'west by sou' to leave the Hebrides to port. They were on the last leg of the voyage, and the wind still held. . . .

"O Shane, it's wonderful . . ." She had come on deck in her man's clothing. . . . She was so tall, so slim, her legs so long, it seemed some pleasant feminine fancy of hers, not a material adaptation to the life on board ship. "The wind will hold until we get there."

"I don't like it," Shane grumbled.

"Why, Shane? Why don't you like it?"

"We're too lucky."

"It isn't luck, Shane. It's the will of God."

"Hmm!"

"Granya!"

"Yes, Shane."

"I've just been thinking. Why couldn't you conspirators have chosen a better time of the year than August for landing your arms? There's only about two hours of night."

"Because, Shane, the arms must be ready for autumn, when the harvest is in. That's the best time for a revolution. And the arms must be distributed. And the men must drill a little. Now is our only time."

"Hmm."

"O Shane, I wish you would be a little enthusiastic.'

"Enthusiastic? At forty-nine!"

"Are you forty-nine, Shane? You don't seem thirty-nine. None could tell but for the little gray in your hair. . . . And Shane . . ."

"Yes!"

"I like your hair rumpled a little with the sea-air . . . much better than when it is sleek in Antrim . . . Shane, you don't know how well you look on board ship."

"Och, be damned to that . . . Mr. Janssen, get them to lay aft, and see if you can't get a little more out of that mizzen . . . A little more pocket in the luff." . . .

§ 14

They passed the Butt of Lewis, sailing due sou'west. . . . . To port they left the Seven Hunters, changing the course to sou'west by sou'. . . . The Hebrides passed them like islands in a dream, purple, gleaming strangely in the sunlight, now a black shower whipping over them, now sunshine pouring in great floods. . . . Lewis went by, and then Harris. . . . North Uist, where the winds blow so hard, they have an old word: *Is traugh fear na droiche air mhachair Uistibh*: 'Tis a pity of the slut's husband on the plains of Uist.

You'll be needing buttons on your coat there. . . . They passed Rona of the Seals, and Benbecula. . . . They passed South Uist and Eriskay. . . . They passed the Ponboy Isles. . . . The Islands of the Cat they called them in Gaelic. . . . Faintly they saw the mists of Hecla . . . heard the curlews. . . . They saw fishing-boats with great brown sails. . . .

Honk-honk of wild ganders in the distance, and occasionally the *chugh* of a diving bird. . . The wind blew from the nor'west. . . . The foam snarled beneath the bows. . . .

"I don't like it. . . . I don't like it. . . ."

"Shane, it is wonderful. . . . God is with us."

"Hunh. . . ." He saw the weather leaches flick. . . . "Don't let her come up," he roared at the helmsman. "Steer her, you Swede bastard. . . . Where the hell did you ever steer before? On a canal?"

"Shane!"

"What is it, Granya?"

"Your language, Shane!"

"Listen, Granya . . . I'm not playing a comedy. . . . I'm sailing a ship . . . that's on an errand I don't like. . . . If you don't like my language, get below. . . ."

"Sorry, Shane!" she said with meek courtesy. She stayed. . . .

They passed Skerryvore. . . . They passed Dhu Heartach, Colonsay, Islay of McCrimmin. . . . Iññistrahull was on the weather beam. . . . They swung eastward. . . . Iññishowen Head showed off the port bow. . . . On an August afternoon, they slipped into Lough Foyle. . . .

§ 15

The soft luminosity of a summer night was in it . . . and a little moon, which Shane damned. . . . Before them rose the outline of Donegal. . . . On each beam they could see faintly the outlines of the bay's arms. . . . . The schooner moved under jibs and mizzen. . . . . From the bow was the splash of the lead. . . .

"By the mark, five!"

"Luff her a little, a little more . . . steady!"

"Four fathoms, no bottom!"

"Keep her off a point!"

"By the deep, four!"

"How's the bottom?"

"Clean and sandy, sir!"

"No bottom at three!"

"Ready for'a'd to let go?"

"All ready, sir!"

"The mark three, no bottom!"

"Lee—o! . . . Hold her!"

The long swish of oars, the rattle of oar-locks. . . . A voice rapping out:

"Rest on the oars!" And then: "Schooner ahoy!"

Shane's heart sank. He gave so answer.

"What ship is that?" The voice rang over the little bay . . . found a grotesque echo in some cliff. . .

"Who are you?"

"Her Majesty's coastguards. Stand by. Coming aboard. Lay on your oars, men!"

And then . . . a long instant. . . . "Toss oars!"

"Bring her into the wind!" Shane ordered. . . . A scramble alongside, and some one was coming over the waist rail. . . . A firm step on deck. . . . Some one was smiling. . . .

"My name's Flannagan, Lieutenant Flannagan. . . . . Sorry, Mr. Campbell, we can't let you land . . . your cargo or your passenger. . . .' '

"I don't understand."

"Well, sir, we know what your cargo is, and my orders are not to let you land. And I was to tell you, sir, that you couldn't land anywhere."

"By God! I knew it would end like this. . . Are we under arrest?"

"No, sir. . . . You are just not to land. I'm sorry, sir, but. . . . Orders!"

"Then what the blazes am I going to do?"

"Jove, I don't know. Can't you bring the cargo back where you got it?"

"I suppose I'll have to do that. But my passenger. . . I can put her ashore."

"I'm sorry, sir. But your passenger can't go ashore, anywhere, any time, in Her Majesty's dominions."

"Hmm!"

He heard her quick step on the companionway.

"Shane."

"Shane, are you there?"

"Shane, Shane, what's wrong?" She came into the shrouded shrouded light of the binnacle. "Shane, who—who is this?"

"My name's Flannagan, Miss O'Malley—royal navy—I'm sorry; you can't land."

"What does it mean, Shane?"

"You're beaten, Granya."

"Are we prisoners?"

" No, Miss O'Malley, just you can't land. And I'm very distressed to tell you. . . . You may not land anywhere, any time, in Her Majesty's dominions."

" That doesn't shut out Mr. Campbell, does it ? "

" I've no orders against him, Miss O'Malley, barring his landing his cargo or you. . . ."

She laid her hand on Shane's arm. . . .

" I'm sorry, Shane . . . I'm very sorry, my dear —dear friend. . . . You were so good. . . . There are few—would have sacrificed their time and profession, and everything—to help a woman on a wild-goose ideal—like mine was. . . . So please forgive me ! "

" There's nothing to forgive, Granya. . . ."

" I want to do this . . ." she leaned forward and kissed him. . . . The lieutenant turned away. " And now good-bye."

" Why good-bye ? I'm not going ashore. I'll stick."

" Dear Shane, you would." She caught his hand, pressed, dropped it. Her voice rang out : " But I'm going ashore. . . ." She had swung over the taffrail and dropped into the water with the soft splash of a fish. . . .

" My God . . . !" Shane swore with rage. " Wait. I'll get her. Will you stand by with your boat ? "

" Right-o ! " Flannagan answered cheerily.

Shane kicked off his shoes, slipped out of his coat. . . . " This damned woman ! " he thought as he dropped astern, came out, began to cast for direction like an otter hound. . . . He heard her soft, rythmical strokes ahead. . . . He tore after her . . . caught up . . . reached her shoulder. . . .

" Come back, Granya ! "

" No, Shane."

He had decided, once he reached her, to turn her back by force, but the strange, gentle voice restrained him. All this matter of Ireland, all this expedition of opera bouffe took on again a strange dimension when she spoke. . . . All the time he had been foolish, he knew, and, worse, looked like a fool, but some strange magic of her voice made it seem natural . . . the naïve brave gestures. . . . One levitated above common ground. . . . Even this moon-madness did not seem trivial and a thing for laughter. . . . A dignity of ancient stories was on it. . . . The blue Irish hills, soft as down, the little moon, and the tide hurrying out of the lough to the great Atlantic. . . A wrench of the will and he gripped her shoulder :

" Shane, please don't ! "

" You're coming back, Granya."

" I'm not, Shane, and please don't hold me. I'm getting weak."

" You'll never make it, Granya. And if you did, where would you go on the Donegal hills ? "

" I don't know, Shane. But please let me go, I implore you. . . . Even if I do go down. . . . Don't you see ? There is nothing for me but this, or death. . . . My life. . . . O Shane, let me go ! "

" Quiet, Granya ! " He caught her wrist.

" Please, Shane. Please, I pray of you. . . ." She began to twist. . . . " O Shane, you hurt."

" Quiet, Granya. Boat-o ! "

The lantern of the coastguards' cutter came nearer.

. . . . The measured swish of the oars . . . the creak. . . . She began to struggle fiercely. . . .

"Granya, if you don't keep quiet I'll have to hit you. . . ."

"O Shane!" she whimpered. . . .

"All right. Get her on board. Steady there. Trim a little. Good!" Flannagan and a great bearded coastguard had her. . . . The silence was broken with her little sobs. . . . He helped her over the waist of the schooner. . . .

"Go below, Granya, and get into some dry clothes. . . . Mr. Flannagan, I'll take the boat back to St. Petersburg. . . . If Miss O'Malley doesn't land, neither do I. May I send a letter ashore? It's only about business, and the place in the glens. . . ."

"I'll take it and have it sent."

"Another thing; we want to get some provisions and water."

"Of course, sir. . . . That's all right."

"Do you think one of the country girls could be persuaded to come on board as Miss O'Malley's maid?"

"I think so. We'll ask the local priest."

"Oh, yes, the priest. . . . Another thing: do you think you could dig out a parson around here somewhere and bring him on board?"

"O Shane, what do you want that for?" She hadn't gone below, but waited in the companionway.

"You don't think you're going wandering around with me, casually, like this?"

"But it's only to St. Petersburg, Shane!"

"And then where do you go? What do you do?"

"I—I—I don't know."

" Better get the parson, Mr. Flannagan."

" Oh, but, Shane——" she protested.

" Go below, Granya, and get those wet things off. . . . . And get into women's clothes. . . . Granya ! "

" Yes, Shane. . . . Very well, Shane. . . ."

BOOK SEVEN

THE KINGDOM, THE POWER AND THE GLORY

§ I

THE KINGDOM AND THE POWER AND THE GLORY

HE felt a little ashamed, a little shy, what with his gray hairs, his paternity, that there should still be a thrill in his heart, a sense of flight in him. At fifty-eight to feel like a schoolboy going home, it seemed—well, not indecent, indecorous. This thing of returning to Antrim had been a matter of pure reason, and then suddenly his heart had spread forgotten wings.

Without, the sound of Broadway had changed subtly, with the coming of the September dusk. The quick-pacing people had given way to the clop-clop-clop of hansom-cabs, and the tramcars with their tired horses came less frequently now. One felt that a giant had been at work all day, and was now stretching himself, not lazily, but a little relaxingly. Soon the great lamps would flare, and the crowds would be going to the playhouses: to Tony Pastor's to see the new play, *Dreams*, or to Harrigan and Hart's to see *Investigation*, or to Mr. Bartley Campbell's latest, *Separation*, at the Grand Opera-house. He would miss all this in Antrim, but Antrim called him. . . . Ulster, our mother. . . .

And three months ago he had never thought this possible. He had drilled himself into a mature philosophy, saying: "It doesn't matter that I never see Ireland again. I am happy here with Granya and young Alan and Robin Beg, little Robin. All the folks are kindly and the country is a great country, and when my time comes to die there are sweet little places on Long Island where they can lay me within sound of the sea, and the gentle snow will come and cover me in winter, and in summer somewhere about me the dogwood will blow, and the very green grass come. And perhaps some young children will come and play around my grave, and I shall hear their little gurgling laughter, sweet as the voices of pigeons. . . . And one day Granya will come. . . . Nothing is more certain than that, that Granya will come. . . ."

But all the philosophy in the world could not shut from his ears the little piping of Antrim. He would say: " 'Tis little thought I gave to Antrim and I a young man! And what is a town or so to me, who have seen all great cities?" And again he said: "Didn't you give up Antrim gladly when you got Granya? Wasn't she worth a hundred Antrims?" And his heart and mind answered: "Yes, a thousand Antrims!" But a very queer thing, the little haunting melody of the glens would not be stilled.

And it came to him thus: I am no longer a young man. For all I look forty-five, as they tell me, yet I am fifty-eight. The life of the body is over now. That has passed, as a mood passes. And the mind is fixed. In what remains of life to me, I must think, divine, weigh. One prepares. . . . And thoughts must not be disturbed. To grow old in a city that is ever young, that is in its twenties itself, as it were—makes an old man cold and afraid. Old buildings he has known come down, old streets are obliterated. It is a very terrible thing to be lonely when old, and to feel everything passes, dies. . . . All I have loved is thrown away, is of no use. . . . Everything old is in the way, and I am old. . . . The hawk-eyed commercial men go about so that the streets are filled with them. . . . And all the sweet things that were said in Galilee seem only a casual all-but-forgotten melody, and no revelation. . . . And then comes a horrible memory of stark Ecclesiastes: "The dead know not anything, neither have they any more a reward; for the memory of them is forgotten. Also their love, and their hatred, and their envy, is now perished; neither have they any more a portion for ever in any thing that is done under the sun." And old men remember the sorrowful things of their life, and how little happiness measured up to the misery and toil of life, and they had hoped. . . . But there were the words of the preacher: "Neither have they any more a reward" . . . And secretly and quietly old men weep. . . .

But to grow old with the mountains and the eternal sea, and to watch the delicate bells of the heather, to know the quiet companionship of dogs—there is a revelation in it. No, nothing dies. And the moon rises and the mountains nod: Yes, I remember you when you were a schoolboy, running to be on time. And the green waves make a pleasant laughter: We are here. When you arise in the morning you may be certain we are here. The friends of one's young days die, scatter, are lost. But the mountains and the water are friends for ever. One can speak to them. One can speak to ancient trees. And the leaves rustle. . . .

And Granya had sensed it. . . . He might have known she would. Conceal it as he might try, a mysterious telepathy was between them. . . . She knew. . . .

It was she who had gone to the British Embassy in Washington, telling Shane nothing. He had heard of it afterwards. She hadn't pleaded or given any promises. She had just flared into the startled envoy.

"I wish to go back to Ireland."

"Unfortunately the Chief Secretary had the matter of Miss O'Malley——"

"I am not Miss O'Malley. I am Shane Campbell's wife."

"But you are a dangerous enemy to the empire!"

"Am I? I had forgotten completely about the empire."

"There was a little matter of a shipload of rifles——

"And now it is a matter of a husband and two children."

"Sure, Miss O'Malley?"

"I am not Miss O'Malley. I am Shane Campbell's wife. And I am absolutely sure."

It had been so easy after all.

And now, when it was true, it was hard to credit. Within two weeks the ship would swing to port around Donegal, and they would enter the bay they had entered nine years ago, nine years and a month ago, to be exact. He wondered whether it would be a foggy morning, or a great golden afternoon. It was a pity it had to be on board a steamship, though. He would liefer have luffed in on board a boat of his own, a great suit of snowy canvas drawing joyously the Irish wind.

§ 2

Upstairs he could hear and distinguish the feet in the nursery. There was the patter of little Alan's feet, and the stumble of Robin Beg's. There was the shuffle of the nursemaid, and the firm, light tread of Granya. Soon she would come down, after the children were safely to bed, and little Alan's prayers were heard. And they would go out to dinner in New York for the last time. It was a little pang to leave New York . . . Ah, but Antrim !

He picked up his paper and read while waiting. . . . It was queer how he could hardly focus his attention on it, impatient for her as a schoolboy for his first love. . . . Always when she entered a room came beauty. . . . Well, she would come. . . . The type took form beneath his eyes. . . . The races at Sheepshead Bay ; Tom Martin had captured the Twin City Handicap. . . . In Ireland they would go to the Curragh and Baldoyle to see the horses, and the Dublin horse-show, and the hunts on a frosty morning. . . . What was this ? Heavy bets laid that Cleveland would be next President. The Irish wouldn't like that. They were all for Blaine. It was only the other night that Mrs. Delia Parnell, Parnell's mother, had attended the great Irish rally in the Academy of Music. . . . That was a mistake, mixing up Irish politics with American statesmanship. There would be folk to resent that, and rightly too. . . . Too much talk of dynamite, and that horrible thing in Phoenix Park. . . . What an involved, emotional affair all this Irish matter was ! . . . To understand Ireland one must understand Irishmen, that either hatred or love rule them. . . . Parnell, though, looked hopeful. No emotion, all brains and will. . . . He could not be side-tracked by preferment, or religion, or love for women. There was a man whose head was firm on his shoulders; he would never be wrecked. . . Ah, here was something Granya would be glad to hear: Margaret Mather got a splendid reception in Pittsburg with her *Lady Macbeth*. . . . Whew! Cholera at Naples. That was serious! Not an over-clean people, the Italians. . . Li Hung Chang degraded of his titles. Who the blazes was Li Hung Chang anyway, and what titles did he have? . . . And Major Kitchener disperses the Berber tribes. . . . How unimportant! Ah, here was something. Great gambling reported on the *City of Rome*. Ah, there was what he always contended, that steam would ruin everything. The great sea a resort for gamblers! In the old days, in sail, when a captain was a captain, he'd have had none of that on board clean timbers. . . . He was a little afraid the world was going to the dogs!

Och! Was that woman never coming down at all, at all?

He smiled to himself at how the Ulster speech came back to him at the thought of Ulster. . . . He turned to the paper with an effort of will. . . . An Indian outbreak feared in Western Montana. . . . Stanley going to Egypt. . . . Policeman beaten up in Brooklyn; a tough place, Brooklyn! . . . American schooner arrested by Russian corvette for selling rum to Bering Strait natives: a very strict modern people, the Russians. . . . Picnics on Staten Island blamed for ruin of young girls. . . And Bismarck and the

Pope still sparring. Did that poor German think he could ever get the better of the subtle Romans. . . ? Och, what was keeping that woman ?

The light had become so dim that he could hardly read. The tempo without quickened. People were hurrying now, on their way to the restaurants for the evening meal. From the restaurants to the theatre. Home to sleep. And a new day with the old work facing them. There was a fascination, a hypnosis to New York. He felt a pang at leaving it. It had been very friendly to him. And he would never see it again. . . . Ah, but he would remember it !

§ 3

It came to him with a sense of revelation that all his life he had been looking forward : always the new thing. And now he would be looking back. Always before guessing. Looking back now, knowing, or not quite knowing, but having before him material from which to draw wisdom, truth. All his life it seemed he had been gathering something. Now was the time to sort it, weave it. . . . And then, what was he to do with whatever he had made ? Toward what end ? The paper he had in his hands dropped to his knees. His eyes fixed on the windows where the lights of the city began to shine, saw a haze, saw nothing. His ears, listening to the *clop-clop-clop* of the hansoms, heard only rhythm, then a faint harmony, then nothing. . . . Himself, within him, seemed to see old scenes, to be in old scenes. The little boy going down to the sea in ships, seeking an island he had seen in a mirage . . . a mood of wonder.

. . . There were feet, there was the world. Every tree was an emerald miracle, every house a mystery, all people were riddles. . . . Come, little boy, come and look ! The instinct of the salmon for the sea. The river where he was spawned hurries to the sea, and his instinct is to go with it, not against it. . . . It deepens and broadens, and ahead is always a clearer pool, a more shadowy rock, a softer water-fern. It is pleasant to swim under the sally branches, and rapids, whip. . . . And there is the lull of an estuary and the *chush-chush* of little waves, and he is in the sea. . . . And now he must lay his own course. . . The lure of the river has brought him so far.

And Shane thought : I was born a salmon in a river. The stupid pretty trout remained in the river, and the secretive eels. . . . And the perch and the roach and the ponderous bream, and the pike that is long of snout, they remained by the grassy waters. . But those that are born salmon must go down to the sea. . . .

A little shadow came into his face, and his breath was caught sharp. He was remembering Moyra, the wife he had, and he no older than a boy . . . Like some strange fascinating, ugly dream that came to him . . . And queerly enough, the picture of Moyra's mother, the old wife of Louth, was clearer in his mind than his wife. . . . Moyra was like some troubled cloud, a thing that blotted out sunshine for a while, through no fault of his own, but the mother was sinister. An old woman keening, and the breath of whisky on her, and her eyes sobering in a bitter greed. . . . Why should Moyra have died ? Fate : the act of God : whatever you care to call it. Why should he have been dragged into it, Shane wondered. If he hadn't, what would have happened ? He didn't know. But he knew this, that in the marriage to Moyra he had been gripped by the shoulder, and looked in the eyes, and a voice had said : " Wait. All is not wonder and mystery. Life is not a child's toy. You must learn."

Poor Moyra, he could hardly remember anything but her pleading, half inimical eyes, her mouth that twisted easily to anger, her shame that her arms and legs were uncouth. And now she had loved him. And now hated him. He remembered one May evening when suddenly she had caught his hand and kissed it, and pressed it to her heart. And later that night she had cursed bitterly at him, saying black was the day she had set eyes on him, and black the day she married him, and her face was twisted into agonized ugliness. And when he went to sea days later he had found a symbol of her religion, an *Agnus Dei,* sewed into his coat to protect him against the terrors of the deep waters.

And she had died, poor tortured Moyra, suddenly. Why ? Had What had fashioned her thought : That's not rightly done ? No. That's poor. Wait. I'll do it over . . .

Ah, well, God give her peace, wherever she wandered ! How many years had it taken to get over, not her death, but their being married ? A long time. Seven bitter years. He might have turned into a bitter, fierce old man, hating all things. The whole thing had been like a cruelty to a happy wondering child. And he had closed his heart, resentful, afraid . . . And then had come Claire-Anne.

Once he had been a child with wondering gray eyes

and life had made him blind as a mole, secretive as a badger, timid of the world as the owl is timid of daylight. The shock of Claire-Anne, and he was cognizant of great enveloping currents of life. Wonders he had known, and bitterness he had known, but the immense forces that wind the stars as a clock is wound he had not known. . . . And with Claire-Anne they had burst about him like thunder. They had played around him as the corposant flickers around the mast-head of a ship. . . . Poor Claire-Anne ! The miracle of her. She was like some flowering bush in an arctic waste. . . . Her wonderful scared eyes, her tortured self. . . . It was a very strange thing that her end did not bother him. . . . A gesture of youth, that sudden snap of the wrist with the poor dead prince's dagger. . . . He had been very honest about it, and it did not bother him, any more than it would have been on his conscience to have shot a crippled horse. . . . Once it had seemed to him unnecessarily histrionic, but now he knew it was merciful. . . . Her spirit had gone too far ever to return to normal life. . . .

But the little woman of the East, that did bother him. In boyhood he had known the wonder of life In youth he had known there existed sordid tragedy. In young manhood passion had crashed like lightning . . . And then he had thought he knew all. He had considered himself the master of life and said : " I will do such and such a thing and be happy. Enjoy this, because I know how to enjoy it. To the wise man, all is a pleasant hedonism." It struck him at the time how terribly foolish and piteous great men were. . . . Jesus dead on a crucifix ; Socrates and the hemlock bowl ; the earnest Paul beheaded at Rome.

. . . A little wisdom, a little callousness would have avoided all this. . . . How satisfied he was, how damned petty ! His little bourgeois life, his harem of one pretty girl, his nice ship . . . smug as a shop-keeper . . . and then life, fate, whatever you call it, had tripped him up, abashed, bested him, through the medium of mountebank wrestler whom he had conquered in a a street brawl . . .

And afterwards, seven years of blackness and despair. The long reach to Buenos Aires, and the querulous sea-birds mocking him : On the land is desolation and pettiness and disappointment. . . . And what is there on the sea ? The great whale is dying ; the monster who ranged the deep must go because men must have oil to cast up their accounts by the light of it, and women must have whalebone for stays. . . . The sleek seal with brown gentle eyes must die that harlots shall wear fur. . . . And there never was a Neptune or a Mannanan mac Lir. . . . They were only stories from a foolish old book. . . . The sun shines for a moment on the green waters, and your heart rises. . . . But remember the blackness of the typhoon, and how the cold left-hand wind rages round the Horn. . . . And the coral islands have great reefs like knives, and the golden tropics lure to black lethal snakes. . . . Fool ! Fool ! We have ranged the clouds, and there is no good-willing God. . . . There is only coldness and malignant things. . . . So cried the querulous sea voices, and they tempted him : " All you have known is desolation and vanity. Better to have died a boy while the meadows they were green. . . . All before you is emptiness," they mocked. And they came nearer : " Behold, the night is black, the ocean is of great depth, immeasurable, the ship plows onward under a quartering breeze. A little step, a little step leeward, a vault over the taffrail as over a little ditch, and there will be peace and rest Look at the water flow past. No problem there . . ." God ! how close he had been to it, in the seven black years, the long voyage from Liverpool, and the sordid town at the end. . . . How close ! And then Alan Donn, God rest him ! had died, and he had gone back to Ireland, and met Granya, and been foolish as a boy in his teens. A shipload of rifles to free Ireland ! What a damned fool he had felt when they had simply shooed him away !

He thought to himself with a little smile that out of the wisdom of his life had always come sorrow, and out of his foolishness had come joy. . . . Granya, and peace, and meaning to his life. . . . A very foolish thing it had been, that expedition. . . . But he wouldn't have it laughed at, nor laugh at it himself. . . . Over the mists of the past the thing took glamour. . . . He had been more moved than he had allowed himself to believe then. And here in his New York drawing-room, remembering the old heroic-comic gesture, and remembering tragedies of material that were glorification of spirit, he thought for an instant he had solved the mystery of Ireland, . . . Ireland was a drug. . . . Out of the gray weeping stones, and the bogs of red moss and purple water, and from the proud brooding mountains, and the fields green as a green banner, there exhaled some subtle thing that made men lose sense of worldly proportion. . . It was in their mother's milk, a subtle poison. It crept into their veins, and hough they might leave Ireland, yet for generations would it persist. . . . It gave them the gift of laughter, and contempt for physical pain, and an egregious sensitiveness. . . . So that the world wondered. . . . their wars were merry wars, and their poetry sobbed, like a bereaved woman. . . . They threw their lives away recklessly, and a phrase meant much to them. . . . Perhaps they knew that action counted nothing, and emotion all . . . Ah, there he was losing himself !

At any rate, Ulster Scot though he was, he didn't regret it—apart even from its bringing him Granya. Perhaps at the news of it, some hard English official might feel a twitch at his heart-strings, and remembering that the Irish were as little children, be kind to some reprobate Celt. . . . An action had so many antennæ. One never knew where it's effects stopped, if ever. . . .

A foolish thing that had brought him joy where wisdom brought him sorrow ! Strange. Until then he had been existent, sentient, but never until then alive. Wonder, disillusionment, passion, tragedy, despair. In each of these moods he had had a glimpse now and then, of an immense universal design, as a bird may have it, and its throat quivering with song, or as a salmon may have it, and he flinging himself tremendously over a weir. He knew it, as a tree knows when the gentle rains of April come. But that he existed, as an entity apart from trees, from salmon, and from birds, he had not known until Granya, broken, had crept weeping into his arms. . . .

" Give me strength, Shane, for God's sake. Give me strength, or I die ! "

And somewhere, out of something, some esoteric where he had plucked strength and given it to her, and he knew it wasn't from his body, or from his mind, or his spirit even, he had given it. He had, from some tremendous storehouse, got life for her, got peace, so that she fluttered like a pigeon and sighed and grew calm. . . . And in that moment he knew he was alive.

He tried to figure it to himself in terms of concrete things, and he said: "If I were on a racing-boat now, I would decide how to make a certain buoy, and my mind would figure how to get there, what tack to make, the exact moment of breaking out the spinnaker rounding the mark. Perhaps my mind is nothing, something I use just now, as I use my body. For the hand on the rudder is not I. It is something I am using to hold that rudder. As I might lash it with a rope, if I were so minded. And my eyes are just something I use. They are just like the indicators on the stays; they and the indicators are one, to tell me how the wind shifts. All that is not I. It is something I use. Perhaps even my mind is something I use, as I use my hands. But somewhere, somewhere within me, is I."

And a great sense of exaltation and wonder and dignity swept through every fiber of him at the thought of this: new-born he was, clean as a trout, naked as a knife, strong as the sea. He was one of the lords of the kindly trees, masters of the pretty flowers: the little animals of God were given him, it being known he would not abuse the gift. . . . And though lightning should strike him yet he would not die, but put off his body like a rent garment. . . . And though he were to meet the savage bear in the forest and have no means of conquering it, yet were he to become aware of this entity of life in him, he would smile at the thought of physical danger, and the great furry thing would recognize that dignity and be abashed. . . . And there was no more wonder, or mystery, or fear, only beauty. . . . The moon was not any more a mystery, but a place to be trodden one day, were his place to be there. . . . And the furthest star was no further than the furthest island on terrestrial seas; one day he would reach that star, somehow, as now he could the furthest island with head and hand. . . . Though death should smite his body he would not die.

§ 4

A strange thing was this, that Granya had always known this life. It was so certain to her that it was no more a wonder than rain is, or sunshine, or the rising of the moon. . . .

He had spoken of it to her one evening in the dusk. She had smiled, her grave beautiful smile.

"Of course I know, Shane. I always knew."

"But how did you know, Granya?"

"I think," she said, "I think all good women know, Shane. Men are so complete, so welded. Mind and body seem to be themselves; the body and mind function so that one doesn't see that there is anything within that directs them. They are compact. But a woman is diffuse, Shane. Her mind is not a man's mind; it is a thing she can use when she wants to and then forget. . . . When women sit and think, you know, they aren't thinking. They are feeling, Shane. It comes like a little wind. There may be a place by the sea-shore, sparse heather and sandy dunes, and the little waves come chiming, and the curlew calls. And you sit. And a very strange peace comes to you, so that in a low soft voice you sing a verse of song. . . . Or it may come on the cold winds of winter, through the ascetic trees. . . . But women are always cognizant of God. . . . Even bad women, Shane, who mistake the Unknown God for the true. . . . And a woman is very much apart from her body. It is just a nuisance at times, or at times a thing of beauty, or at times a thing one expresses something with, something that is too deep for words, as with a violin. And to some it is a curse. . . . But a body is always apart from one, and a mind is, too. . . . Shane, you have seen very beautiful old women. . . . Women with a beauty that is like a flame that does not burn, that have a light within them somewhere . . . that is not of the mind or of the body . . . that is of these things worn thin so that they themselves show . . . See, heart ? "

" But, Granya, why must a man find out, and a woman know ? "

" Shane of my heart, because it is necessary to women that they may live. A man can live without knowing God, as blind men live without ever seeing the moon. For they have minds, Shane, pursuits —the amassing of money, the little light of fame, that is only a vanity—not real. . . . But Shane, no matter how hard a man has to work, a woman has more terrible things. . . . There is no man on earth can understand the bearing of children. . . . And there is no man, were he to think of it, try to know, but would rather die than submit to what he thinks that terror. . . . And yet, Shane, it is not so much. . . .

After a little agony, when one goes into the dark, olive valley, and strength seems to go from you in great waves, until you are robbed of strength as a man may be robbed of blood. . . . Then one goes out of one's self and gets it. . . . The beauty in the face of young mothers, of brides. That is not body or mind, Shane, that is their selves. This was the Eleusinian mystery, Shane, that women know that God lives, and that they cannot die. . . .

" See, Shane, the stars are out. The dew is falling. And on the morrow you must be afoot early. Shall we go in ? "

" Come."

Once, before Alan Oge was born, a wave of panic swept over him, and he caught her hand and looked at her :

" What is it, Shane ? "

" If—if you should die—"

" I shall not die, Shane. I know. I shall not die."

" But how do you know ? "

" I just know, Shane. That's all."

" O Granya, it seems very terrible, that one day one of us should die."

" Dear Shane, it is not very terrible. If I should die, my heart, I should know I would not have long to wait. And I should be with you, Shane, even dead, when I could. . . . And after days of trouble suddenly one morning you would know you had had a good night's sleep, and that would be because I had come to you in the night and had kissed you, and laid a dim hand on you . . . And sometimes, in difficulties, you would feel a sudden rush of strength, and that would be because I was beside you . . . dear heart, dear Shane."

"I am so much older Granya. I shall be the first to die."

"If you are the first to go, Shane, I shall be like some wife of the Crusades, of an old time when a dream meant more than a pocketful of money . . . and men were glad to go, and women glad to send them. I shall sit by my fire, and when you come I shall talk to you in my heart . . . saying little foolish sweet things. . . . And when I need you, I shall go out into the soft night, and call, and you will hear my voice in the Milky Way . . . and God will let you come . . . my darling . . ."

"Granya!"

"And maybe—sweet, sweet thought—He will let us go together. . . ."

§ 5

Here was a great fact, that he lived, but with the fact came a problem: Why? If within him there existed this sentient, supple, strong thing, and it did exist, for what end was it designed? It was not enough to have faith, to know one lived to save one's soul. . . . That was selfish, and selfishness was an unpardonable thing, the sin against the Holy Spirit, which has ordained there should be one occult purpose. . . . . No, everything had a reason. . . . . The sheltering trees, the ocean from whose womb came the great clouds that nurtured the green grass: the winds that were like gigantic brooms. The wise and the good laboured, and never shirked. . . . Each man must give according to his station, the strong man of strength, the wise one of wisdom ; the one who knew beauty must give it somehow, not huddle it like a miser's hoard. . . All men must work ; that was as natural an instinct as the law that men must eat : and work did not mean grinding, but justifying one's existence fully. . . . None may hold back, for that is ignoble, and all that is ignoble dies, dies and is used again. . . . The murderer's dead body may nurture a green bay-tree, such beautiful economy nature has. . . . And it seemed to him that the souls of dark men were used too, but used as negations, and that was death. . . . Perhaps they provided the sinister thunderstorms, the terrible typhoon, the cold polar breezes, the storms off the Horn. . . . They might be the counterpoint of nature's harmony. . . . But this was going past knowledge, and past knowledge of heart and head one must not go. . . . But of one thing he was certain ; all that is ignoble dies. . . .

He had always known from the time he was a young boy that man must do something. . . . It was not sufficient to make a little money and sit down and spend it, as a dog finds a bone and gnaws it, or buries it, in a solitary place. . . . For a long time he had thought it sufficient to do the little commerce of the world. . . . But that was not sufficient. . . . In Buenos Aires he had felt ridiculous, as a giant might feel ridiculous carrying little stones for the making of a grocer's house. . . . Ashamed, a little resentful ! He was like a dumb paralytic with flaming words in his heart and brain, and he could not write them, not even speak them aloud. . . .

But all his life this had worried him, the getting of work to do. And when he came to America with Granya he had come with great plans. Ships and ship-building were the only things he knew, and he had thought with others that the great clipper days might be revived. Iron steamships were grasping the swift commerce of the world, but there were errands great wooden ships under skysails might yet be supreme in; the grain trade of San Francisco, for instance. And it might be possible, so he had dreamed, that once more the great pre-war clippers should be the pride of the new idealistic commonwealth . . . and what had come from his hand ? A half-dozen three-masted schooners, and not very good schooners either, being too long in the hull for strength. . . . And nobody seemed to care. . . . From Belfast and the Clyde, iron boats swarmed like flies. . . . And people were impatient. . . . They did not care to wait if a ship were blown from her course. . . . They wanted ships on time. . . . People had laughed at him, calling him crazy, and saying he was trying to stem progress. . . . And then they had done worse. . . . They had smiled and said it was a hobby of his. . . . He knew it was no use. He quit. . . . And Granya had been very tender.

"You mustn't mind, Shane. It was very lovely of you to dream and act. . . . But it is not intended. Don't take it to heart, dearest."

"All my life, Granya, I have been trying to do something, and I always fail."

"Dear Shane, you never fail. The success is in yourself, not outside of yourself. That is all."

"Ah, yes, Granya, but that is not enough. That seems so selfish. So many men have done so much for the world, and I have done nothing. Even the old charwoman on her knees scrubbing floors has done more. She has given her best, and her best has been useful."

"But Shane, you must wait. Have patience."

"I am old, Granya, and have done nothing."

"Wait, Shane, wait. I am going to dim the light, and blur all these things around us, and tell you a secret thought has been deep in my heart for years. There will be we two just in the room—absolute. And come nearer the fire, dear Shane, where I can just see where your hand is, and put my hand on it when the thought makes me feel like a child in a great wood. . . . Shane. . . .

"You know your charts, the charts you use and you at sea, the charts of the heavens, where what stars we know are marked, the sun and the moon and Venus and Jupiter, and Sirius the dog-star, and Saturn, and the star you steer your ship by, the polar star. . . . And all the constellations, the Milky Way, and the belt of Orion, and the Plow and the Great Bear and the great glory you see when you pass the line, the Southern Cross . . . and the little stars you have no names for, but mark them on your chart with quaint Greek letters. . . . Our little world is so little, so pathetically little in this immensity. . . It is as though we were living on the smallest of islands, like some of the islands you have known and you on board ship following the moon down the West —Saba, where the Dutch are in the Caribbean, or Grenada, the very little island. . . . And on that island they know only vaguely that such great lands as Africa and Europe and Asia are. . . . They don't know it from experience. . . . But Peking of the bells exists, and stately Madrid, and Paris that is a blaze of light, and London where the fog rolls inland from the sea. . . . Heart of my heart, how terrible it is that folk cannot, will not see, understand. . . . And they say: Well, we don't see it. Here we were born and here we die. . . . And they say: Show us somebody who has been there. . . . They forget how long is the journey and how a man may have affairs in the crowning cities. . . . Dearest, I am losing myself, but I know.

"And this is what I want to tell you, Shane, that when you die—oh, such an ugly word that is, Shane, for the bud bursting into flower—when it is your time to leave here, Shane, there will be a place for you, not idleness at all. . . . All the stars, Shane, the valleys of the moon. . . . There is work, Shane dear. Nothing is perfect, else there should be no reason for life. There must be stars that are old, as Dublin is old, and need vitality. . . . There must be stars that are young and cruel, as this city is young and cruel, and need sweet strength. . . . But I am very presumptuous, Shane, to try and fathom the Great Master's plan. . . . It is so colourful—oh, there is no word or symbol for it, Shane. . . . But there is a Great Master and there is a Plan. . . .

"Heart, I tell you this, showing all my weakness of thought. You know it is the truth, too. . . . But I tell you I know, so that our two selves' knowing may make it a little stronger in us. . . .

"O Shane, I have no logic, I know. . . . And all

the logicians in the world could not shame me to myself. All the reason in the world could not shake me. It would be artillery shot against the wind. . . . A star is a promise to me, Shane, and the wind a token, and the new moon just a pleasant occurrence, like the coming of spring. . . .

"Shane, I know all this. I know it not for myself, but for you. . . . I know three things: I know God lives, I know I love you, I know we shall not die. . . . I love you, Shane, and there is no shame on me telling it to you, for you are as my heart and I am as yours. . . . When I see you at times there comes over me a sweetness from head to foot, and at times when I see you, a great dignity comes to me, because you love me, and your love is good. . . . I know there is a place in the coming days, and I know I shall be with you, wherever you go. . . .

"Here in this dim room, Shane, I know these things. Outside is the world, that is forgetting or that doesn't care, or will not see. Here in this dim room, with the red of the fire turning to a gentle yellow, I know it better than the people in churches, that kindly God lives, that I love you, Shane, and that we shall not die. . . ."

§ 6

It seemed to him that he must have been in reverie for ages, so much had he thought sitting there, so much felt. . . . He had been like a gull poised on the wing, and now he dropped gently to the calm waters. . . . . New York to-day, and in two weeks Antrim, and then a rest. . . . And then wider spaces than he had ever known, greater adventure. . . . A day would come when he would be called, as though some one had said : Shane Campbell ! and then a gesture that made a horse stumble, or a flaw of wind that would turn over a boat. . . . Click ! . . .

And it seemed to him that it would be not only sweeter, but wiser to die in Antrim. . . . New York was no place for a man like him to die. For an old man, weary with life's work, there would be gentle hands, and soft caring, and guidance for tired eyes. . . . But for a man young spiritually, strong, there would be no coddling. . . . He would be expected to jump forward at the call. . . . And to go through the maze of smoke and dust, and the evil jungles of the air one sensed in a great city would be—waste of time and energy. . . . In Antrim when the call would come there would be the clear high air, the friendly glens, the great encouraging mountains, and the Moyle laughing in the moonlight : Don't be embarrassed ! Don't be afraid !

Above, he heard a door shut. There was no longer the patter of the boys' feet on the floor, nor the drag of the maid's shoes, but Granya's firm, light step he could sense somehow, and then came a little sound to him, that he knew was her dropping to her knees by Alan Beg's bed, while she recited for him, taught him, the great prayer. . . . Shane bowed his head in reverence. . . . He could see the dim beauty of her face, her great trusting eyes, her sweet hands. . . . Almost could he hear her voice, so close was she in his heart. . . .

§ 7

"Our Father, . . ."

He could see the symbols that were in her mind, because they were in his too, the gentle pictures that translated the thought these words evoked: the great majestic figure with the strong hands and gentle eyes, the eyes that smiled when colts gambolled, or a rabbit flashed across the grass, that loved the beauty of the garden when He walked in it at the close of day. One felt Him now and then as He went through His smallest world, perhaps in the evening when the crickets sang, perhaps over the moonlit waters, or with the little winds of dawn. . . . Such strength and kindliness. And the majestic eyes were troubled for, sympathetic toward the wayward, the bothered, the weak. . . . They only hardened with the promise of terror for the hypocrite, the traitor, for those who devoured widows' houses. . . .

"Which art in heaven . . ."

He smiled to himself at the thought of heaven. There was where one's fancy was free, to realise all the sweet desires of what was good in one. . . . To those who deserved it God would not begrudge His heaven. . . . A quiet place, Shane thought, a hushed place, a place of rest. . . . Whither one might go to realise again all the beauty one had ever known. . . . All that one had held sweet and wonderful would be there—they had not died. . . . A white magic would bring back the laughter of babies, and kisses gently given . . . and all estrangements of friends and lovers would be eased there, and they would be brought together in a magical trysting-place, and there would be no unharmony. . . . All the horses one had ever loved would take shape in the air, with necks stretched and whinnying recognition. . . . All the great ships one had wondered at would appear when called, their spread of snowy canvas, their tapering spars. . . . All the dogs one had had would be there . . . their yelps of joy, their sweet brown eyes, their ears up, their tails wagging . . . all the dogs would be there!

"Hallowed by thy Name . . ."

The head must bow there. The name evoked a thought, and the thought was ineffable, such glory and sweetness and strength it had . . . . Names brought pictures. When the word "Helen" was uttered, one saw the burned towers of Troy. . . . And "Venice," massive shadows and great moonlit waters. . . . And Genghis Khan brought the riot of galloping horses and the Tartar blades a-flash. . . . Such power great words had, and this was the greatest word, so great as to be terrible, and not to be mentioned by petty men, who cheapen with their grudging tongues. . . . No picture there, but some great anthem of the stars. . . . Not as yet could our ears hear it. . . Nor would they ever hear it, if we had not reverence.

"Thy kingdom come . . ."

Some immense plan existed, which human mind could never see. No practical wisdom could ever grasp. Were all the sum of practical wisdom gathered in a little room, and infused with spirit until it burst the four walls of the world, yet it might not grasp it. . . . . Yet all things worked that this plan should come to fruition. The stars rolled in their courses.

The great winds came. There fell the rain of April and the soft December snow. . . . And the kingdom was a good kingdom, for nothing evil conquered ever. . . . It died and was eliminated, and when it was all as nothing then might the kingdom come; no arbitrary blowing of Gabriel's trumpet, but that foremost sweetness that comes from the west wind. . . .

"Thy will be done on earth . . ."

It was always done on earth, but the ignoble, the inglorious, the small, put their petty obstacles in its way, and delayed the coming of the kingdom. . . . Men grew engrossed in their affairs, grew self-sufficient. A little money in their pockets, and God was forgotten. A little more and they despised their fellow-men, and hatred arose. And evil wars came, and years were lost . . . Cunning men put the emotions, the ideals, the actions of glorious men up for barter. . . . And the men took the land and the waters and the light, and worked tortuously until they could sell them at a price. . . . And the things God had made for his people were the means to procure these dark folk wine and mistresses and the state of kings. . . . Such was not the doing of the Will. . . . But one day it would be worked out by men how these things could not ever again be. . . . The slow, certain coming of the kingdom. . . .

"As it is in heaven . . ."

From the green resting-place came all that was sweet and harmonious, the shape of clouds, the high spirit of horses, the loyalty of dogs, the graceful movement swans have, and the song of the lesser birds. From that green resting-place came the gold of the gorse, and the sweet line of trees, and the purple the heather has—the loved heather. Thence came the word that set the friendly moon on high, and put out the white beauty of the young and alternated sunshine with the rains of spring. All was done there according to wisdom and beauty.

" Give us this day our daily bread . . . "

That was no whine for the prisoner's dole. That was the simplicity of asking that the moon and the sun still rise. Give beauty to women, and grace to children, and songs for poets to sing. Let not the green tree wither, but send it rain. And give a little softness to the hearts of callous men. And remind us that widows live, and that there are fatherless. Teach us how to heal sickly children, and be easy on horses. And give us gentleness. And when roses grow on the walls in June, put a bud in our hearts. . . .

" And forgive us our trespasses . . . "

The picture that came into Shane's mind then was not the picture of an abased man beating his breast, but the thought of a mature man clanging through the halls of heaven past every guard until he came where wisdom and beauty was, and standing and throwing back his head : " I have done wrong," he would say, " rotten wrong, and I'm wretched about it." And there would be an answer : " You did right to come."

"As we forgive them that trespass against us . . . "

Ah ! That was hard ! That was the most difficult thing in the world, the Celt in Shane knew. The horripilation of the skin, the twitching nostrils, the feeling for the knife in the armpit. . . . When one was young, the careless word, the savage blow, the brooding feud. . . . But men grew better with the increase of the years, and with maturity came the sense that not every one could insult or hurt a man. The jibes and trespasses of petty people meant so little, and one sensed that Destiny, the strange veiled One, balanced in His own wise time the evil done a man with unexpected good. . . . One grew wiser even yet with the years and knew that a great wrong was outside one's personal jurisdiction. . . . One had to leave that to the broad justice of the High God. . One could appeal there, as with the old *cri de haro* of Norman law. . . . *Haro! haro! A l'aide, mon prince. On me fait tort!* Hither! Hither! Help me, my king; one dropped on one's knees in the market-place: I am being injured overmuch! And it was the prince's duty to help feal men. . . . To forgive trespasses—only one understood in maturity, one grew to it. . . . The strong and wise were the meek, not the weaklings . . . the men who knew that justice was absolute . . . the men with the calm eyes and the grim smile, they were the terrible meek. . . .

"And lead us not into temptation . . ."

A little cry of humility that was a very human reminder to the Only Perfect One that we in this very small world were weak. Work we had to do, destinies to fulfil, but under weakness, or from false strength, one might wander from our appointed path. . . . The power of office, let it not breed arrogance . . the sense of money, let it not bring smug callousness. . . . And the singers of the world be proud only of the trust, but humble in themselves as the birds are among the trees. . . . And let not strength have contempt, but gentleness. . . .

" But deliver us from . . ."

There were dark places in the world, and one needed guidance there, protection. . . . From Satan, who is not a spirit, but a horrible miasma, that floats in little vapours here and there, when the clean winds are resting . . . from the warm inviting and evil jungle where one might seek relief in distress, or having been overlong in the high air . . . from the twisted souls of dark men and women who seek to sully as with writhing, piteous hands . . . from deep sinister pools we know are thick with horror, but feel charmed toward, as one feels like plunging to death from the summit of some building terribly high. . . . From these, Lord God, deliver us !

" For thine is the kingdom, The power, And the glory.

" For ever and ever."

America, 1920–1922.